Slave Girl

in the Harem

By

Sheniqua Waters

Slave Girl in the Harem by Sheniqua Waters is a second edition of Slave Girl by Sheniqua Waters.

This novel is a work of fiction. Events, locales and incidents described herein are done so fictitiously. Any similarities of names or characters printed herein to persons living or dead are completely coincidental.

TheWorldsBestBook.com

Second Edition of Slave Girl by Sheniqua Waters.

ISBN: 978-0615888262

Thank you for purchasing this book.

Chapter One

Cairo, Egypt – 1452 A.D.

She was being watched. The tiny goose bumps that covered her arms and the prickly hair that stood up on the back of her neck told her it was true. She stopped walking, turned and looked over her shoulder. Behind her was a long winding path with thick grass growing beside it. The sun shone warmly over the earth and the cool fingers of the wind brushed against her cheeks. Sounds of sunbirds chirping, and the sight of a colorful butterfly fluttering by, spoke of a normal calm. But an instinctual feeling inside her insisted something was wrong. She did not move from her stance for a moment. With a squint, she inspected the dirt pathway as far as she could see.

There was no one there.

Laila took a deep breath. Why did she feel so uneasy?

She stepped off the dusty trail onto the lush green grass and continued to walk toward her destination. The Nile River came into view, its massive expanse displayed like a silvery blue silk spread across the earth. The sun's rays reflected off the water like shimmering diamonds bobbing upon the river. Laila picked up her pace. Her hideout was near.

At the water's edge, Laila looked over her shoulder again. There was nothing but fields of grass and open sky. She told herself to relax. She had been to the river many times over the years. Nothing bad had ever happened. Why should today be any different? She needed to cleanse herself of the eerie feeling that captivated her imagination.

She knelt beside the water and looked into it. Her reflection shown back at her. Placing her hand in the water, she splashed the cold liquid on her face causing her image to distort into ripples. Refreshed, she walked to her hiding place, a large rock formation that jutted out over the river. Its smooth sides made it impossible for animals to climb and the rock formation curved at the top providing much desired shade.

Laila hoisted herself onto the rock. Before she sat down on the stone, she looked out over the river. There was a Red-Billed Ibis balanced on one leg. In the distance, there were men on boats fishing for their catch of the day. Downstream, women busily washed clothes along the bank. Upstream, rows and rows of wheat grew in fields. Beyond the fields of grain was a thicket of trees. Everything appeared as it should be. Laila eased down on the cool stone and relaxed. The sound of the river and the hum of insects helped to create a peaceful oasis.

Gradually, Laila's thoughts began to drift to the issue that weighed heavily on her mind. Her betrothal. She had been promised to a boy in the village when she was very young. Now, however, she did not want to marry him. A witness to her parents' loveless arranged marriage, Laila did not want to endure the same fate. It had been devastating when her father eventually left her mother for another woman. As a result, Laila decided she would only give herself to a man who committed himself to love her and no one else...forever.

"Your marriage shan't be postponed any longer," her mother had announced that morning. "I can't continue to give in to your excuses. The villagers are starting to talk. They say you too old to be unmarried. Since you will not protect yourself and your reputation, I will."

Laila remembered shouting, "You're not listening to me! I already told you! I'm not going to marry a man I don't love! You can't force me to marry anyone!"

"Don't speak to me with such disrespect!" her mother scolded. "And, don't go to the river today!" she ordered.

But, a few hours after her mother left for a day of shopping in the city, Laila made her way to the river.

6

She headed to the river because she needed to think and being alone near the serene waters of the Nile helped her relax. Besides, Laila had told herself, she would be back home long before dark, before anyone returned and missed her.

Now, as she stared up at the blue sky, a tinge of remorse nestled in her heart. She regretted shouting at her mother. She should not have lost her temper. But how else could she make her mother understand the way she felt?

As her thoughts wandered, Laila's eyelids became heavy. Her eyes closed a couple of times. Each time she managed to pry them back open. Eventually, however, her eyelids became so heavy it was impossible to fight it any longer and she fell asleep.

She had to be dreaming. Why else was there a black man with fiendish dark eyes and an unkempt beard looming over her?

Laila sat up, instantly awake.

The man stepped toward her and she noticed he had a jagged scar running from the side of his nose to the middle of his cheek.

Her heartbeat quickened.

Anxiously, she glanced over the water which now reflected dim splashes of pink, purple and yellow light from the evening sky.

She looked upstream.

The fishermen were gone.

She looked downstream.

The women were nowhere to be seen and the sun was quickly slipping behind the horizon, soon to be replaced by dark gray night.

"Who are you and what do you want?" Laila demanded, trying to hide the panic she felt.

The stranger did not answer.

Laila sprung to her feet but was shoved down onto the rock. "Yer not going anywhere!" the man growled.

Sprawled across the rock, Laila stared up in bewilderment at the intruder. She managed to gather her wits and attempted to rise again.

The man thrust her down once more and straddled her as he untied the rope that was around his waist.

Laila let out a deafening scream. "Let me go! Let me go!" she screeched, punching wildly at the assailant. Her arms flailed about, weaving up and down, in and out, to evade capture and inflict pain on the intruder. Her captor, undaunted by her jabs, grabbed for her arms. Laila tried to kick her feet, but the man's weight stifled her efforts. With a churlish grunt, she clawed at the man's face. She sank her nails into the assailant's cheek. He roared from the pain then knocked her hands away.

"Ye shouldn't have done that!" he hissed and leaned forward.

His hot stale breath stung her nose as he caught her left arm, pinned it down and quickly tied one end of the rope around her wrist.

Laila screamed in tortured protest as the rope tightened around her wrist and bit into her skin. The man released her left arm and tried to seize her right arm. Lifting her left arm, the coarse rope dangling from it, Laila brought her hand to her opponent's face. She clasped her fingers tightly over the attacker's left eye and savagely burrowed her nails into the muscle. Her adversary yelped in anguish. He released his grip and both of his hands went to his injured eye.

Without hesitating, Laila shoved the brute off her and rolled away from him. She attempted to scramble to her feet but lost her footing. She tried to stand once more. Still, she could not find her footing. Ripped by fear, she whimpered and tried again. This time, she made it to her feet. In a flash, she jumped down from the rock, stumbled, then ran to the fields toward the thicket of trees. Her heart pounded rapidly in her chest. Her breathing was so loud it echoed in her ears. She heard an angry shout behind her. But she did not look back. Instead, she quickened her pace as she sprinted through the stalks of wheat. The forest of trees was not far ahead, she had to make it. *'Legs, please don't give out!'* she prayed as she ran. She was so close. Almost there...

She entered the thicket of trees just as the sun's remaining light disappeared from the sky and an ominous darkness took its place.

It was dark. Too dark. Only a minute amount of moonlight shimmered through the leaves of the towering trees to reach the forest floor. The moon's rays dissolved into a dim vapor that cast gloomy shadows on the trees and turned the trees into frightening-looking monsters. Laila could barely see a few steps in front of her as she raced further into the darkness. She had been in these woods before. But now, as her heart pounded and her blood pulsed through her veins, she lost her sense of direction.

Still she ran.

Wind whipped against her face. A pain grew in her side. It was hard to breathe. She darted to a large wide tree and stood behind it panting. That man had tried to tie her up! Who was he? Why had he assaulted her? Had she lost him? Or had she been running in circles? She looked into the darkness but saw nothing. Somewhere in the distance, a wildcat's eerie cry sounded. An owl hooted. Laila shivered as uncertainty flexed into fear.

She was alone in the dark and she was being hunted.

Leaves crackled and the sound of heavy footsteps floated to Laila's ear on the wings of the wind. Instantly, she flattened her back against the enormous tree she had been leaning on and wished she could melt into the hard bark. The snap of branches under heavy footsteps revealed her assailant approached behind her. The clearing was up ahead. She had to keep moving. She lifted her foot. Too late she realized a twig was on the ground in front of her. Her face contorted in horror as her foot landed on the twig loudly snapping it into two pieces. Terror exploded inside her when she heard, "Ye there! Stop! Ye can't get away slave!"

She was moving again. She wasn't about to look back. One foot in front of the other and she was flying like the wind. When she entered the clearing, she became aware of a whirling noise behind her. As she ran, the sound barreled upon her in a race to overtake her. Suddenly, a coarse binding snaked around her ankles slamming them together moments before her feet wrenched upward. Laila felt herself falling forward. She hit the ground with an agonizing thud. Air smashed out of her chest. Laila whimpered in immobilizing pain when she regained her breath. Desperate, she tried to spread her legs but found her feet bound by a long cord with weights on the end. Terror snaked from her toes and lodged in her throat as she watched the stranger approach her.

"It's no use. Ye can't get away," the man bellowed down at her.

His menacing words were the impetus Laila needed to try her escape again. She clutched at her restraints then tried to crawl away.

The man lunged forward, grabbed her feet and pulled her to him. A sharp rock scraped her legs and belly. She spat dirt and leaves from her mouth.

"No! No!" she screamed. "Let me go!"

The assailant flipped her over and sank his weight on her chest cutting off any chance of escape. Laila found it harder and harder to breathe. She squirmed, gasping for air. In response, her foe pressed his girth more firmly upon her. Frantically, she slapped at him but her head was swimming.

"Ye shall bring me a good price," she heard the man jeer.

Then, with one crude punch, he hit her across the face and everything went black.

Chapter Two

She would be missed by now, Laila was sure of it. She was also sure no one knew she had walked to the river that afternoon. No one knew she had been captured and no one knew to come after her.

Her captor had taken her to a ship anchored in the waters outside of the city. The ship was filthy and smelled of human waste. Anguished moans and sorrowful wails echoed through the wooden walls. The captain strode on deck and when he neared Laila, she shouted to him that she was being held against her will. She informed him she wanted to be released so she could return home and see her mother again. But the captain never acknowledged her. Instead, she was locked in the bottom of the ship with the rest of the human cargo who had been captured by slave traders.

Laila thought about the times she had come to the city with her mother and saw the stream of slave traders pass through the markets of Cairo. She had seen the look of their human bounty and remembered it well. The captives always had the same haunting look in their eyes. Never had she imagined she would become one of them.

As the sorrowful souls bound beside her wailed in anguish, cold tears crowded into Laila's eyes. Someone's sharp elbow jabbed into her side. Someone else coughed in her face. Unable to fight the desolate feeling that lodged in the pit of her stomach, tears began to spill down her cheeks. Where was she going? How could she find her way back home? Oh, why hadn't she listened to her mother and stayed away from the river that day?

Crippled by fear, Laila began to tremble as the ship quietly sailed away from Cairo out into the tranquil waters of the Mediterranean Sea.

✖

Laila looked at the deckhand walking toward her holding a tray of bowls. She clutched her stomach as excruciating hunger pains gnawed her insides. When the deckhand tossed a bowl in front of her, she looked into it and her stomach turned in revulsion. The very thought of placing the burnt slop in her mouth made her want to heave.

Despairingly, she raised her head and looked at the resplendent sunlight that streamed between the wooden floorboards of the deck above her. She was not sure how many days the sunlight had teased her tattered senses. She had lost track of time inside the cavern of the massive ship. She could not remember how many nights she had sobbed herself to sleep and prayed for an opportunity to return home. Could she find her way back home? She wasn't sure.

Laila lay her head against the beam that supported her and fruitlessly tried to ignore the pangs in her belly. She had to eat. If she didn't, she feared she might succumb to the sickness that permeated the cramped pit of shackled captives.

Hesitantly, she picked up the bowl of rations. After a sharp intake of breath, she closed her eyes and tilted the dish toward her lips.

There was a loud shout.

Immediately, Laila opened her eyes and hastily lowered the bowl.

A sailor stuck his head into the hull and yelled, "Land's been spotted ahead! We've reached our destination!"

At his words, the bowl slipped from Laila's fingers and she let out a terrified whimper.

❈

The ship docked in a city called Constantinople a few hours later. Now accustomed to the constant rocking of the ship, Laila's feet felt wobbly aground. She was pushed into line with the rest of the human cargo and led inside the city's triple walls. The captives marched along the streets of the city's bazaar, which was alive with potent energy. Each corridor was crowded with masses of inhabitants bustling about.

Numerous street merchants bellowed entreaties to potential patrons jaunting by. Other vendors raucously negotiated the pricing of their merchandise with shoppers. Artists, strategically positioned on street corners, gathered small crowds as they busily painted replicas of architecture crafted with detailed carvings and Byzantine crosses. Musicians congregated along the cobblestone streets and belched out vibrant music. The talking and haggling, combined with the reverberating music, mixed into a deluge of noise. Men, whose *dalmatics* denoted they belonged to religious orders, weaved slowly through the streets seemingly oblivious to it all.

Laila did not have time to be too impressed with the sights and sounds of the Byzantine Empire for she, along with the others from the ship, was marched to an auction house near the edge of the city. The females were separated from the males and put in dingy holding cells.

Laila wanted to scream in protest against her unjust kidnapping and imprisonment. She had to escape. But, even as she thought it, she knew it was impossible. Far away from home…two seas away…she was in a new land, unable to speak the language, and unable to return home.

A door across the room opened. A short man with a flat nose entered. He wore a red robe that trailed behind him as he walked to the holding cells and began to speak. Laila did not understand the language he spoke. Some of the women present must have because they began to cry. When the man turned to leave, Laila found her tongue.

"Wait!" she called out in Arabic, hoping he would understand her. "I have something to say to you."

The man turned and looked at her.

Afraid it could be her last chance to free herself, she spoke, "Please listen to me. I am not a slave."

"You're not a slave," the man repeated in Arabic.

He understood her! Relieved, Laila quickly answered back, "That's right!"

"Do you speak Greek?" he asked.

"Nay. And I don't belong here," she protested. "I should be free."

The man walked back to the cell.

"Let's look at you." He leaned forward to study her heart-shaped face and copper colored eyes. "My...my. You are very beautiful. Very exotic."

Oh, why wasn't he focusing on what she was telling him? Desperate, she tried again. "Are you listening to me? I said I don't belong here. You've got to believe me."

"I believe." The man unlocked the cell door.

"You believe me?" Laila sighed with relief as she walked out of the cell.

The worker closed the door behind her, then continued, "Aye, I do believe. I believe you will yield a very high price on the auction block today."

"What?...No!"

The man took a step back and clapped his hands.

A middle-aged woman, dressed in a well-worn linen *tunica,* appeared. She had white hair and premature wrinkles etched in her face.

"Get this wench ready to be sold," the man instructed caustically.

"You can't do this! No!" Laila argued as the woman advanced forward with a look that warned her to silence her objections.

The older woman clutched Laila's upper arm, pushed her forward, and led her behind a tall wooden wall in the far corner of the room. The white-haired woman began to tug at the strap of Laila's *kalasiris.*

Laila wrenched away from the servant. "What do you think you are doing?" she hissed.

"Ssshh. Child," the older woman whispered in Arabic. "Don't cause problems for yerself."

"I shouldn't be here!" Laila countered. "I am not a slave!"

"Make it easy on yerself and don't fight it. I've seen what they do to those who resist them. The gold coins ye will bring them are all they care about. They don't care about the truth or yer feelings. If they even think ye will cost them coin, they will not hesitate to punish ye," the seasoned woman explained.

"But–!"

"No buts, sweet child. Ye best forget yer old life. Ye are a slave now. There's naught ye can do about it. The sooner ye accept it the better." The timeworn servant shuffled her calloused hands as she concluded her counsel.

As a demoralized frown enveloped the woman's face, the preponderance of impotence obtained in her new reality hit Laila and the hope she clung to began its retreat. Disheartened, she offered no resistance when the woman once again reached out and began to undress her.

Laila's clothing was quickly removed, a jar of warm water was produced and the servant began to wash her dry skin with a small cloth. As water tumbled down her body, Laila felt the remainder of her resistance melt away. All of the pain from her emotional and physical turmoil faded and the scant hope that tarried completed its retreat.

A short time later, the woman draped a long yellow cloak over Laila's shoulders. Then, she tied the drawstring around Laila's throat into a loose bow. "Ye look beautiful," she said sadly.

Just as she finished speaking, the man in the red robe snapped orders to remove all of the female captives from their holding cell. Sniffles and wails permeated the room as the females were lined up by a back door. Laila was pushed into the line and one by one, each female was led outside. When it was Laila's turn, the worker in the red robe nudged her forward. "Get going!" he ordered.

Wearily, Laila stepped through the door of the auction house and into the unknown.

Laila walked nervously down a small walkway. She stepped into an enormous courtyard which was immersed in sunlight. In the center of the courtyard was a large wooden dais. Men who appeared to be Greek, Venetian, French and Turkish milled restlessly around the staging area. Unlike the others present, there was a man who stood patiently near the steps of the platform.

He had olive colored skin and his hair and beard were liberally sprinkled with gray. Attired in a gold caftan that did little to hide the bulge of his stomach, a silk green robe that was trimmed in gold, and a *kavuk* on his head, the gentleman created an imposing impression. The man exuded an air of prominence flanked by a guard with two scimitars tucked in his girdle and a gangly black man wearing a *takke*.

Laila turned her attention to the overweight auctioneer with flushed cheeks standing on the dais. The auctioneer looked at her, nodded his head in approval and spoke in a language she did not understand. When she did not acknowledge his words, the man impatiently motioned for her to come to him.

The courtyard fell silent.

Laila felt every pair of male eyes shift to her. She stood for a moment and wondered if she should run back inside the auction house. However, she wasn't sure she could make it back inside because her legs felt as if they were made of molasses. Casting a look the way she had come, Laila saw the worker in the red robe poised by the back door with a grimacing scowl on his face. She turned her gaze away from him, and though fear imbedded itself in the pit of her stomach, she lifted her chin and stepped forward.

As Laila made her way to the platform, the crowd murmured excitedly. When she neared the steps, she felt someone's audacious gaze devouring her. Laila glanced up and realized it was the man in the silk green robe watching her. Quickly, she climbed the few steps to the top of the dais. As she turned to face the men, she lowered her head. Suddenly, she could not bear to look into any of the prying eyes. She didn't want to see the faces of the men who bought and sold humans as if they were buying and selling animals.

The auctioneer once again spoke in a language Laila did not understand. Then, he said in Arabic, "Whatever your needs are, be sure this slave girl will fulfill them. Whether it's cooking, cleaning for your family, or a maid for your wife, you've come to the right place."

The men present began to converse with one another.

"Gentlemen," the auctioneer continued. "Not only will she work for your family...she will work for *you*. Her beauty is undeniable. She's a jewel plucked straight from the Nile and brought here to service *all* of your needs. Just take one look at her and you will know any price you have to pay for her is but a bargain."

As her raven colored hair flowed in the wind, Laila managed to stand majestic and valiant as the buyers inspected her.

"Let's get a better look at her!" one of the men called out even as the breeze pressed the yellow cape against her slender body, revealing her round curves.

There were murmurs of approval when the auctioneer stepped forward and tugged on the tie around her neck. As it unraveled, he pulled on the cloak.

Realizing the cape was tumbling down her shoulders, Laila grabbed for the material. She managed to catch the edge of the cloth in time to prevent her chest from being exposed.

The men present began to grunt and heckle in opposition to her actions.

The auctioneer reached out and tried to pull her cloak again. Laila defiantly shifted her body away from his grasp. When the auctioneer came toward Laila again, she lifted her foot and kicked him in the calf. He let out a boorish curse.

Raucous laughter erupted from the crowd in response to the antics playing out on stage.

The auction worker with the red robe appeared, the scowl still on his face. He stomped up behind Laila, clutched the cloak at her shoulders then brazenly tore the cape from her body.

Laila let out a horrified gasp as the garment was ripped from her naked frame. She tried to cover her most intimate parts with her hands, but it was futile. Catcalls and cheers of elation went up from the onlookers as her nude form was bared for all to see.

Laila's heart plummeted to her feet.

Somehow, her feet found wings and with tears in her eyes, she fled from the spot of her degradation.

Instead of heading back into the auction house, she found herself running down the steps of the dais toward the entrance of the courtyard. Just as her feet stepped in the entryway a figure appeared. Propelled by her own speed, Laila slammed into the rock hard chest of a tall male. In the next moment, she felt his strong arms encircle her waist as she tumbled forward against his broad rugged frame. The startled man fell backward hitting the ground first. Laila landed on top of him and gasped as her breasts flattened against the massive wall of his chest. She felt his fingertips move to the base of her spine in an attempt to steady her against his frame.

Laila was vaguely aware of the collective grumble from the assembled crowd. It took a moment for her to catch her breath. When she did, she lifted her head, brushed back the hair from her face and found herself gazing into the eyes of the most handsome man she had ever seen. He had amber colored eyes, a chiseled chin, skin that looked as if it had been lightly kissed by the sun and a full head of sable colored hair that started to curl near the end.

The handsome man took a deep breath then with a concerned expression spoke to her. However, Laila did not respond because she could not understand his words.

There was a rustling sound. They both looked up as the red robed worker appeared above them. The worker grabbed Laila's arm and yanked her to her feet before quickly turning his attention to assisting the fallen male to his feet. Both men exchanged words then the auction worker turned to Laila and said, "This is Master al Numan. He wants to know if you're all right."

Laila nodded and looked at the attractive man again. She saw an amused grin curl over the man's lips and followed his gaze until she realized he was staring at her nude body. With a huff, she grabbed the yellow cape out of the auction worker's hand and securely wrapped it around her body.

The worker spoke to the man again before pushing her back toward the auction house.

As she entered the auction house, the auction worker grabbed her arm and swung her around to face him. He clutched her shoulders and began to shake her. Laila's stomach, which was already in knots, began to churn violently.

"You fool!" the man shouted at her. "You knocked over a very important man! How dare you!"

"Let her go!" a cacophonous male voice interrupted the worker's aggression.

Laila and the man looked up and saw the gangly man from the courtyard who wore the *takke*. He had a stern look on his face. He glanced over at the people in the stalls, then looked back at Laila and the auction worker. The man said something to the auction worker. The auction worker lowered one hand, but still clutching one of Laila's arms tight, he answered back. The stranger took an inspecting glance at Laila. She lowered her eyes. He spoke again. This time his voice was even more strident. The worker replied in a similar tone and for a few minutes, there seemed to be a debate. Finally, the auction worker threw up his hands as if in surrender and shoved Laila toward the stranger.

"Fine! You can have her!" the auction worker spat in Arabic. Then, he said to Laila, "This servant says his master is looking for a handmaid for his daughter and he wants you. It is I who should be paying them to take you away from here because you are too much trouble. I am glad to be rid of you."

The tall stranger handed the worker several coins.

"Now she's your problem!" was the retort from the auction worker as he left them to return to the auction.

The servant looked down at Laila and smiled. "You speak Arabic?" he inquired.

Laila nodded her head.

"You look like a frightened doe," he commented before saying, "Let not your heart be troubled. You have been sold to Ibrahim, the Emir of Karamania. The Emir is a very influential and wealthy man. He and his daughter have come to the city for a visit. The Emir bought you to be a handmaid for his daughter. He has spoiled your new mistress beyond belief. I hope she likes you. Although I cannot be sure she will. Either way, you will serve her diligently. Have you eaten?"

Laila shook her head.

The servant handed her an apple.

When she bit into it, her stomach growled appreciatively.

"Where are you from?" he asked.

"My home is in Cairo," Laila replied between bites.

"Cairo? I am from Sudan. The Emir and his daughter can speak Arabic but their native tongue is Turkish. You will have to learn it. My name is Jamal. What do you call yourself?"

"My name is Laila."

"Lay-la." Jamal rolled her name slowly off his tongue. "That will not do. Your new name will be….Kalilah."

"Ka-lee-la?" Laila repeated the name. It sounded foreign to her. "I don't like that name. It is not my name. My name is Laila!"

"Do not fight me on this, little one. You are a servant now. Your old life is over. So is your old name. I have been a servant of our master for many many years. I know what is expected. I know what it will take for you to fit in. From now on, you will be known as Kalilah," Jamal insisted.

He stopped speaking as the white haired woman who had prepared her for the auction approached. She walked to Laila and handed her a brown linen *tunica*.

"Put that on," Jamal ordered. Then, without waiting for a response, he nodded for Laila to follow him and started to walk away.

✂

When Kudar al Numan stepped into the auction house, it had been to deliver a message to his father's friend, Ibrahim, the Emir of Karamania. His mission had been interrupted when without warning, a beautiful female collided into him. Instinctively, he encircled his arm around the girl's tiny waist as they both tumbled to the ground.

He remembered how the beauty's long black hair had fanned across his face and how frightened she looked when she brushed her hair from her eyes. More than that, he recalled the sight of the pretty girl's curvy figure. The tiny mounds of her breasts had jiggled in his face when the auction worker pulled her upward. As she was righted to stand on her feet, he could not help but notice her shapely legs which led up to a perfectly rounded bottom and equally curvaceous hips.

After speaking to the girl in Arabic, the auction worker said to him, "So sorry, Master al Numan. Please accept my apologies for this girl."

"Who is she?" he had asked, once he was on his feet.

"She is of no importance. Just a dimwitted slave who thought she could escape. I assure you, she will no longer be a problem," the worker stated before leading the girl away.

Kudar glanced into the courtyard and saw the Emir, dressed in a silk green robe, walking toward him. Impetuously, he turned his attention back to the girl and found himself watching until she disappeared inside the auction house.

�෴

The moment Laila walked out of the auction house, she was immediately engulfed by the sounds of streets bustling with chaotic activity. She followed Jamal to a camel. He helped her on the back of the animal then climbed on a second camel. As they rode through the streets, they passed vendors peddling beautiful handmade rugs and saw schoolboys scurrying through crowds of patrons milling by fruit stands. They also smelled the sugary smell of delicacies and the poignant smell of herbs and spices that wafted through the air.

When they reached the top of one street, the vast blue sea came into view, showcased in majestic splendor just beyond the city. However, Laila was too exhausted to be impressed. Slowly, the riders made their way around the winding cobblestone streets and out of the city.

While they rode, Laila thought about her family and how useless it seemed to hope she would be released and somehow find her way back home.

Seeing her unhappiness, Jamal spoke, "You are now a handmaid to the Emir's daughter. It is useless to fight it."

"I have never been a handmaid in my life and I don't want to start being one now," Laila retorted.

"Being a slave is your destiny," Jamal surmised.

But even as Laila heard his words, there was a glimmer of hope inside her that refused to die. In her heart, she knew she was not a slave and she promised herself she would return to her home as soon as she had the opportunity.

⚜

Laila and Jamal traveled until a huge palace came into view. The palace, a magnificent stone structure, stood proudly on a hill surrounded by a wall.

"It's magnificent," Laila blurted out, unable to hide her amazement.

"This is the al Numan compound. Amir al Numan, the Sultan's Ambassador to Constantinople, lives here, as does his son, Kudar al Numan. Amir al Numan believes it's time his son finds a wife. He wants his son to marry a nice Muslim girl of Turkish descent with honorable breeding. Ibrahim, the Emir of Karamania, was asked by the Ambassador to bring his daughter, Zora, to visit in hopes she will be able to entice Kudar. That is why the Emir and Mistress Zora are visiting Constantinople and staying at the al Numan palace," Jamal said informatively.

"Amir and his son are very influential people," he revealed. "They work closely with our current Sultan who is called Mehmed II. Amir personally served Sultan Mehmed's father. The old Sultan was called Sultan Murad. It is said Amir was once a slave to Murad but found favor with the old Sultan and worked his way up the ranks. Not only was he given an ambassadorship and allowed to build this palace, he was also given a stipend which he still receives every month from Sultan Mehmed."

Jamal paused briefly, then continued, "I was in Adrianople with Ibrahim at the reception Mehmed held after Murad's death. Though Mehmed appointed some of the ministers elsewhere, he confirmed most of his father's ministers in their places. Amir was one of the ministers allowed to keep their positions."

Jamal nodded his head. "Kudar will inherit Amir's wealth one day though he won't need it. Kudar has amassed much wealth on his own due to his talent as an architect. It's rumored the Sultan has promised Amir he will use Kudar to build a building for him."

The camels came to a stop at the palace gates just as Jamal finished speaking. Moments after they dismounted, a black man with a goatee and dreadlocks tied away from his face exited the palace and walked to Jamal. The two men exchanged words.

Laila followed the men as they entered through the palace gates and stepped into a large courtyard. It was then Laila saw that the courtyard separated two grand palaces. Their guide led them to the mansion on the right side of the courtyard.

When Laila stepped inside, she found the coolness refreshing. As the trio walked through the mansion, Laila couldn't help but be amazed by the grandeur of the place. Marble floors covered spacious hallways and cozy rooms. There were huge columns with decorative candles strategically spaced on them. Beautiful painted scenes were on the ceiling above the window lined walls. Sweet smelling flowers were arranged on tables and shelves. As they walked, their escort gave a brief history of the more important pieces of artwork they passed, including the prestigious statues.

"Here we are," the escort said, once they had climbed a flight of stairs. He turned to a door on their right and opened it. "Since Mistress Zora is occupying these quarters during her stay, her handmaid will reside with her. As you know, Ibrahim is set up with quarters in the Ambassador's palace across the courtyard.

Mistress Zora returned from the city early today and decided to go riding before dinner. She should be in soon. Until then," the escort turned to Laila, "you may rest and refresh yourself. There is a bit of fruit left," he pointed to a nightstand beside a divan with a pitcher of water and a platter of food on it. "If you need more, ask and refreshments will be sent to you…and…oh yes…" He walked to the curtain and pulled it back. "Out here is the garden."

The garden their escort alluded to was a balcony with colorful flowers along the wall. A breathtaking view of the city could be seen in the distance. There was a huge lounge chair in the middle of the balcony.

"Everything is nice," Laila admitted approvingly.

"Very well, I will take my leave," the man said. "My name is Omar if you need anything."

"Thank you, Omar. She will be just fine," Jamal assured.

Omar left and Laila walked around the spacious living area.

"Freshen up then meet me outside," Jamal instructed, before he left the room.

Laila hungrily ate the last of the melons, figs and bread drizzled with honey that remained on the platter. To refresh herself, she splashed water on her face. As she headed outside, she noted how tired she felt and hoped for a chance to lie down soon.

When she stepped into the courtyard, she saw Jamal standing just outside the palace gates and walked to him.

He cast a quick glance at her then called out to a female who rode a brown horse in the distance and waved his hands in the air. The female rider looked in their direction, but continued to ride the horse a few minutes longer. Finally, she directed the trotting horse toward them.

As she neared, Laila saw the female wore a dark blue *ferace* as an overmantle and a light colored *basortu* covered her head. When her features crystallized, Laila noticed that the woman had olive colored skin, brown eyes with thick lashes and mahogany colored hair, which peeked from beneath her *basortu*.

"Whoa now!" the young woman said briskly to her horse before bringing the animal to a stop in front of Jamal and Laila.

"Merhaba," Jamal said in greeting as the woman dismounted. He then snapped his fingers and a stable

25

hand ran out, took the horse's reins and led the animal away.

Jamal and the female exchanged several words before he began to speak in Arabic. "Well, Mistress Zora, now you have your maid. It's the new handmaid your father purchased today. Her name is Kalilah. She is from Cairo. She doesn't speak Turkish. But she does understand Arabic." He looked at Laila. "Kalilah, it's your new mistress."

"Kalilah, huh?" Zora took a brazen look at Laila.

Laila was a little perplexed at the young woman's churlish nature, but she did not have time to be affronted. Now that she was in the presence of someone who seemed to hold a position of power, she had to try and explain the mistake that led her here.

"Mistress Zora," Laila began when Zora started to turn from her. "My real name is Laila and I am not a slave. This whole thing has been a mistake. You have to listen to me. I should be free. I want to go back home."

Zora stared at Laila without speaking.

Laila continued, "I was abducted by a ghastly man. It was horrible. I was taken to the auction house. I tried to explain to them that I am not a slave. But no one listened to me. I want to go home more than anything in the world. You have to release me. Let me return to my home," Laila pleaded and stared at Zora expectantly.

Zora looked at Laila for a moment with a contemplative expression on her face. Abruptly, her expression hardened and her eyes became tiny slits. In a scathing tone she remarked, "Jamal, see to it that this slave never gives me orders again."

With that said, Zora pivoted poignantly and strode into the courtyard, leaving Laila to fight back the tears that crowded in her eyes.

Chapter Three

"See that my *cizmes* are cleaned," Zora ordered and pointed to her riding boots when Laila entered Zora's quarters several minutes later.

Immediately, Laila began to clean the boots.

"Not so loud. I am going to see Kudar again tonight so I must be well rested. I can't rest with you making so much noise," Zora revealed from where she lay on the divan. A smile graced her lips. "He is the most attractive man I have ever seen. Being married to him would be paradise..." her voice trailed off.

Grateful that Zora had stopped speaking, Laila worked quickly to clean the boots.

"I'm hot. Fan me," Zora said to Laila, once Laila had finished her chore.

Laila's heart sank. "My feet..."

"What are you complaining about?"

"I'm very tired from the journey. I don't want to stand on my feet."

"I am the master here. You are my slave. You will do as I say when I say. Now do it," Zora instructed in a captious tone. "Don't try to get out of work. I don't know why my father chose you. You don't even make a good slave," Zora sneered.

Laila lowered her head and looked around for something to use as a fan. She found what she needed and began to fan her new mistress.

"Faster!" Zora demanded after a while.

Laila's arms felt heavy and her legs and feet ached. But without a word, she began to move the fan faster. With a heavy heart, she remembered the time when she was free...when there was no one telling her what to do or when to do it. She thought about how she had been loved by her family. Her feelings mattered...back home.

As Laila remembered the past, silent tears stung her eyes. She knew she would never forget her home or her family.

She looked at Zora and saw she had fallen asleep. For that, Laila was grateful because her tears were threatening to spill over like a raging river.

Finally, they did.

They streamed down her face burning a trail of heat. Laila stopped fanning, sank to the ground and lifted her hands to her face as silent sobs shook her body.

⚜

"Oh, Father, I can't believe how magical Constantinople has been!" Zora squealed when she met her father in the sitting area of Amir's home late that afternoon.

"Daughter, I am glad you are enjoying your time here. On the other hand, I have not been as fortunate this trip. I thought coming here was a great opportunity for you and me. I'd hoped I could persuade Amir that the Sultan, at nineteen, is too inexperienced to lead. Our Sultan, Mehmed II, is a young arrogant whelp who will not listen to reason. I received a message from his Grand Vizier that stated he refuses to meet with me to discuss any military campaigns."

"You're boring me, Father."

"Oh, all right. No political talk. Have you met the new handmaid I bought for you?"

"Yes. She was asleep when I left the room. I am going to have her help me dress for dinner in a little while." Changing the subject Zora said, "I am so glad Amir asked you to bring me to see Kudar."

"Well, it was only logical Amir ask you to bring you here. After all, he knows you have the qualities that will make a good wife for his son."

"I remember the first time I saw Kudar. It was years ago when he and his father came to our home. You were working with the Ambassador and he and Kudar came over for dinner several times."

"Since that time, Amir's son has grown into a nice young man. Kudar al Numan is arguably the most illegible bachelor in the territory."

Zora batted her eyes demurely. "I deserve to be married to someone like Kudar. He is talented and very attractive. He is part Turkish but his mother is English, right?"

"Yes, that is true. She is a lovely woman."

"His lighter skin he gets from his mother. His hair and his features he takes from his Turkish father. We'll make beautiful children together," Zora sighed wistfully.

Ibrahim chuckled at his daughter's antics. "It could happen. Though I might remind you, he no doubt has many young women competing for his attention. But have no fear. You have the best chance to charm him for you, daughter, are the prettiest girl ever born."

Zora laughed lightly. "Thank you, Father," she said sweetly.

※

"Kalilah! Kalilah, wake up!"

Laila opened her eyes with much effort. She wanted to continue to sleep. But that was impossible as Zora's voice sounded again. "Kalilah! Finally, you're awake."

Laila slowly stood to her feet.

"I want something to eat. Go let the cooks know I want some food. I have to eat now so I don't eat too much in front of Kudar tonight. After I'm done eating, you need to help me get ready. I have to look my best if I am to get Kudar to fall for me. Step to it, skinny girl!"

Laila left the room and walked downstairs. She started to retrace her earlier steps but realized she had not seen anything resembling a cooking area when she arrived. So she turned and walked in the opposite direction down a long hallway.

The faint murmur of voices reached her ears. She walked toward the sound drifting from behind a slightly opened door. She approached the door and looked inside. The room was a study and across it, directly ahead of her, was a door that led to the courtyard. Realizing the voices were originating from the courtyard, she stepped into the room. Her attention was immediately drawn to a huge drawing that hung on the wall. It was a drawing of a large fortress on what appeared to be rawhide. She walked closer to the drawing to get a better look at it.

"That drawing is of Rumeli Hisari, a fortress that I helped design. I'm rather proud of it," a sultry tenor sounded behind her.

Laila gasp and quickly turned around to find herself looking at a man whose presence had been hidden behind the door. He was in the process of pulling a *gomlek* over his shoulders. For a few seconds, she was able to view his tantalizing bronze colored chest which rippled with muscles.

He lowered the shirt and fastened the ties, concealing his enticing physique.

Laila lifted her eyes to his face and found herself staring into the same amber colored eyes she had looked into earlier that morning. Spellbound by his mesmerizing gaze, she once again took in his chiseled chin and had to fight back the urge to run her fingers through his full mane. The attractive rake grinned a lopsided grin as if he could read her thoughts.

Both parties examined each other for a moment without saying a word.

Finally, the man continued, "Rumeli Hisari is being built approximately six miles south of Constantinople. Sultan Mehmed wanted the new fortress built in addition to the old fortress, Anadolu Hisar, on the Anatolian shore. The Sultan is having it built so Turks can control the straits."

Laila was not sure she was listening for she was too busy noticing the man's perfect lips.

The tempter continued, "Emperor Constantine sent a message to Sultan Mehmed protesting the fortress. Sultan Mehmed's answer was to cut off the heads of the couriers sent to deliver the message. Since then, all ships intending to enter the Black Sea must pay tolls. If not, their ship will be sunk. But enough about that. I'm glad to see you on your feet."

"You speak Arabic?" she asked shyly.

"Of course. I am the Ambassador's son. I heard that worker at the auction house speaking to you in Arabic. So when I saw you walk in, I figured I should speak it. Everyone who lives here knows Arabic because of my father's position. Now, tell me, are you looking for someone?"

"Nay. I'm not lusting...I mean, *looking* for anyone." Laila blushed at her verbal mistake.

The man laughed, very amused. "Well, can I be of help to you?"

Laila shook her head timidly. "Probably not," she managed to say.

"Considering this is my study and I live here, I am sure I can be of some assistance. My name is Kudar al Numan."

"I didn't realize this was your study and I didn't..." Kudar? *The Kudar?* Yes, he had said Kudar. It was unbelievable. The same man she had knocked over that morning and was currently staring at was the same man Zora hoped to attract. If Zora found out that she had disturbed him..."I was looking for...never mind... I shouldn't be disturbing you..." mumbling, Laila headed for the exit.

"What's your...?"

Laila did not hear the rest of the question because she rushed out of the room and to the courtyard.

Kudar had been in his study working on drawings for Sultan Mehmed. As dinnertime neared, he debated whether to change out of the plain *gomlek* he had put on that morning into one that was a little more formal for dinner. He knew, if he didn't change shirts on his own, his mother would suggest he change when she saw him before dinner that evening. So he stood up and walked behind the open door of his study and pulled off his shirt. That was when the enchanting female entered into the room. Though she was dressed in a simple brown *tunica* made of linen, he recognized her curvy figure right away.

She was beautifully alluring as she stood staring at the drawing that hung on the wall. The way her shimmery black hair fell down her back captivated his gaze. When she turned around to face him, there was no hiding the sensuality of her copper colored eyes, slightly rounded nose or her luscious full lips that seemed to be made for kissing. He remembered seeing her in all of her nude glory and a grin spread over his lips.

She seemed a little shy, which for an unknown reason, he found appealing. Normally, it bored him whenever females acted that way around him. To him, it always seemed like a pretense. But this girl…this girl was different.

She spoke and Kudar could not recall ever hearing such a captivating voice. He couldn't help but laugh when she said 'lusting' instead of 'looking'. Obviously, he had an affect on her. He expected no less. After all, every girl was impressed by him. Whether it was his good looks or charm, he couldn't be sure.

The moment, he told the girl his name, however, was the moment she became frightened. Before he knew it, she hurried out of the room.

He had rushed to the door, stepped outside and looked around the courtyard. All he saw was his father and Ibrahim sitting on a bench smoking a *hookah*.

She had gone just as mysteriously as she had come.

A platter of mulberries, figs and nuts arrived for Zora. While she ate, Laila prepared a bath in the huge clay tub that had been brought into the room after Zora insisted she was too tired to go to the *hamam* to bathe. After Zora bathe, Laila helped her dress for the evening. Zora stood completely still as Laila adorned her in a carefully selected *bindalli* made of red velvet then fastened a gold *kusak* securely around her waist. At Zora's insistence, Laila also brushed her hair until it shone then placed a sheer veil over her head.

"We are all attending a camel wrestling tournament tonight. Maybe tonight will be the night Kudar falls for me. I hope I capture his heart," Zora murmured wistfully.

Laila swallowed the lump in her throat. Kudar was just as handsome as Zora said he would be. She hoped he wasn't angry about what happened that morning or that she had intruded in his office, and she hoped the occurrences didn't get back to Zora. She could only imagine Zora's reaction if Zora found out.

"How do I look?" Zora asked then scoffed, "Why am I asking you? You know nothing about what's fashionable. You are just a slave girl."

Zora's words cut Laila to the quick. However, she refused to let her mistress see. When Zora finally left the room, Laila was glad. There was no one to order her around. No one to insult her. "I know about fashion!" Laila explained to the empty room.

She walked over to the garments Zora left lying on the divan and picked out one she thought would look pretty on her. She slipped out of her *tunica* and quickly bathed herself. Refreshed, she slid into the beautiful garment she had selected. It was too big for her but Laila smiled. She pressed the soft cloth to her skin and twirled around in a circle. Oh, what she would give to own such nice things. To be a wealthy lady going to meet a wealthy prince.

Laila curtsied in front of her imaginary prince. "My prince, aren't you glad you could meet me?" She laughed to herself.

She took off the garment and sat down on the divan. It was soft compared to the pallet on the floor she was expected to sleep on. Pushing the garments to the side, she lay down. Maybe now she could get some sleep. The evening was young and it was sure to be hours before Zora returned.

Laila let out a sigh of relief when Zora returned in the wee hours of the night bursting with excitement and made no mention of Kudar being disturbed.

The next morning, Zora left to go to the city's *souk*. Laila spent her morning resting in the garden. She looked out toward the city and wondered about the activities going on there. As evening approached, she was overcome with boredom and set out to investigate the palace.

Laila tried to stay out of sight as she went from room to room admiring the richness and opulence.

"You open that door and you'll be in the harem," a voice startled her.

Laila turned and saw a pretty young girl with fiery red hair standing behind her.

"My name is Vashti. I saw you when you arrived with Jamal."

"You did?"

"Yes. I don't miss much of what goes on around here. For instance, I know you speak Arabic and I know you were bought for Mistress Zora."

"Do you think Master Kudar and Mistress Zora will wed?" Laila inquired.

"His father has tried to make him choose and many beauties have tried. Women are always throwing themselves at Master Kudar. Unfortunately for them, Master Kudar will never succumb. He's a man with a heart for pleasure who has no desire to settle down and why should he when he has me?"

Laila could not help but hear the resentment in Vashti's voice when she spoke the last sentence.

"I thought only Sultans had harems."

"Most of the time that's true. But if they can afford them, wealthy men have been known to have harems as well. Ambassador Amir has his and there are those of us that belong to Master Kudar. I was given to Master Kudar by the Sultan himself as a gift. I am the Master's favorite," Vashti assured in a wistful tone as she spoke of Kudar.

"Master Kudar has a harem?"

"Yes. Come. I will show it to you."

Vashti took Laila's hand in hers then pushed open the solid oak door with her other hand. A thin white curtain hung in front of them, allowing them to see into the harem. Vashti pushed back the drapery and they stepped inside a huge room. It was a living area decorated in warm soft colors and beautiful oriental rugs topped by large plush pillows.

A brunette and a woman with cream colored skin and shimmering black hair sat in the room supervising angelic little girls who scampered about.

"This is the common area," Vashti began.

"Are these all of the women that live here?" Laila inquired.

"Not all of the women you see live here. Some of the women you may see live in the Ambassador's harem which is in the palace across the courtyard. His women come and visit us all the time. Sometimes we go visit them. They bring their children, which is always nice."

"What countries are the women from?" Laila asked.

"There are some Circassians, Georgians and an Abkahasian. Some were brought as slaves and some had poor families who sold them to the Ambassador so that they could have a better life."

"They seem happy," Laila commented.

"Of course. What is there not to be happy about?"

"The women are all so beautiful. Are they all treated the same?"

"We are all treated well. Though here, just as in the Sultan's palace, there are ranks. There are concubines, *ikbals*, which are the master's favorites and a *kadin* who is the favorite wife. The Ambassador's *kadin* is Master Kudar's mother."

"You said some of these women belong to the Ambassador and some belong to Master Kudar. Why doesn't Ambassador Amir let his son choose one of the women from the harem to marry?"

"That is a good question. It is because none of us are Turkish and none of us were bought up Muslim. Though his *kadin* is an English woman, the Ambassador has decided he wants his son to embrace his Turkish and Muslim roots."

"What does Master Kudar want?"

"From what I've seen, there has been no one who has caught his eye. If there were, I would be the first to know because I know the Master very well."

"Who stays in those rooms?" Laila asked, as they walked past private chambers that lined the common area.

"In the Ambassador's harem the rooms go to the women who have given him children. He has many daughters. The little girls you see running around the harem are his youngest daughters. Kudar is his only son."

"What about those of you who belong to Kudar?" Laila asked, looking at her guide.

"I have the biggest room. But none of us are his wife and none of us have had any children. His father has seen to that. You see, until now, Master Amir has been content to let Master Kudar sow his seed. But Amir al Numan, with his wife's approval, has ordered all of us in Master Kudar's harem to take a potion so we will not conceive. Master Amir does not want his son to become a father until he has wed. He does not want his first grandchild to be conceived by a woman who is not Turkish and does not have a Muslim heritage."

"I see." Laila frowned.

"Why the frown?" Vashti asked.

"I must admit, I am not used to the idea of so many women for one man. I find it rather unsettling."

"You shouldn't. We women are very content to be here. It is the way things are. It is our way."

As Vashti's words settled in Laila's mind, they came to a door that led to an outdoor patio. Laila saw a peacock lounging in a corner by a garden overflowing with tulips and crocuses. There were a couple of women exercising and two blondes sat weaving in the sun.

Vashti pointed to two lounge chairs. "Come, let's talk in the sun," she said with a smile.

"The harem is amazing!" Laila exclaimed as Vashti led her back into the hallway a few hours later. "But, don't you ever wish you could go back to your homeland?" Laila asked the redhead.

"This is my home. I belong here," Vashti responded contentedly.

"I'm glad you're happy. The harem is very intriguing. Thank you for the tour."

"It was no problem. It was my pleasure," Vashti replied with a smile.

✂

Laila made her way back to the room she shared with Zora. When she got there, she found Zora had not returned. She tidied up the chamber then ate some of the leftover fruit on the platter near the divan.

The sun was beginning to set.

Laila slipped into the nightdress Vashti had given her. The garment was white with a faint hint of gold thread weaved throughout the material. It fit her tightly around the bodice and hung loosely to her ankles.

As evening set in, Laila poured herself a drink and walked to the garden. She looked over the balcony and saw several servants walking below. Turning from the view, she walked to the lounge chair in the middle of the balcony. She placed her cup on the ground by the legs of the chair before settling into the seat. As she sat back, the huge comfortable chair seemed to swallow her up. Laila relaxed in the cozy seat and curled her feet under her before looking up at the sky. The sky was stained with orange, purple and yellow light as the sun kissed the earth for the final time that evening.

Her thoughts drifted once again to her home just as they did every time she had a moment alone. She really missed her mother and wondered what her mother was doing at that very moment. Probably cooking dinner no doubt. Laila wiggled her nose as if she could smell the meat cooking on the hearth.

When she came back from her trips to the river, she could always smell the meat roasting over the fire even before she walked through the door of the hut. As she stepped inside the hut, her mother would look up from her preparation and smile. "Welcome home, my angel," she would say.

Chapter Four

She heard a murmur of voices and struggled to open her eyes.

"I know we are not supposed to be alone together. But I want to talk to you. I had a lovely evening," Zora's voice sounded.

"So did I," came the reply of a subdued male voice.

Laila opened her eyes and noticed the full moon high in the night sky. Now fully awake, she realized she recognized the subdued voice. That deep timber belonged to Kudar.

"This whole trip has been absolutely wonderful," Zora was saying.

"That's good. My father's goal is to make sure you have a good time."

"Your father has been very generous...so many gifts. My father is impressed at how much the city has grown and changed since his last trip."

Laila felt uneasy listening to the pair. She was sure they were unaware of her presence since she was sitting in the oversized lounge chair.

Footsteps approached but stopped at the open door that led to the balcony.

Zora's voice sounded again. "I've shown you the real me. I want to know if you were impressed. I think I have made it clear I would be a perfect match for you," she confided to her companion before the footsteps trailed back into the room.

"Zora, you're sweet. But as I've said, matching me with someone is my father's idea. I'm not sure I am ready to settle down."

"Your father said you have to choose."

"He's been very adamant about that lately. He won't relent at all."

"So will you choose a bride?"

"Do I have a choice?" Kudar's voice held a hint of frustration.

"A man of your position has many maidens vying for you. I suspect you feel like a fortunate man."

"You would think so though sometimes I'm not so sure."

"Will you choose me, tell me?" Zora pleaded breathlessly.

At Zora's words, Laila straightened her legs and sat up to listen more intently to the couple's conversation. When her feet fell to the ground, her toe bumped the cup she had placed by the leg of the lounge chair. The cup fell over with a clank. She heard Zora gasp. Laila peered over the top of the chair into the room and saw Kudar and Zora standing inside.

"Well...well. Who do we have here?" Kudar asked inquisitively.

"She is just my maid," Zora answered curtly.

As they both stared at her, Laila stood up and stepped beside the chair. When she did, the moonlight behind her caused the outline of her figure to be seen through the nightdress she wore. Every curve on her body seemed to be accented and Kudar did not have to imagine what the small mounds of her breasts looked like as they pressed against the soft material. He looked her over from head to toe.

He took in the way her hair fell free, her dark mysterious eyes, and he noticed that the way she stood caused her nightdress to rest against her shapely legs. In that moment, Kudar thought she was the most seductive woman he had ever seen. His body had a primal reaction to the arousing sight before him. He felt a stirring in his loins and found he could not take his eyes off the beauty in front of him.

The way Kudar gazed at her handmaid was not lost on Zora. At first, she wanted to deny what she was seeing. However, it was impossible to ignore the way Kudar's eyes were leisurely roaming over the slave girl's body. Suddenly, jealousy reared its head in Zora, and in that moment, she hated the beautiful girl.

Kudar rubbed his chin, the sapphire from the ring he wore sparkled in the light. "Have we met before?" he asked Laila with a light knowing smile.

"No. You've never met her." Zora found her voice.

"Does your maid have a name?"

"Her name is Kalilah," Zora snapped impatiently.

"Kalilah? Well, Kalilah, it is very nice to meet you." Kudar continued to grin.

Laila lowered her eyes and curtsied to the Ambassador's son. She thought she should be a little more unnerved by Kudar's bold stare, but found she wasn't. What she was more unnerved about was Zora's anger.

"Zora, be a dear and bring Kalilah to dinner tomorrow night, will you?" Kudar asked gently. "Such a lovely thing should not be shut away. She should get out more."

Zora bit her bottom lip to keep from protesting. "As you wish," came her stiff reply.

Kudar took his eyes off Laila and turned to Zora. "Until tomorrow night," he said. Taking her hand, he bought it to his lips for a kiss then turned and left the room.

Laila stared after Kudar. His lopsided grin still pressed in her mind.

Without warning, Zora's hand slammed across Laila's cheek. The loud smack echoed against the stone walls as Laila's head lurched to the right. Laila brought her hand to her burning cheek. Stunned, she looked at Zora through watery eyes.

"You little tramp!" Zora yelled. "How dare you throw yourself at Kudar! He doesn't want you! You can never mean anything to him! He is a noble wealthy man! You are a lowly servant! You won't be able to move beyond your station! You are a lowly slave and that will always be! Just you remember that, for I will not be outdone by a slave!"

❁

The next night Zora insisted she be dressed in her finest for dinner. After Laila finished assisting her mistress, she started to prepare herself for dinner. She put on her *tunica* which she asked Jamal to have cleaned then returned to her. Then, she put her hair up in a neat bun and held it in place with a hairpin made of ivory.

"You're not going," Zora announced, when it was time to leave the room.

"But, Master Kudar said—"

"Don't worry about Master Kudar. He will be in good hands with me. You will not be there to distract him," Zora replied. "I have worked too long and hard to get Master Kudar's attention to let you steal him away from me."

"What do you mean?" Laila asked.

"Don't play innocent with me," Zora snapped. "There's no way I'm letting you go tonight."

Laila turned from Zora. She couldn't believe she was actually disappointed by Zora's words. She had no intention of trying to seduce Kudar as Zora had accused. It was not as if Kudar was actually interested in her. That was ridiculous. Sure, she had noticed the way he looked at her. But he probably looked at all of the females that way. The facts were he was handsome, rich and obviously used to being forward and getting what he wanted. Laila was sure he was not really interested in her. After all, he was looking for a bride. Someone with wealth and breeding. Since she had neither, she was sure he would never consider her as a potential partner.

Laila turned back to Zora. "Mistress Zora, I am not trying to steal Master Kudar from you. You are overreacting."

"Overreacting?" Zora mocked. Reaching out, she yanked the pin out of Laila's hair, causing the carefully placed locks to fall in disarray about her head. "You've got to learn to respect me and you've got to learn your place! You are not going tonight and that's final!" Zora shrieked, before stalking out of the room.

After Zora left, Laila wanted to cry. However, she did not. She told herself she had to get used to Zora's outbursts. But in truth, she knew she would always hurt inside every time Zora berated her. Laila picked the hairpin off the floor and held it in her hand. An idea came to her. She had someone to talk to now. Vashti would help her find a way to cope. There was no reason why she should be alone instead of with a listening ear. With that in mind, Laila set out to find her new friend.

⚜

Wine flowed freely. Smoke from *hookahs* curled and circled lazily toward the ceiling. Musicians played lively music though no one seemed to be paying attention to them. Kudar took a moment to look around the eatery. He saw his mother was already seated at the women's table on one side of the room. His father sat at the head table talking intently to Ibrahim. He wondered where Zora and her handmaid were as dinner was going to be served soon. He had to admit, for some reason, he could not wait to see how Kalilah would look all dressed up in fancy attire. She had looked so very attractive in only her nightdress.

There was a tap on his arm. He looked down. It was Zora. He took her hand in his. "You look lovely," he said and it was true.

"Thank you." Zora smiled. "I'm glad you approve."

Kudar looked around. "Where is Kalilah?" he asked, scanning the doorway.

"She's not feeling well and cannot be disturbed. She asked that I send her regrets," Zora said smoothly.

A shadow came across Kudar's face. Zora noted it and the fact that he seemed satisfied with her explanation because he did not press the issue further.

Dinner began. It consisted of lamb, beef shish kebab grilled on a skewer, fish, stuffed vine leaves, meze, rice and vegetables prepared in olive oil. After dinner, *muhallebi* was served. Drinks known as *kahve* and *raki*, a grape-flavored brandy, was served as several dervishes appeared and began to perform.

During the performance, Zora looked at Kudar and she thought of her handmaid. Why did Kudar appear attracted to her maid? What did the girl have that she didn't? Zora clutched her fists. There was no way she would be bested by a slave. Not now. Not ever.

✼

When Kudar saw Zora at the next few outings, he suggested she bring her handmaid with her when she had a chance. But, each time, Zora made an excuse as to why her servant could not join them. As her excuses grew, so did her resentment towards her slave and Kudar. While they were attending a javelin tournament, Kudar inquired about her maid once more.

"Why are you so interested in Kalilah?" Zora asked.

"She seems sweet and I hate to think of her confined in that room all day every day," he replied.

"I don't care. Why should you?"

"Zora, what a horrible thing to say. You shouldn't treat her badly," he admonished.

"Maybe you should remember that she's only a slave," Zora snapped back.

"She may be a slave. But that's no reason to treat her badly," Kudar countered.

"Well, she's my slave. I don't see why you're so concerned," Zora bristled.

"It shouldn't matter if she is a slave, should it? She still has feelings. I care about that."

Zora frowned. It was clear there was a female on Kudar's mind. However, it was not her and the very thought of it was humiliating. In that moment, her time with Kudar was no longer enjoyable. Although there were only a few more days until she and her father were to return to their home, Zora decided she wanted to leave the palace right away.

After she left Kudar's side, Zora went to her father and informed him she was ready to return to Karamania immediately.

"Why can't we wait a few more days until–"

"No, Father. I want to leave now," Zora insisted.

"It's such a long journey home."

"That's why we need to start now."

"All right. All right," Ibrahim conceded.

When Zora told Laila they were leaving, Laila was a little surprised. She knew Zora had been excited about having a chance to win Kudar's hand. Now Zora seemed determined to have things packed as soon as possible. Laila wondered what disagreement had come between the two.

Ibrahim's household prepared to depart the palace the very next morning. The caravan contained numerous slaves as well as oxen purchased in Constantinople to help clear and cultivate fields for planting. The cargo consisted of additional items also purchased in Constantinople such as beautiful hand woven rugs, and ceramic plates and bowls with bright mosaic prints. Armed guards encircled the convoy to keep it safe.

Laila watched the Emir impart final orders to the servants and the servants scramble to obey his commands. As if feeling her eyes on him, the Emir turned to her. He peered at her with a lecherous gaze and scanned her body from head to toe. As he examined her, an instinctual foreboding coursed through Laila. Unnerved, she hastily climbed on one of the camels.

As the entourage rode away from the beautiful mansion, Laila couldn't believe she actually felt a twinge of sadness. She had met a nice friend in Vashti there and spent many hours talking with the girl.

Laila thought of the long journey ahead and settled in for the ride as the city slowly faded then disappeared into the distance. Her thoughts soon turned to her family and the fact she was traveling even further from her home. With each passing mile, the hopelessness she felt grew.

"The homesick feelings you feel will fade in time," Jamal predicted.

"I hate living like a slave. Always at someone else's mercy." Laila's voice held a hollow tone.

"You are too delicate emotionally. You are one who is not made for a life of slavery. I see that now. I will watch out for you and try to make things easier for you so that you are not so sad all the time," he promised.

Laila turned from Jamal. She was not interested in any of his promises. What she wanted was to return home and no amount of words were going to change that.

Zora began the trip in a pleasant mood. However, as the day dragged on, her amenable manner deteriorated. Traveling was slow going because Ibrahim had the entourage stop frequently to accommodate her whims. In an attempt to avoid Zora and never be alone with Ibrahim, Laila mingled with the other servants. However, Ibrahim's voice drifted to her ears. She heard him tell Zora the Ambassador had refused to side with him against the Sultan.

As she listened to their conversation, Laila reached in the satchel Jamal had given her and took out a water pouch. She drank from the pouch in order to sooth her parched throat. Afterwards, she rummaged through her satchel and pulled out a *basortu*, which she used to cover her head and protect herself from the sun.

Just before sunset, the caravan stopped for the night. Cramped due to the travel, Laila's feet were wobbly when she stepped to the ground. Some of the servants scurried about putting up tents while others worked to build a fire and make dinner.

Finally, dinner was served.

After dinner, Zora called for Laila, saying she needed assistance. Laila picked up her satchel and entered Zora's tent. It was sweltering inside the tent so Laila took off her head covering, placed it in her satchel then sat the travel bag in the corner.

"It's hot in here," Zora complained. "Come brush my hair. After that, fan me until I fall asleep," she instructed.

Laila brushed Zora's hair then fanned her until she drifted off to sleep.

After Laila was sure Zora was asleep, she left the tent.

The sun had set and a cool breeze started to blow over the earth. Laila walked to the area where the other servants slept and unrolled a pallet on the hard ground. She lowered herself onto the pallet and relaxed.

Just as she was about to drift off to sleep, the sound of horse hooves pounding the earth reached the retired camp. Several servants scrambled to their feet and looked into the darkness for the advancing riders. Ibrahim exited his tent moments before Zora exited her tent.

"What is the meaning of this?" Zora demanded.

"Someone's coming," Ibrahim explained.

Three riders appeared through the night shadows. As they approached, it became obvious that two out of the three were guards from the palace. The rider who was not dressed like a guard was the man Laila remembered seeing the day she arrived at the Ambassador's home. He was Omar, the escort who led her to Zora's quarters. The riders neared those assembled and stopped their horses. The burly men dismounted and walked to Ibrahim.

"What's the meaning of this?" Ibrahim asked.

"We are here on orders from the Ambassador's palace," Omar announced.

"Amir? What does he want?" Ibrahim asked.

"The orders are not from Ambassador Amir. They are from his son, Master Kudar."

"Kudar?" Zora's demure lightened immediately at the mention of Kudar's name. For a moment, she imagined that he had sent for her. After she left the palace without saying goodbye, he must have realized he cared for her, she thought with a sigh of relief. Why had she doubted herself? Why had she doubted Kudar?

"A ring is missing from the palace," Omar stated.

"A ring?" Ibrahim repeated.

"It's a sapphire ring that was personally given to Master Kudar by Sultan Mehmed. Now, it's missing."

"What do you mean? You don't think I took it?" Ibrahim questioned.

"Nay. The palace would never suggest that you personally took the ring. The palace believes that someone in your caravan may have taken it without your knowledge."

"That's outrageous. No one from my contingent would do such a despicable thing. No member of my household would dishonor me or my daughter in such a manner," Ibrahim insisted.

"Then, you won't mind if we search your caravan." Omar nodded toward the guards. "We have our orders."

"But...but..."

Before Ibrahim could finish his protests, the guards began to search the satchels and bags lying around.

Omar walked over to Laila. "Where do you keep your belongings?" he asked her.

"In my travel bag."

"What does it look like?"

"It's brown with carvings etched on the handles."

"Where is it?" He wanted to know.

"In Mistress Zora's tent, in the corner," she answered.

Omar headed for the tent where Zora stood.

"What do you think you're going to find in my tent?" Laila heard Zora question Omar as he approached.

Omar called a guard and the guard walked over to them. "I have my orders," Omar said evenly before disappearing into the tent.

The guard stepped to block Zora when she tried to follow Omar.

"This is outrageous!" Zora protested. "I have never been treated this way in my entire life!"

Ibrahim walked to his daughter and gathered her in his arms. "It'll be all right, daughter. They won't find a thing."

"How could Kudar think that I would ever–?"

Omar exited the tent, causing Zora to stop speaking.

"The ring has been found!" Omar proclaimed boisterously.

"How? Where?" Zora questioned.

Omar pulled his hands from behind his back to reveal the bag he held in his hand.

Laila immediately realized he was holding her travel bag. She watched speechless as he reached into the satchel and pulled out her head covering, followed by a shiny sapphire ring. Her eyes filled with shock and denial as everyone present gasped in unified astonishment. "No... No..." Laila sputtered. "I didn't do it. I didn't steal that ring," she protested as all eyes turned to her.

Zora looked at the ring then at her servant. She could not believe what she was witnessing. How could the girl be so cunning? How dare her maid cause shame on her father and his household? Anger erupted in Zora. As her thoughts shifted from shock to outrage, she reached out, snatched the whip from the holster of the guard who stood in front of her and rushed toward her slave.

"You deceitful thief!" she fumed. Raising her hand above her head, she lifted the whip then brought it down with all her might.

The whip whistled in the wind before its talons curled across Laila's back. Laila stumbled forward. Zora repeated her actions. The whip whirled through the air before its tail once again scratched across Laila's back. She fell to the ground with a horrified scream. Enraged, Zora meted out one stinging blow followed by another. Laila let out a shrill wail of pain as the whip continuously burrowed into her back.

Omar authoritatively pointed to Zora and one of the guards quickly stepped forward. When Zora started to bring her hand down yet again, the guard grabbed her wrist and yanked the whip from her fist.

Breathing hard, her face flushed red, Zora promised, "She will be punished for her thievery. Tell Kudar and his family my father and I are mortified by her actions. I will see to it that she pays dearly for this incident."

"She's to be taken back to the palace to face punishment for her crime," Omar replied.

"What?" Ibrahim cut in.

"I will see to it that she pays for her thievery," Zora protested.

"It's already been decided," Omar countered abruptly.

"I didn't steal anything!" Laila shrieked as she scrambled to her feet. Pain wracked her back. It felt as if she had been stung by a thousand bees. She told herself not to dwell on the ache because she had to make sure the truth was known. "Please listen to me!" Laila stepped toward Ibrahim. "I didn't take that ring! I know nothing about it!"

"Silence!" Zora's answer was followed by a sharp slap across Laila's soft cheek.

The first time Zora had slapped her, Laila had not cried. This time, however, she could not hold back the tears that ran down her face.

"You've ruined everything for us," Ibrahim accused. "Now, neither Amir nor Kudar will send for us again. We will never be asked back to the palace."

"We must leave now," Omar interrupted.

One of the guards came up behind Laila and took hold of her wrist.

"I've been instructed to give you this," Omar said, producing a small pouch from his cloak before handing it to Ibrahim.

Ibrahim opened the pouch and poured several gold coins into his hand. His eyes grew as big as saucers.

"Payment for the loss of your slave," Omar revealed.

Ibrahim passed the bag of coins to Zora who shook the bag then looked inside it.

"Kudar is most generous," she admitted.

"Please express our regrets that this incident happened. We will just brush this nasty event out of our minds." Ibrahim smiled agreeably.

Reaching out, Zora placed her hand under Laila's chin. She tilted Laila's chin upward and peered down her nose at Laila's ashen face. "What is to become of her?" she inquired.

"That will be for Master Kudar to decide," came the answer.

As Zora looked at Laila, a smile curved her lips. "You will get exactly what you deserve," she taunted.

A chill went through Laila at the venom in Zora's tone.

Without further hesitation, the guard nudged Laila forward.

Laila pulled against his grip.

"No! No!" she screeched.

The guard, being stronger than her, dragged her to his horse. Effortlessly, he tossed her on the animal's back before climbing on behind her. He tugged the horse's reins decisively and spurred the steed forward. The horse bade the command and within seconds, Laila found herself heading back the way she had come...back to the palace.

❉

Fear began as a tiny seed in the pit of Laila's stomach. However, it swiftly spread like a deadly sickness until it was practically consuming her insides. The sound of horse hooves hitting the earth was nothing compared to the sound of her own heartbeat. As sand scattered underneath the horses' hooves, Laila realized her hopes and dreams were like the sand, dashed and spread into the darkness...gone forever.

She had heard about Islamic justice. She had heard people could get their hands chopped off if they were caught stealing. Was she to suffer such a fate? She could only imagine the torturous punishment she would receive. Everyone believed she was a thief and wanted her to be punished. No one would care enough to listen to her claim of innocence. How had this happened? How had the ring gotten into her bag?

Laila looked at Omar, who rode on the horse beside her. The moonlight blanketed his stern and emotionless face. It did not seem like he would be interested in hearing her pleas of innocence. In spite of this, Laila felt she had to explain she was not guilty of theft.

"I did not steal that ring!" she blurted out as more tears ran down her face. "There's no way I would do such a thing! I would never steal that piece of jewelry. I swear it!"

He did not acknowledge her.

She tried again. "Please let me go! I did not do this! It's a lie! It's all a big lie!"

Her answer was the steady beat of the horses' hooves.

Laila lowered her head. Her back felt as if it was on fire and throbbed with pain. Suddenly, she was very cold. The night air from the plains whipped across her face, cooling her tears and chilling her to the core. She closed her eyes, wiped away her tears and managed to whisper a prayer for her safety.

On horseback, and with no caravan to slow them, the posse set an incredible pace back to the palace.

Each stride of the horse brought Laila more and more fear, for she was once again leaving the past and heading toward an unknown future.

The palace came into view. It looked magnificent on the hill. Its stone wall seemed to have an alabaster glow against the black night.

Finally, the small band arrived at the palace gates. Laila was assisted off the horse when the animal came to a halt. Several guards walked out. Words were exchanged. The gates opened. Omar took her by the elbow, nudged her forward and they proceeded into the courtyard. He led her through the side door of Kudar's home.

The palace was dark. The click of their shoes echoed on the marble floors. Omar led her down an obsidian hall. As they walked up the flight of stairs, Laila realized he was taking her to the room she had shared with Zora.

Once they made it to the room, Omar opened the door then looked at Laila. Laila stepped into the room. He closed the door behind her leaving her alone in the darkness. Laila leaned against the wooden door. She did not trust her feet to move. When she thought she could move, she slowly walked to the divan and sat on it. The bed was soft and sagged under her weight.

The door to the balcony was open and light from the early morning sun as it slowly awakened the day crept in. A cool breeze gently glided around her. One million terrifying thoughts flashed through Laila's mind. Her thoughts were interrupted as the door creaked opened to the shadowy hallway. After a moment, a figure stepped into the entryway filling it. The early morning light outlined the monumental silhouette of a male. Instinctually, Laila knew it was Kudar.

She felt his gaze on her before she could see his eyes clearly. An uncontrolled shimmer went through her in response to the heat of his predatory scrutiny. When he stepped forward, most of the dark shadows fell away from his face and she was able to see him clearly. He looked exceptionally polished and very pleasing to the eye. He shut the door behind him and took another step into the room.

"Welcome back."

Too much cheerfulness sounded in his voice, Laila thought, though his tone was low and gentle.

"I didn't steal that ring! I didn't put it in my bag!" she started to protest.

"You didn't?"

"No! I don't know how any of it happened! All I know is, I did not put that sapphire ring in my bag!"

"I know," Kudar answered, halting any further assertions.

"What?" Laila asked confused.

"I said, I know you didn't do it, I know you didn't do it because it was me. I am the one who had the ring placed in your bag."

Chapter Five

Wanting to dispel some of the shock in her gaze, Kudar repeated himself. "I know you didn't steal the ring. So you can relax." He sat down on the bed next to her. "The truth is, I am the one who sent Omar and those guards after Ibrahim's caravan. I told Omar to find you and place the ring in your bag. I had to find a way to get you back to the palace. I wanted to see you again."

Kudar expected his revelation to ease Laila's mind. But as he looked at her, it was obvious her mind had not been eased at all. He tried again. "I didn't know you had left the palace until Vashti told me. When I found out, I thought I should do something. You don't need to go back with Zora. I know she doesn't treat you well. I talked to her and she seems very heartless." Kudar stopped talking. He looked at Laila, now covered by soft golden sunlight. She looked very young and extremely vulnerable.

Suddenly, he wanted to take her into his arms and assure her everything would be all right. He wanted to wipe the fear and pain from her expression. He reached out so he could put his arm around her. When his arm touched her back, she pulled away with a soft cry of pain. She turned her back to him as a tear slipped from her eye. In the next instant, she was crying.

"My dear, what is the matter?" Kudar asked, concern evident in his voice. Suddenly, he noticed tears all over her *tunica* and he could see dark bruising on her back. In one quick motion, he ripped her *tunica* apart. "What the...?" Kudar's voice faded as he viewed the sight before him. It was evident why she pulled away when he tried to touch her. Her back was a bed of bruises. Small welts protruded from her skin. It was obvious she had been beaten. Instantly, anger swelled

55

inside him. "Who did this to you?" he demanded. "Kalilah, answer me!"

Laila managed to control her tears. "Zora," she whispered.

"Zora! How could she be so cruel?"

"She thought I stole the ring and that embarrassed her," Laila answered.

"Oh no!" Kudar groaned, realizing the pain his scheme had caused her. "Kalilah." He placed his hands on her upper arm and turned her to him.

She held her head low.

He put his hand under her chin and gently lifted it.

She slowly raised her eyes to his.

"Listen to me, Kalilah. You will never have to be afraid of a beating ever again." Decisively, he stood up and walked to the door. "Omar!" he called loudly.

Instantly, Omar appeared.

"Go get Bella and Yasmine!" he ordered.

A few minutes later, two young maidens appeared. They bowed quickly when they saw Kudar.

"I am putting Kalilah in your care," he told the young women. "Make sure she is well taken care of. See that she is fed and bathed. See that her wounds are tended. Keep me posted on her condition," Kudar instructed as the women motioned for Laila to come to them.

Laila stood and clutching her *tunica* so that it would not fall from her body, she walked to the young women.

"You are excused," Kudar said to the small group.

The maidens bowed and headed from the room.

Laila slowly followed them, leaving Kudar staring after her.

✾

The halls of the palace were still dark as the three women made their way down the corridor. The ladies turned down another hall before heading for two huge wooden doors. Laila remembered seeing the doors before and knew that they led to the harem. One of the doors was opened, the silk curtain pushed aside and the trio stepped into the common living area.

"First, you must refresh yourself," one of the girls began. "I will prepare your bath. After which, we must feed you. I am sure Cook can prepare something–"

"No worries," Laila interrupted. "It is still very early. I don't want you to go through the trouble or get the cook out of bed. I am fine. I am tired though."

"Of course you're tired," the other girl said. "Follow me."

Laila followed her guide to a small room where she was presented with several blankets.

"You can sleep here," the girl whispered, pointing to a bed.

"Thank you," Laila said.

The young maiden smiled then walked away.

Laila arranged the blankets on the small bed and settled into the bedding. She could not help but think about the events of the day. She remembered the wide range of emotions she felt when she saw Omar pull the ring out of her satchel. She commiserated on how terrified she had been as she rode back to Kudar's home. She remembered the feeling of dread she felt as she waited in the dark room.

Then, Kudar walked in.

Despite it all, Laila had to admit, he looked very attractive as he stood before her. He revealed he ordered the ring placed in her bag. He thought he was being clever. Well, as far as she was concerned, he was too sure of himself. Who did he think he was? How dare he put her through such torment!

Laila relaxed a bit as she thought about Kudar's reaction when he saw the bruising on her back. He had informed her she would never have to worry about being beaten again. Laila realized she believed him. At the revelation, calm enveloped her. She turned on her side in the cozy pallet and pulled the sheet to her chin. She yawned and closed her eyes.

As the sun began to peek its head over the horizon…as birds began to chirp their morning chorus…she slowly drifted to sleep.

⌘

Laila was surprised at how she felt about staying in the harem. For the first time in a long time, she felt she could relax – really relax. Bella and Yasmine buzzed about hoping to assist her. However, she sent them away so she could continue to slumber. She woke long enough to eat the nutritious meals they served her before she went back to sleep. She slept for hours at a time, resting her body so it could heal. After a few days, she finally awoke refreshed and ready to face the world.

Vashti, happy to see Laila and eager to help, guided Laila around the harem. As they strolled through the living area, the pair stopped to listen to the music lessons that were in progress. Beautiful music from a lute called a *baglama* and a long-neck lute, similar to the *baglama*, called a *tanbar* reverberated throughout the entire harem. Laila stopped to play with the little girls while their mothers finished the music class. That evening, for the third time that day, there was a call to prayer and Laila watched the women pause to pray.

Laila was so enthralled with settling into her new surroundings, it seemed the next few days flew by. One morning, as she sat in the garden sunbathing, Omar, who she now knew was the chief eunuch in charge of the harem, appeared and announced he had a note for her.

"I wonder who it is from," Laila mumbled to Vashti who lay beside her.

"Read it," Vashti prodded Omar.

Omar unfolded the paper and began reading the document. It was a letter from Kudar requesting Laila's presence in his chambers for dinner that night.

"He wants to see you!" Vashti exclaimed. "Fortune has been favorable to you. You don't have much time to prepare."

"Dinner is not for hours," Laila asserted.

"It takes a lot of time to be properly beautified," Omar acknowledged.

"I'll help her dress. Tell Master Kudar she will honor his request," Vashti assured.

Omar nodded. "I will return for her when it is time. Have her ready."

When Omar left, the women in the harem gathered around her.

"There is nothing to get excited about," Laila declared in response to their chatter.

"There is a lot to do to prime you for a night with Master Kudar," Yasmine spoke up.

"She's right," Bella agreed. "In the harem, our focus is taking care of our Master. It's our only duty and we take it seriously."

"How often do you see Master Kudar?"

"Omar keeps a schedule for us. We take turns. That way it is fair and everything remains even," Vashti explained.

"You will have your night. Then, we will each have a night before you get another audience with him. That is our way," one of the ladies said.

A schedule? What was this, a prison? She had to go to Kudar when she was told it was time? She couldn't see him when she wanted to or not see him if she didn't want to?

"What if I don't want to go and I am scheduled?" she asked the women.

All of the women looked disturbed at the thought.

"Not want to go? You must go. No one has ever said no to the Master."

"We wouldn't dare," was the reply.

"You've only been here a short while so you haven't been taught the rules on how to please the Master. Just be quiet. You don't have to talk much. You are not in his room to give your opinion," one of the women gathered around her spoke.

"Listen to him," Yasmine chimed in. "Even if you are thinking of something else. Act like you love everything he does."

"You pretend with the Master? How could you not love what he does?" Vashti demanded.

"I…I mean…I was just trying to tell her to be very giving in bed," Yasmine stammered.

"I don't think I can do it," Laila revealed.

"First time nervousness," Bella speculated.

"Don't be shy. We've all gone through it. It will be nice. Master Kudar is a very giving lover," Vashti confessed.

If it were possible, Laila turned beet red at Vashti's words.

Vashti led Laila to a table and gave her a small snack to eat.

Once the food was consumed, Laila's nails were trimmed. Next, she was taken to a table in the corner of the patio and instructed to lay across it in preparation for a massage. Lavender smelling lotion was applied to her body and she was given a deep tissue massage that melted away all of her tension.

Following the massage, Laila was taken to the *hamam* and a bath was drawn for her. The water was sprinkled with lavender and lilacs. The soft fragrance filled the room as Laila disrobed and stepped into the luxurious bath. She soaked in the bath and her hair was washed and her body scrubbed.

When the bath was over, she felt refreshed and clean. Her hair was dried, straightened then styled into a ponytail that flipped at the end.

Once that was done, Vashti took her to a room filled with beautiful clothes. Laila was in awe when she saw the many beautiful garments made of silk, cotton and satin. She let her hand run over the material. There were shirts called *gomleks*, vests called *cepkens* and pants called *salvars*. There were caftans and outergarments known as *uceteks*. All were different

sizes and available in a beautiful rainbow of colors –
some red, green, purple.

"You may choose anything from this room," Vashti
revealed.

After browsing through the garments, Laila chose a
silk *gomlek* and a green *cepken*. The *cepken* was
embroidered with blue thread and had tiny strings that
tied it together in the valley between her breasts. She
chose green ankle length *salvars* which she belted with
a gold *kusak* before sliding her feet into slippers called
cariks. For the final touch, her eyes were outlined with
a thin charcoal colored liner. Balm was applied to her
lips just before Omar appeared.

"Very impressive," the eunuch said when he saw
Laila. "I trust you are ready."

Laila nodded her head.

Omar led her out of the harem and up a flight of
steps to a part of the palace she had not seen before.
The chief eunuch stopped in front of a door, opened it,
then nudged Laila inside the room.

Though her head was bowed, Laila managed to
notice details of the room. The chamber was spacious
with several columns separating the large opulent
space. There was an enormous bed in the middle of
the marble floor which Laila could not ignore. Across
the room, an open door led to a balcony. In the corner
of the balcony, there was a table set with food. Plush
red pillows lay around it.

"You may rise," a deep male voice rumbled.

Laila straightened herself and saw Kudar standing
at a table in a small alcove in the corner of the room.
He seemed even more handsome than she
remembered. He wore a white *gomlek* which was open
down the front exposing his muscular chest, and he
had on a pair of loose fitting trousers.

"You look beautiful," he commented. "Would you
like something to drink?" Without waiting for an answer,
he picked up a chalice and began to pour the drink into
two goblets. "Come," he instructed.

A lump caught in Laila's throat when Kudar turned to look at her.

"You're not afraid of me are you, Kalilah?" he asked.

Laila shook her head, walked to him, then took the goblet from his outstretched hand. She raised the cup and wine touched her lips.

"Are you hungry? I am famished. Let us partake of the meal," Kudar suggested.

Laila stepped forward and walked to the balcony. Kudar followed her. They sat on the lush pillows around the table and looked toward the city, which could be seen the in the distance. When Laila began eating, she found the food tasted as delicious as it smelled and the meat was so tender it practically fell off the bone. Kudar attempted small talk during the meal. However, Laila had a hard time focusing on any of his words. Her thoughts lingered on what the maidens in the harem told her about their nights with Kudar.

"Has everything here in the palace been to your liking, Kalilah?" Kudar asked her after the meal.

"Aye. Everything has been wonderful. I have never seen such beautiful clothes in my life. It took me forever to choose a garment to wear to dinner tonight."

Kudar chuckled. "I'm glad you were impressed. I wanted to wait until I knew you were feeling better before I called you. How about your back? Has it healed?"

"Aye, I think so."

"Let me see," Kudar prodded.

Laila looked at him for a moment before she turned her back to him. She untied the tie of her *cepken* then slowly unfastened her *gomlek*. Careful to keep her chest covered, she let the vest and shirt fall down her back.

"Um…Everything looks all right," Kudar said as his fingers lightly traced her back. After a short pause, he added, "You are as beautiful as the first day I saw you."

Laila turned her head to look at him. "You remember seeing me at the auction house?"

"Of course. I remember seeing a lot of you that day," Kudar replied as a mischievous grin spread over his inviting lips.

In response, Laila's expression turned to a scowl and Kudar felt her stiffen then start to pull away from him. Impulsively, he slid his arm around her waist and pulled her to him. She fell back into his arms. He bent his head and kissed her gently on the mouth.

When his mouth touched hers, an explosion of heat oozed through him and an uncontrollable moan escaped from his throat. He had been dreaming about this moment since the day she had been brought back to the palace. Now that his lips were on hers, his body reacted strongly to the touch of her soft, yielding lips.

"Don't be afraid," he chided when he felt a shudder go through her. "It will be nice for the both of us," he whispered, then kissed her again expectantly.

In Kudar's imagination, she had been very willing. In his imagination, she had responded with a moan and eagerly wrapped her arms around his neck. Now, however, she lay completely still in his embrace. Lifting his head, he asked, "Why won't you kiss me back?"

Laila did not answer. Instead, she pushed away from him.

Quickly, tying her vest together, she rose and walked to the balcony wall. She turned her back to him and looked out toward the city at the pink and purple light that canvassed the sky in wake of the setting sun.

"Answer me," Kudar demanded.

At the sound of his impertinent tone, Laila turned to face him and found her voice. "Why are you pretending this is about me?" she questioned.

"What?"

"Look. I've faced it. None of this is about me. "It's about you and what you want. I do not have a say. You wanted to kiss me. So, I let you kiss me."

"You *let* me kiss you?

"What more do you want from me?"

"I want you to kiss me back. I want you to enjoy it as much as I do."

"Enjoy it? I don't know you. Why would I want to kiss you and make love to you? If you want someone who feels privileged to be in your bed, you want one of the other women in your harem. You don't want me."

For a moment, Kudar was taken aback by Laila's frankness. But he decided he wanted to hear what she had to say, even if he may not like it. After all, she was now talking which was more than she had done during dinner.

"I've been told I'm a very giving lover," Kudar admitted. "I'm sure you will like it."

"If I don't have a choice, does it matter? How is being here in your palace any different than being a slave to Zora? I didn't have a choice then, and I don't have a choice now. You want me to be like one of your many love slaves who give you their bodies when you want it. That's not what I want. When I make love, I want to be in love first."

Kudar chuckled. "That's nonsense. What does love have to do with anything? I see to it that you have a place to live and nice things to keep you comfortable. In return, we give each other pleasure. That makes the most sense."

"If I wanted that kind of relationship, I would have married the boy my parents picked out for me back home," Laila protested.

"You compare me to a boy?" Kudar scoffed as he stood to his feet. "You compare *this* to what you have back home." He swept his arms about. "You had nothing this nice at home and no boy can treat you as good as I can."

"I want to choose who I love. I want to choose who I kiss."

In a few strides, Kudar was at her side. He turned her to face him. "You should want to kiss me," he explained.

"Well, I don't!" Laila retorted. Why did he think she would be so eager to jump into his bed? His arrogance was beyond belief! "Why should I want to kiss a man who's kissed a multitude of girls before me?" she countered in a steely voice.

"This is why..." Kudar grumbled as he drew her hard against his chest and lowered his head to her.

This time, when his lips met hers, an unexpected bolt of heat seared Laila's lips. Her legs suddenly felt weak. She could not help but lean into Kudar for support as a wave of untamed attraction coursed through her being. As her body melted into his, she felt the evidence of his desire.

"You can't tell me that kiss did not affect you. I know you felt what I did," Kudar rasped when their lips parted.

Laila shook her head breathing deeply. "No. It did not affect me," she managed to say.

"You're lying," Kudar countered, now that his prowess had been challenged.

"I'm not lying!"

"Oh? Just *lusting* for me?" he questioned.

Laila blushed and pulled away from him. She had to step away from Kudar. Being so close to him was clouding her thoughts. Not only was she having trouble thinking, she was having trouble taking her eyes off his enticing lips. She stepped sideways in an attempt to move past him. But Kudar stepped to block her path.

"I can see it in your eyes," he noted. "The truth is, you want me just as much as I want you."

Laila shook her head in repudiation. "Why should I want you? You don't even know my real name," she bristled.

"Well, what's your real name?"

"Laila," she replied.

"Lay-la, huh?"

She nodded.

Without warning, Kudar scooped her into his arms. Laila gasped in astonishment as her slippers fell silently from her feet and her arms settled around his neck. With long strides, he made it to his enormous bed in the middle of the room then dropped her on it. A moment later, he stretched out over her. Through the dim light, he looked down at her with a smoldering gaze. Her vest, which had been hurriedly clasped together now fell open, partially exposing one of her cinnamon colored breasts.

"Well, Lay-la, I want you," Kudar whispered, before crushing his lips over hers. His hand, which had been on her leg, slid over her thigh and stomach, then under her vest to the silk that covered her breasts. His large hand cupped one of her small breasts as he caressed the material draped over the soft mound. He felt her nipples hardened under his palm.

Once again, Laila lay completely still beneath him, refusing to respond to his touch. He held her for a few seconds more before he released her with an irritated curse. "I won't force you," he explained solemnly.

Laila hastily clutched her vest together.

"One day, you will come to me and admit that you want me just as much as I want you," he vowed.

"No, I won't," Laila managed breathlessly as she sat up.

"The day will come when you will choose to give yourself to me. You will beg me to make love to you."

"Never!" Laila insisted as she slid from the bed and rushed toward the door.

"Why do you think you were brought back to my harem?" Kudar called after her.

His answer was the sound of her bare feet against the marble, then the slam of the door as she made her exit.

✄

Kudar was alone and he did not like it. Her lavender scent still lingered in his bed. Since the day Laila fell into his arms, he had not expected it, but his mind had been invaded by thoughts of her. During her recuperation, each day that passed increased his anticipation to see her again. Finally, after Omar reported she was up and about, he waited one more day, then he summoned her. He planned an evening of drinking, eating and seduction. Followed by a night of loving. But, it had not work out that way. Laila had different ideas.

Kudar brooded. How could she resist him? She should have been melting underneath him. Didn't she know she belonged to him and he had the power to make her succumb to him whether she wanted to or not? Even as he thought it, he knew that wasn't what he wanted. He didn't want Laila to give herself to him out of fear or obligation.

Earlier, she had revealed what it would take to make her consent. She said she wanted to be in love first…to choose who she made love to. Where had she gotten such crazy ideas? He didn't know. But it was obvious, if she could not choose for herself, she would not be willing. Truth be told, Kudar did not want her unless she was willing. He had never forced himself on anyone before and he wasn't about to start now.

For Laila the answer was, *She had to be in love.* For Kudar the question was, *What was he going to do about it?*

Chapter Six

Laila touched her lips. She was still reeling from the effects of Kudar's kiss as she hurried back to the harem. Why was she so flustered by his touch? Laila shook her head. She didn't want to ponder the question too long because she wasn't sure she was prepared to deal with the answer.

The women in the harem were surprised to see her return that night. They swarmed around her and began asking a million questions.

"Not to worry. You'll have plenty of time to get your bearings. You won't be called to see Kudar for at least a week," Vashti assured.

As Laila settled in her pallet for the night, she tried to push thoughts of Kudar's kiss out of her mind. Those tasty lips...she must forget them. Those smoldering brown eyes...the touch of his hand as it trailed up her thigh... She had to forget about the moment he touched her breast...and she especially had to forget the way her body wanted to react to his touch.

But, as the night deepened, Laila found it impossible to ignore thoughts of Kudar.

✄

The next morning as Laila ate breakfast, Omar appeared with a note from Kudar. The note requested her presence again that evening. Word of Kudar's invitation to Laila spread like wildfire through the harem. Vashti, Yasmine and Bella appeared to investigate.

"This is highly irregular. You must have really impressed him in bed last night," Yasmine deduced. "Why else would Master Kudar call you again?"

"It wasn't like that," Laila protested.

The other girls did not say a word. They just looked at her suspiciously.

Laila was dressed and waiting when Omar came for her. The eunuch led her from the harem to Kudar's chambers as he had the previous night. Laila entered Kudar's room and bowed.

"You may rise," he said to her.

When she did, approval shown in his eyes as he took in the sight of her. She had on ruby colored *salvars* with burnt orange thread woven through the material and a matching top. Her onyx colored hair fell about her shoulders.

"Laila, you do not have to bow when you enter my chambers."

"Yes, Master," she replied as she straightened herself.

"I hope I didn't offend your sensibilities last evening," Kudar began. "Let's begin anew. Come," he took her hand in his. He led her through the palace to the place where the food was prepared. "I've sent the servants away. The cooking area is completely ours for the night," he revealed.

"Why?" Laila asked.

"Because I'm going to make dinner for you."

"What? *You* make dinner for me?"

"You sound surprised."

"I am."

"Well, you shouldn't be." Kudar rolled up his sleeves. "I'm a great cook," he explained.

Kudar quickly took charge of the dinner preparation. Laila offered to wash and chop the potatoes and onions while Kudar seasoned and grilled the meat. Soon, the whole room smelled of the spicy meat that simmered over the fire. The couple talked and laughed as the food roasted.

Laila's stomach growled. "Everything smells so good. It's making me hungry," she declared.

"I hope you enjoy the meal," Kudar said as he began to cut fruit and place it on a platter.

"Do I need to put the plates and bowls on the table?"

"I've got all of that taken care of...you'll see." Kudar grinned cryptically before he picked up a chalice and poured the wine. "Would you like something to drink?" He held out a goblet.

Laila walked to him and took the goblet from him. Their fingers touched briefly.

As she sipped her drink, Laila realized Kudar was devouring her with his gaze. That knowledge sent an unexpected spark of attraction to her toes.

"You look absolutely beautiful," he said, after studying her curvaceous body.

Laila let her eyes roam his body for a moment and thought she could say the same thing about him.

"I hope you're hungry because dinner is ready," Kudar announced sometime later. He held out an arm for her. Laila wrapped her hand around his upper arm and he led her to the courtyard.

When Laila stepped into the courtyard, she saw that one of the tables had already been beautifully set. It was covered with a plum colored cloth and decorated with colorful flowers. Two candles flickered in the center of the table.

"Master Kudar, this is so nice. Did you do this?"

"For you, I did. Do you like it?"

"Aye," Laila assured.

"I'm glad you like it," Kudar admitted. "Have a seat," he instructed.

After Laila was seated, Kudar returned to the cooking area and reappeared carrying food on serving platters. When he sat down, he said, "*Afiyet olsun*. May what you eat bring you well being."

Laila smiled and they began to eat.

As they had during the meal preparation, the pair talked easily to one another and found themselves laughing over the smallest things. Their easy conversation continued while they devoured the meal and the warm evening evolved into night.

"*Elinize saglik*," Laila replied, repeating the words Vashti had taught her. "Bless your hand. Everything was wonderful. Thank you for cooking dinner for me," she purred sweetly before she ate the last bit of fruit off the platter.

Kudar reached his hands across the table and beckoned her to place her hands in his. She did. He closed his powerful hands over hers and looked into her eyes.

As their eyes met, Laila felt a flutter in her stomach. She looked away.

When she did, Kudar raised his finger and traced the outline of her lips. He whispered, "You have beautiful lips. I like kissing them."

"I don't go around kissing strangers," Laila replied.

"Then you should get to know me. That way, I will no longer be a stranger."

"You think it will be easier to get me into your bed that way, don't you?" she prodded.

"You catch on fast," Kudar responded.

"It's going to take a lot more than dinner to get me in bed with you," Laila retorted.

"Too bad," he answered with a piteous expression.

Laila couldn't help but laugh. "I don't want to go to bed with someone unless we love each other and are committed to one another," she explained, after she had recovered enough to speak.

"I faced it a long time ago. No relationship lasts forever," Kudar affirmed.

"How can it if you're sleeping with more than one woman?" Laila countered. "Besides, you don't want to be committed to just one woman."

"I don't?"

She shook her head negatively.

"You think you've got me figured out, don't you, Laila?" he grimaced.

71

"Well, let's just say, I had a lovely dinner and I thank you for it. But, I'm looking for more than you can offer me."

"Because you want your man to be exclusively committed to you?"

Laila nodded affirmatively.

Kudar smirked. "I can't believe you really think that kind of a relationship is actually possible."

"It's not possible for me and you. I can assure you of that," Laila declared.

Kudar was silent for a moment, then he said, "Who knows. Maybe I'm willing to try out this new type of relationship you speak of. Maybe I am up for the challenge." Truth be told, Laila was already a challenge...a very attractive challenge with a sharp wit, which he found very appealing. "You say we can never be because I can't offer you what you want. However, I don't think you honestly believe that," he mused.

"Aye. I do."

"Really? Then why won't you look into my eyes?" he wanted to know.

Laila cleared her throat.

"You don't have to answer. Just be ready tomorrow at noon," he instructed.

"Tomorrow at noon? Why?"

"Because we are going to spend some more time together...so you can get to know me." Kudar paused. After a moment, he said, "You know...I think I am going to like letting you get to know me."

"Why do you say that?"

"Well, once you get to know me, you'll learn some interesting things about me."

"Like what?"

"Like, I don't clear away dishes. Do you know what that means?" he asked standing to his feet.

"No, what does it mean?"

"It means, you'll have to clear away the dishes all by yourself," he said with a wink. Then, he disappeared inside the palace before Laila could utter a word of protest.

The next morning, another note arrived for Laila. This time Kudar requested she join him for lunch in his study. When Laila arrived in Kudar's office, he was sitting at his desk working on a drawing.

"You are very good," she said, as she viewed his work.

"Thank you. I find my work very fulfilling," he replied with a smile.

"I was a little surprised that you called for me again," she admitted as she settled in the seat in front of his desk and curled her feet in her lap.

"I told you I would."

"Vashti and the girls were shooting me dirty looks when I left the harem. I think they are officially jealous of me. Omar keeps a schedule which charts the days we spend with you. By sending for me so many days in a row, you are messing up the schedule."

"I don't care about that damn schedule. This is my life. I should be able to spend time with the woman I want. If I want to spend time with you, I will."

As Kudar finished speaking, lunch arrived.

While they ate, he said, "Tell me about yourself. Where are you from?"

Laila sipped her drink then began to tell her history. "I was born in Egypt. Cairo is my home. I lived with my mother. She has two sisters." After Laila said the words, she realized she hadn't thought much about her home since she had been brought back to Kudar's abode. She lowered her eyes. "I wonder if they still think of me. My fondest memories are of the hours I spent at the Nile River. There was a place there; I called it my hideout. It is by our village along the river where the river starts to bend. There is a huge rock formation that jets out over the water. I use to go there to spend time alone and think. It was definitely my favorite place." As memories came flooding back to Laila, her heart became heavy. "That abductor took it all away from me."

"What happened?"

"I was at the river…at my hideout. I fell asleep and when I woke up, the slaver was upon me. My mother told me not to go to the river that day, and I had a feeling something was wrong, but I went anyway. I was taken from my home and put on the auction block. It was horrible. I was stripped and humiliated on that block."

Seeing the expression on Laila's face made Kudar determine to erase all of her bad memories.

She continued, "As you know, I was sold to Ibrahim and became a handmaid to Zora, which was dreadful."

"What do you mean?"

"I'm not sure why. But Zora never liked me. She treated me very badly from the first day I met her. Whenever she had the chance, she would try to humiliate me. She told me I was a slave and would always be a slave."

"You poor thing," Kudar comforted. "Zora is spoiled, smug and vain. You never have to worry about her again," he promised, deciding he would protect Laila from any further hurt or harm.

✄

A short time later, they retired to Kudar's chambers and talked the afternoon away. That evening, Kudar said, "Come, there's somewhere I want to take you."

"Where?"

"You'll see. Follow me."

Kudar led her out of the palace to the courtyard. When they exited through the gate of the compound, they were met by a stable hand holding the reins of two horses.

"What's going on here?" Laila inquired.

"We're going to ride into the city."

"What?"

"You heard me. Can you ride a horse?"

"Yes."

"Then hop on," Kudar instructed.

Laila took the sash that was around her waist and tied her hair into a ponytail. The stable hand helped her on the smaller horse while Kudar climbed on the larger one. Kudar spurred his steed forward and Laila followed.

As the sun started to set, the pair rode over fields as warm wind curled about their faces and through their hair. Kudar rode ahead of Laila then brought his horse in stride alongside hers.

"You're a good rider," she acknowledged.

"I've been riding since before I can remember," Kudar answered.

As distance continued to separate the riders from the palace Laila asked, "Why wasn't your family's home built inside the city? Why was it built so far out of the city?"

"That was my father's decision. He said he didn't want to make his home inside Constantinople since it's a Christian city and does not fall under Ottoman rule."

"I am a Christian."

"Are you?"

"Um hum. Some missionaries came to our village when I was born. I was even named after one of them."

"Interesting. My mother was a Christian," Kudar revealed.

"Really?"

"Yes."

"I heard your family is close to the Sultan."

"My father was close with the Sultan's father, Murad. He was a slave of Murad's but worked hard and became very successful. It's because of him I work as an architect for the current Sultan, Mehmed. One day, I hope to be as successful as my father."

"You seem to admire your father very much," Laila noted.

Kudar shrugged his shoulders. "He's a good man." Then, changing the subject he called out, "Last one to the city is a loser!" before prodding his horse into a gallop.

"Master Kudar!" Laila squealed as she started her horse into a sprint after him.

※

Laila and Kudar made it to Constantinople as the moon settled in the sky. The couple tethered their horses and began a leisurely stroll down the cobblestone streets. The first time Laila had arrived in Constantinople, she had been too preoccupied to enjoy the scenery. The last time she passed through the city, she had not been able to really look around. Now, for the first time, she had a chance to appreciate the surrounding splendor.

Massive walls surrounded the city. Christian flags undulated in the breeze from tall towers spaced at intervals along the walls. Kudar pointed out the fashionable blachernae quarter that had been built between the Great Wall and the harbor. As they strolled along the street, he also pointed out the Greek and Roman influences in the city. Kudar led her by one of the city's most prominent Byzantine structures, a church called St. Sophia. He talked about the unique architecture on the building, noting the Christian crosses and impressive frescoes and mosaics. After a while, he led her to an inlet of land by the harbor.

As they looked out over the vast green blue water, he said, "This harbor is called Golden Horn."

"It's beautiful," Laila remarked of the ships that floated lazily by.

"The calm before the storm. It's said Sultan Mehmed will one day declare war on this city. The emperor, Constantine XI Dragases, seems to be too young to realize he should take the threat seriously."

"If there is a war, who do you think will win?"

"There have been many attempts by different forces to besiege Constantinople. None of them succeeded. But this time, I think the Christians may be underestimating Sultan Mehmed. After all, he is not called The Conqueror for no reason."

The couple walked to an eating establishment by the sea and ordered dinner. During the meal, the conversation flowed smoothly. After dinner, the pair continued their scenic stroll along the streets. When they stopped to listen to a musician play, Laila realized she and Kudar were holding hands. It had been such a natural occurrence she had not realized when it happened.

While the pair rode back to the palace, Laila thought about the evening she had shared with Kudar. She realized she felt a twinge of regret that their time together was coming to an end.

They made it back to the palace and dismounted. A stable hand appeared to take the horses' reins.

"I had a very good time," she admitted, after the horses were led away.

"I'm glad," Kudar answered as they stepped in the courtyard which was washed in light from the buildings surrounding it.

"I can only imagine what the girls in the harem are thinking," Laila commented as they strolled toward the house. "They probably think we were rolling around in bed this whole time."

"If I had my way, that's exactly where we'd be."

"Master Kudar!" Laila exclaimed. "You don't know me well enough for that."

"I hope to remedy that soon."

When Laila reached out to open the palace door, Kudar clasped her arm and turned her to face him. Embraced by shadows, Laila looked up at him and she felt her heart skip a beat. Kudar leaned forward. Laila stepped backward, only to have her back bump against a cold stone wall. She pushed her hands against Kudar's chest to halt his advance.

He abandoned his advance and gazed down at her. Smiling, he reached for the sash that held her hair and gingerly tugged it. When the sash unraveled, Laila shook her head, causing her locks to untangle and fall about her shoulders. A look of desire emerged in Kudar's eye, and without a word, he slid his arms around her waist. Tenderly, he pulled her to him. Laila wrapped her arms around his neck before she realized it.

Kudar smiled then lowered his lips toward hers.

Laila quickly turned her face from him and his lips brushed her cheek.

Slowly, his lips trailed across her cheek and down her neck. "Let me kiss you," he whispered.

Laila shook her head. "I'm not ready for that."

Kudar kissed her neck again. His touch stirred an unexpected craving deep within her. Unnerved by the feeling, Laila pulled away from him. However, Kudar prevented her exit by placing his hands on the wall, entrapping her between his arms.

Leaning in so that his lips were very close to hers, he said, "We kissed before and it was nice. Let's do it again."

"I'm not the type of girl who gives herself without requiring anything in return," Laila reminded him.

"You're a strange creature. You know that? Beautiful but strange." His finger trailed up the side of her arm and traced a lock of hair at the side of her face. "I will have you."

Laila swatted his hand away and shook her head. "You're so sure of yourself."

Kudar nodded his head in agreement. "In time you will choose me. One day you will want to make love to me."

"Will I?"

He didn't answer her. Those amber eyes of his just looked hungrily down at her.

Laila lingered a moment more. Then, she slid underneath his outstretched arm, turned and sauntered inside as Kudar's gaze followed her.

The night air felt placating to Amir al Numan when he exited the massive doors of his home. Light from the surrounding buildings illuminated the cobblestone courtyard forcing shadows against the palace walls. Cloaked by darkness, Amir leisurely sipped wine from his goblet and stared up at the brilliant stars in the blue black sky.

After a while, he heard the compound's gate open. He looked toward the entryway and saw Kudar and a female companion walk into the courtyard. In an attempt to get his son's attention, Amir raised his hand and opened his mouth. Instinctively, sound died in his throat and he lowered his hand when he saw Kudar reach out and caress the female's arm.

Amir backed deeper into the shadows and silently watched the pair. Even from his vantage point, he could see the enraptured desire in his son's eyes. He watched his son reach up and tug the sash that held the girl's hair away from her face. Then, he saw Kudar slide his arm around the female's petite waist and draw her to his chest.

A glower enveloped Amir's countenance when he realized Kudar's consort was the handmaid he had heard so much about. The female's name had flown around the compound like wildfire the moment Kudar began to spend every day with her. Amir shook his head in disapproval as he watched the couple immersed in an embrace. The vixen. She was a new unwelcomed distraction that needed to be dealt with.

Amir let his thoughts wander for a moment. He thought back to the days when he had been a slave. As a slave, he experienced prejudice and discrimination but managed to rise above his station to gain riches and respect. He did not want Kudar to ever experience the prejudice he experienced as a slave.

So far, he had succeeded in preventing Kudar from being stigmatized by his past. To ensure that never happened, he wanted his son to find a Turkish bride…one whose family had a long history of freedom and affluence. By joining the families, Amir was certain that then and only then would his dishonorable past be fully erased.

Amir brought his attention back to the present. His eyes narrowed as he focused them on Laila. He had to stop this infatuation before it began. No one could get in the way of the plans he had for his son. No one. Not even the curvaceous beauty from the Nile.

"Father? How are you?" Kudar asked in greeting when his father walked into his study the next morning.

"I'm fine, son. How are you?" Amir inquired.

"Great!"

"You've been working hard?"

"Yes."

"Let me see some of your latest sketches."

Kudar picked up a few drawings from his desk and handed them to his father. "What do you think?" he asked eagerly.

Amir was silent as he mulled over Kudar's work. Finally, he said, "These are really good, son. You are very talented."

Kudar smiled, encouraged by his father's words. "It pleases me to know you approve."

"Of course. I know I can count on you to bring honor to the al Numan name in your work...and in your personal life. You make me very proud. Kudar, you have been a good son. The son of my dreams. One day you will have many strong sons of your own who will carry on our family's name. Once that happens, I will be content.

Before any of that can happen, you must choose a proper bride, a Muslim girl of Turkish descent. A wife who will bring honor to our family by her impeccable breeding and commitment to the Ottoman way of life. I look forward to that day..."

Amir let his words trail off when he saw the contemplative look on his son's face. It appeared his

words were having the desired affect. So there was no
need to continue.

✂

Laila fell back on the soft scarlet pillows with a
playful sigh. Kudar followed her lead and settled next to
her. The couple had finished eating yet another tasty
dinner together on the balcony off Kudar's room. They
had spent hours talking as the sun set. Now, the moon
was high in the sky.

"Look at all the stars in the sky. I think it's a
beautiful night," Kudar commented as a soothing
breeze caressed them both.

"Me too," Laila agreed.

Kudar raised himself on his elbow and looked down
at her. She looked beautiful and inviting as he peered
into her captivating eyes. He leaned down to kiss her.
She turned her face from him.

"Why won't you give me a kiss?"

"Because we can never be," Laila replied.

"If that's true, then one kiss won't change anything,
right?"

"I…I guess not," Laila acceded.

"Well, then, I'm going to kiss you now…" Kudar's
voice trailed off as he pressed his lips against hers.

When Kudar lowered his head this time, Laila did
not turn away. She shyly accepted his kiss. Slowly, a
searing heat built between them and flickered into a
red-hot flame. Its hypnotic power caused Laila to
submit to its alluring intensity. She returned Kudar's
kiss, wrapped her arms around his neck and pulled him
to her. She ran her fingers through his curly hair just as
she had been wanting to do.

"I want you. I have to have you," Kudar's voice was
husky when their lips parted. Intertwining his fingers in
hers, he lifted her arms above her head before he
lowered his lips and grazed at the base of her neck.

Laila felt Kudar's manhood harden against her thigh. She heard a moan and realized the sound had escaped her throat. She writhed under him. His lips hungrily met hers again, heightening an unexpected yearning within her. She pushed against Kudar's chest to stave the amorous fervor that heated her flesh.

"Let's not stop." Kudar nuzzled his nose against hers.

"We should not be doing this," Laila whispered.

"You kissed me back and it was nice."

"Too nice."

"I always enjoy it when we're together, Laila. The more I see you, the more I want to see you. The more I touch you..." He tenderly caressed her arm before placing a soft kiss on her shoulder.

"You're not making it easy," she acknowledged.

Kudar raised his head and looked down at her. Long lashes covered sultry eyes. Her lips were swollen and slightly moistened from their kiss. He kissed her one last time then started to raise himself to a sitting position.

Laila tugged on his wrist causing him to turn back to her.

"Where are you going?" she asked.

"Sweet one, you win. If you want me to continue to act honorably, we'd better call it a night."

Laila glanced down and viewed the evidence of his discomfort.

When he turned away from her again, she said, "Don't go."

"Lovely Laila, I can't kiss you and touch you all over and expect myself to stop. If I stay here next to you, I am going to want to make love to you. I know that's not what you want," he explained.

"You think you can't stop yourself? That's because you're not used to being told no. But, you can control yourself, if you try," Laila declared.

"You think so, huh?"

"Yes. You just have to put your mind to it. You can learn that you don't have to give into temptation," she assured.

"Why do I have a feeling you're going to teach me?" Kudar replied with a grimace.

Chapter Seven

In the months that followed, the couple relished the hours they spent in each other's company. Kudar spent hours during the day teaching her to speak Turkish. In the evening, they took long leisurely walks. During this time, Laila continued to open up to Kudar. She shared more information about her old life and he listened intently. She told him the name of her village and described in greater detail the location of her home. Kudar pulled out a map, and based on her description, he showed her where she lived in relation to Constantinople.

One morning, after an enjoyable horseback riding excursion, the couple stopped along a secluded area by the sea. Kudar helped Laila down from her horse. A blanket was spread out and the couple prepared for lunch. As they ate their food, they admired the chromatic water that sparkled as blue as the sky. After the meal was consumed, the duet was lulled to sleep by the sound of the somniferous waves.

Laila woke before Kudar and lured by the amethyst water, shed herself of everything but her undergarments and walked into the warm, soothing water. Smiling, she waded out a few feet then ducked underneath the refreshing balm.

Kudar awoke a few minutes later and seeing Laila's discarded garb lying next to him, he reached out and picked up an article of her clothing. Looking out over the water, he smiled when he saw her treading near the shore. Without taking his eyes off her, he quickly shed himself of his attire and headed into the water.

When Laila saw Kudar wading toward her, she smiled at him.

"You're seducing me. You know that, don't you?" he called to her.

"What?" she called back.

"I said, you're seducing me. You know that, right? Of course you do."

"What?" she called out again.

Knowing Laila could hear him perfectly fine, Kudar sighed, grinned amiably then submerged his body below the water's surface. Moments later, he emerged next to her and pulled her gently into his arms. Laila squealed in teasing protest and squirmed playfully in his embrace. Her breasts brushed against his chest.

He moaned. "You know you are seducing me...and I'm letting you do it," he affirmed.

"I know no such thing," Laila replied.

"How could you not know it? You are a beautiful woman, Laila. Inside and out. I've never met anyone as interesting as you. There's no other person in the world I would rather be with."

"You're just saying that," Laila accused. But in truth, she couldn't help but acknowledge to herself that Kudar did indeed care for her.

At the dawning of this revelation, Laila placed her lips timidly against his. In response to her provocation, Kudar drank from her lips.

After several moments, Laila pushed away from him slightly, realizing she was finding it hard to catch her breath.

Kudar looked down at her with a playful grin. "Don't worry. None of the girls I kiss can catch their breath either. It's due to the fact I'm such a good kisser," he explained with a cocky air.

Laila squealed and splashed water on him.

He laughed merrily and lovingly drew her back to him. As their bodies pressed together, there was no mistaking the craving that arose in him.

Laila felt butterflies in her stomach in response to his body's reaction. It was her turn to moan. Blushing, she stepped from him. "Oh my. I shouldn't kiss you. It's getting harder and harder to resist you."

"Then don't resist me."

"I don't want to send you the wrong message."

"You've made your views on my advances perfectly clear. I've always respected your wishes, haven't I? Today will be no different. Nothing will happen unless you want it to happen. I promise."

Abruptly, Laila turned from him and waded back to shore. Dripping with water, she knelt on the blanket then turned and lay on her back. In an attempt to block the brilliance of the resplendent sun, she draped her left arm over her eyes. Kudar approached and she felt the sandy ground sag as he knelt on the blanket beside her.

"May I see your hand?" he asked, before taking her right hand in his.

Laila opened her eyes and saw Kudar looking down at her with a pleased smile on his face. He began to knead the palm of her hand.

"I want to help you relax," he explained as his hands leisurely eased their way up her arm. After a few minutes, he took her left arm and affectionately caressed and stroked her limb. He transitioned to her neck and applied moderate pressure with his fingertips. "Relax," he whispered.

Laila closed her eyes and listened to the sound of the serene waves as Kudar's fingers continued to knead her body with exquisite skill. Slowly, a peaceful sensation engulfed her and all remaining resistance dwindled away.

"Turn over on your stomach."

It took a second for Kudar's voice to cut through the haze in her mind. When it did, she opened her eyes and sat up.

"Your top needs to be taken off," he said, pointing to the upper half of her undergarment, then quickly added, "So I can rub your back."

Laila eyed him suspiciously.

Noting her hesitation, Kudar dramatically turned his back to her. "As you can see, I have my back to you. I promise I won't turn around until after you tell me you're ready."

Laila paused for a few seconds before she quickly discarded the material confining her breasts. The cool air felt good as it whisked against her skin. She settled on her stomach. "All right, I'm ready," she announced.

Kudar turned to her, swept her hair to one side, then began his ministrations on her back.

The subdued touch of his masterful hands once again lulled her into a euphoric stupor. She felt herself drift into utopia as she accepted the bliss his intoxicating hands granted her. Kudar's tranquil strokes offered paradise...an enchanted dreamland she hoped would never end. That was why she couldn't bring herself to move the first time his fingers glided along the sides of her breasts. The second time his fingers stroked the sides of her breasts, she managed a weak rebuttal. "Master Kudar, I know that was no accident."

"You're right, lovely Laila," he conceded. "I was hoping you'd let me get away with it."

She shook her head negatively.

"All right," he said matter-of-factly before he transferred his soothing fingers to the back of her lower legs.

His hands ebbed down her legs then ascended to her thighs. His tantalizing fingers maneuvered higher and higher, until they were between her legs. She felt his hand brush the material that covered her most intimate treasure. At that moment, Laila couldn't imagine heaven being more sublime than Kudar's touch. Her only reply was a moan.

Encouraged by Laila's response, Kudar's fingers grazed the cloth again. The third time, his fingers slithered beneath the obstructive barrier. They glided between swollen folds where he felt a welcoming wetness. Brazenly, his finger slipped inside her forbidden treasure.

Laila gasped, but did not pull away.

"Finally, you allow me the honor of touching you in a more intimate way," Kudar remarked. "This is what I've wanted to do since the first time you came to my room."

Laila was too placated to reply.

His response was to move his fingers in her.

Laila bit her lip to stifle the moan of pleasure that rose in her.

"Turn over, Laila, I want to look at you," Kudar coaxed.

Laila heard his request and knew exactly what he wanted. He wanted to look at her nude breasts. She should scold him for requesting such a liberty. She had specifically told him she didn't want to send him the wrong message...the message that she wanted to be intimate with him...have him make love to her...have his hands fondle her body for a reason other than a massage. Oh, why was she laying still, considering his request for one instant? Where was her chastity? Where was her virtue?

At that moment, both were nonexistent.

Unable to resist her enraptured state, she rolled over exposing herself to him. As she looked into his eyes, she was rewarded with a reverent look of appreciative veneration.

He was silent for a short while, as if entranced by her sun-bathed beauty. Finally, he spoke. "You're absolutely divine," he said, bent his head and kissed her as a groan of insatiable yearning rumbled in his throat.

Laila ardently returned his kiss. Running her fingers through his hair, she pulled him down to her. His fingers slipped easily between her thighs once more. She arched her back, pressing her body against his as pleasure consumed her whole being.

She should stop this, should have stopped this long ago. But as she thought it, his fingers began to rub the nub of her maidenhead and any remaining thoughts of resistance faded into oblivion. As he continued to longingly rub her crown jewel, she felt his mouth trail to her breast. She felt his hand grasp her round bottom as he suckled on her plump nipple.

"Master Kudar," she moaned, engulfed by delirious torment.

Kudar's response was to kiss her, swallowing up any sound. In that instant, nothing mattered to him except he bring her satisfaction and release the constrained need imprisoned within her.

"Master Kudar," she mumbled again, just as her insides melted into a delicious explosion of smoldering wantonness and ecstasy. She felt herself float to heaven on the wings of angels. Several exhilarating moments later, she felt herself flutter back down to earth and gracefully land on the soft blanket.

Her body was sweaty and she was breathing hard as she tried to come out of her rapturous haze.

Kudar pelted light kisses on her shoulder. "I am assuming you enjoyed that. It's my desire to please you. Shall we do it again?" he asked as he looked perspicaciously down at her.

The stimulating look on his bronzed face brought Laila's senses back with a cold splash. She shook her head in an attempt to restore her sensibilities. There was no way she could let Kudar touch her down there again. If he did, there would be no stopping what would happen next. Today would be the day he would have her...the day he owned her. She was not ready for that to happen.

Unnerved by the fact she had lost total control of herself, Laila captiously responded, "No!" and tried to sit up. But too weak, she slid back on the blanket.

"Take that look out of your eyes," Kudar bid as Laila stared up at him. "We did nothing wrong here."

"You promised me you'd respect my wishes," she protested.

"I promised nothing would happen unless you wanted it to happen. You wanted what just happened to happen, didn't you, my love? Tell me you did."

Laila looked into Kudar's beseeching gaze and her resolved evaporated. Suddenly, she could not remember why she did not want to give herself to him.

Decisively, Kudar scooped up her top then stood. Reaching out, he helped her stand on her wobbly feet. "You've had enough for today," he stated, pulling her top over her shoulders. "I don't want you to do more than you want to do," he asserted, then started to turn away.

Hastily, Laila reached out and caught his arm.

Slowly, he turned to her.

"I did want what happened to happen," Laila confessed before she stood on the tip of her toes and leaned forward. She placed a kiss on his cheek before demurely raising her eyes to meet his affectionate gaze.

"I'm glad," was his reply.

※

As fall approached, Laila and Kudar, along with five of Kudar's young sisters, decided to enjoy the balmy weather by having a picnic. The little girls, chased by Kudar, squealed gleefully while they ran near Laila who busily unpacked the food onto a blanket under a cypress tree. After the food was ready, Laila called to the siblings.

When Kudar approached Laila, he growled and reached out his hands as if he were going to seize her. Laila scrambled to her feet with a yelp and started to run around the edges of the blanket. The sisters giggled boisterously at the antics playing out before them.

Kudar quickly captured Laila and began to tickle her. Laughing uncontrollably, the two tumbled onto the blanket. Delighted at the sight before them, the young girls pounced on top of the pair.

Finally, the joyous group managed to compose themselves enough to eat lunch. After the meal was consumed, the ensemble stretched out on the blanket to bask in the sun-kissed breeze. When Kudar's sisters fell asleep, Laila sat up and began to put away the remainder of the food.

Kudar crouched next to her and took her in his arms. "I want you," he whispered.

"As soon as you get me, you will tire of me I fear." Laila shook her head. "I am in no rush for that to happen."

"I could never tire of you. I love being around you too much," Kudar assured. "Remember that sapphire ring you were falsely accused of taking?" he asked, suddenly becoming serious.

Laila nodded.

"Every time I looked at that ring, I was reminded of the injustice I brought upon you. I decided to have a new ring made. I had the sapphire from the old ring placed in a new setting." As he finished speaking, Kudar dug into his pocket then brought his hand forward.

Laila saw he held a ring made of gold, crowned with a brilliant sapphire, which was encircled by sparkling diamonds.

"It's for you. A new ring to represent a new beginning," Kudar stated. "I no longer want to be reminded of the past. Only a future with you."

Laila couldn't believe Kudar's words or thoughtfulness. She blinked back the unexpected tears that crowded in her eyes.

Kudar slipped the ring on her finger. It was a perfect fit. "It's beautiful and I want you to have it," he explained. "Now, every time you look at it, I want you to think of me."

Laila was speechless. Never had she been given such a thoughtful or expensive gift. She started to protest. Kudar quieted her by pulling her to him.

They lay side by side in contented silence.

✼

Fall reluctantly departed and winter arrived, as did a summons from the Sultan. After reading the summons, Kudar and his father left the palace almost immediately.

With Kudar gone, most of the women in the harem did not hold back their resentful feelings toward Laila and all the time she spent with him. They showed their discontentment by completely ignoring her. Because of this, the wintry weeks were lonely and dragged by for Laila. Her mind was filled with thoughts of Kudar. She realized she missed the time they spent together...missed the conversations they shared...the touch of his hands...his arms around her...his lips...not to mention his goddamn cocky attitude. She missed that too.

She realized her heart ached for him and she could no longer deny her susceptibility to him. Yes, she had to admit it. She wanted to be with Kudar...to give herself to him. She wanted to have Kudar make love to her, just as he predicted she would.

Laila let her mind wander for a moment and imagined herself in Kudar's arms. She imagined hearing him say, "I love you and no one else. I want you to be my wife, no matter what anyone says."

As if reading her thoughts, Vashti sneered, "What you have with Kudar won't last. One day you'll be like us...on the outside of his life looking in."

Laila brought her attention back to the present as Vashti's words stung her heart. When Laila looked at Vashti, she could see the anguish in the redhead's eyes. She reached out to touch her old friend.

Vashti pulled away and hissed, "Don't you dare touch me!" before she pivoted and stormed away.

When Kudar and Amir returned to the compound, they were accompanied by Ibrahim and a few Ottoman magnates. The men brought word that they had met with the Sultan and the Sultan was beginning to prepare for war against Constantinople. They revealed the Sultan ordered a Venetian ship sunk by cannon fire when it tried to run a blockade. The ship's crew, which consisted of thirty men, was taken prisoner. The Sultan then ordered the executions of the Venetian sailors and had their captain impaled.

At the behest of the Sultan, the men had return to the palace to continue discussing strategies for the upcoming war. Amir ordered a lavish dinner prepared for the guests.

Upon arrival to his chambers, Kudar immediately sent a note to Laila requesting she accompany him to his father's house for dinner that evening.

When he saw her, she rushed to him.

"I missed you," she admitted breathlessly as they embraced.

"Not as much as I missed you," he replied and kissed her cheek. "You look bewitching dressed as you are," he said of her embroidered caftan. "I wanted to see you tonight because there is going to be war and I have to leave again very soon."

Kudar watched as Laila frowned.

"We will make the most of every minute," he promised. Covering her hand protectively with his, he led her across the courtyard to his father's abode.

They walked to a large living area that had been rearranged for the lavish dinner. There were lush pillows encircling tables aligned around the room. Nearly all of the seating was taken by the boisterous guests who had already begun to eat. Kudar led Laila to a corner in the back of the room, which was partially cut off from the main room by a thin white curtain. The pair sank into luxurious pillows as a servant arrived with the drinks, followed by another servant with food.

"I've got to go mingle. It would be impolite if I totally ignored our guests," Kudar said before he excused himself.

As he made his way around the room, he stopped briefly to talk to Ibrahim and several men who were in the midst of discussing the impending war. When Kudar saw his mother, he walked to her and gave her a hug.

93

"You brought your friend," his mother said, casting a glance at Laila.

"I hope you like her," he confessed.

"I will have to make an effort to get to know her. From what I hear, you have made the women in your harem envious of her."

"You arrived late," a deep voice interrupted mother and son.

Kudar and his mother looked up as his father approached and stopped next to them.

"You should have come alone," Amir remarked with a dismissive nod toward Laila.

"I brought the person I wanted to be with," Kudar bristled.

"A harem girl in front of these important men? How do you expect to remain part of the proper circles or pick a proper bride if you bring your whore with you?"

"*Father!*" Kudar snarled curtly. "You are out of line!"

Amir raised his eyebrow at the tone of his son's voice. Undeterred, he placed a hand on Kudar's shoulder and said, "I know what it's like to be infatuated with a pair of tits. But you must keep your head about you. It's time you start taking your life seriously. You can't be a goddamn woman pleaser all your life. I'm respecting you enough not to arrange a marriage for you. Don't make me regret that decision."

As his father finished speaking, the music started. Kudar left his parents' side and returned to sit next to Laila. Without speaking a word, he began to gulp wine from his chalice.

"Are you all right?" Laila asked him after seeing the grimaced look on his face.

He nodded quickly then turned his attention toward the entryway as a small group of hired entertainers sauntered to the center of the room. Music began to ring out and the spirited performers began a lively dance. After the first routine ended, a new one began. Kudar was uninterested in the performance, and took another swig of wine, then another, as he contemplated his father's reprimand.

His father's request that he get married had been easy to dismiss in the beginning. Now, it was a demand that was becoming harder and harder to ignore. Kudar respected his father and did not want to deliberately disregard his parent's wish.

But truth be told, he was not interested in living life exactly as his father wanted him to. For years, he had been told to settle down and get married. The problem was, his father wanted him to marry some well-bred girl who would no doubt be ugly and boring. He, on the other hand, wanted a woman who challenged him. Someone he could talk to. He already had the perfect companion in his life. And as an extra benefit, she never failed to stir his loins.

Kudar reached out and touched Laila's hair. She turned and looked at him with a smile. The gentleness in her smile melted his heart. She was the one person who had managed to touch his soul. How it happened, he wasn't sure. By Allah! He certainly had not planned for it to happen. Didn't think it could happen. But now, the thought of being with another female was not remotely appealing. At least his mother was willing to get to know Laila. Why couldn't his father be the same way? Why did his father have to be so worried about bloodlines? And, why did he feel so much guilt at the idea of letting his father down?

Kudar's thoughts were abruptly interrupted as the lights dimmed and the music began to wail an exotic tone. A young girl walked in and glided to the center of the room. She was dressed from head to toe in brightly colored veils. As the music churned, the girl began to slowly move her hips. She let her arms glide across her body. Then, she skillfully began to remove her attire. One by one, her veils were discarded, revealing chestnut colored hair and soft bronze skin. When the veil covering her chest was removed, oiled shoulders and blossoming cleavage were exposed. Next, the maiden peeled away the chiffon sheath that covered her face. Smoky eyes and full red lips were unmasked.

Turning gracefully, the sultry female shed the overlay that was around her waist.

The music ended.

When the music started again, it was much faster. The lissome beauty jiggled her body invitingly then tossed aside the final veil that covered her legs. Churning her hips seductively, she began a belly dance. She fluttered leisurely about the room oozing sensual energy. The beat of the music accelerated as the young dancer continued to gyrate. She made her way to Kudar and Laila and stood in front of them. The seductive siren brought her hands in front of her chest and clasped them together. Then, she trailed her fingers alluringly down her body. Finally, the vixen wiggled her bottom provocatively before slithering back to the center of the room.

Kudar couldn't help but be affected by the sight of the girl's erotic movement. It had been some time since he had been intimate with a woman. Now, the sight of a sweaty female body inflamed his senses. He reached for the white curtain and tugged it closed. Hungrily, he drew Laila to his chest and kissed her passionately. With his arms enveloping her, he gently lowered her so that her back rested on a pillow.

Laila wrapped her arms around his neck.

"I would have never believed it possible. But I want you now more than ever," Kudar mused, gazing down at her ethereal beauty.

"Master Kudar…"

Suddenly, Kudar wanted to hear her say his name. "Don't call me Master. Call me Kudar. I want to hear you say my name."

"Kudar," Laila spoke his name.

Hearing his name on her tongue was harmony to his ears. Kudar nestled his head on her shoulder.

"Kudar," she murmured again.

"Laila, I missed you so much. I think about you all the time. I want to touch you." His hands touched the material covering her breasts. Gingerly, he unfastened the ties of her caftan which loosened the material enough to reveal the cinnamon colored skin between the valley of her breasts. Kudar slipped his hefty hands under the material. A groan escaped his lips when he squeezed her succulent breast. Laila's euphoric sigh reached his ears. He curled his lips over her right nipple and felt her body rouse in response to his touch.

"Are you sure they can't hear us?"

Kudar released the nipple that was in his mouth. "If they can, let them!" he mumbled, turning his attention to her left nipple while his hands traced the curve of her hips, then found their way under her garment.

Laila inhaled sharply as slowly...ever so slowly...his fingers grazed her womanhood. A guttural sound came from her throat when his fingers found their way inside her. As he continued to feast at her supple breasts, she writhed in rapturous bliss underneath him.

Enchanted by her seductive movement, Kudar spoke. "Lovely Laila, you have utterly defeated my patience and self control. I have to have you. All of you."

"I can't wait either," Laila admitted demurely.

"Let's make love. Right here, right now."

"Right now?" Laila questioned. "What about the people? They are just on the other side of the curtain. They might hear us," she whispered.

"No one can see us, and with all the music and talking going on, no one will hear us."

"Oh, Kudar, we shouldn't."

"I've played your game long enough. You have utterly seduced me. Don't make me wait any longer."

"Oh Kudar..."

"Make love to me, silly girl, before I explode."

Laila ran her fingers through his curly locks. "I'm not sure... Vashti and the others are a part of your life..."

Kudar quelled her words with a voracious kiss. "There's only one thing that matters and that's, do you want to make love to me? Say you do."

"I do want to make love to you, Kudar. More than anything."

"Then, stop talking and make love to me woman," he chided.

"It's just... I don't know if I can ever be enough for you."

"What do you think has been happening between us all this time? Laila, don't you get it? Before you walked into my life, I didn't know what real love was all about. I didn't think true love between one man and one woman was possible. I thought sharing my wealth with a woman was enough. You showed me there's more to love than that. You didn't want my wealth and riches. You just wanted my heart. Well, lovely Laila, I'm giving it to you. Please be gentle with it."

Laila's response was to kiss Kudar ardently.

When their lips parted, Kudar said softly, "You told me before you wanted to choose who you made love to. Tell me, do you choose to make love to me?"

Laila looked longingly into his eyes and whispered, "You predicted the day would come when I would want to make love to you. Well, that day is here. I do want to make love to you. I want it. I want you. Please make love to me," she pleaded, as she unbound his shirt and rubbed her fingers over his expansive chest. She boldly slid her hands in his trousers and encircled her fingers around his hardened tower.

"Oh my god," Kudar rasped.

Laila glided her hand up and down his manhood. "I do want you, Kudar. I can admit it now."

Kissing her lips one last time, Kudar stretched over her. He lowered his trousers before heaving up her caftan so that the garment bunched around her waist. She spread her legs apart. He settled between them. She wrapped her legs around him. He began to press his rigid member into her and did not stop until he was submerged within her tight wet walls. Her breathless gasp met his ears as she accepted his immense girth. When she quieted, he began to slowly move inside her.

"O my god!" Kudar moaned as previously denied pleasure mounted in him.

Nearly overcome by its affect, he quickened his pace, kissed her feverishly and caressed her velvet skin. "I've dreamed of making love to you since the day I met you," he managed to say. "You were well worth the wait. You're so beautiful. I don't want this to end."

Just as he finished saying those words, there was a rustling sound. In the next moment, the curtain that concealed them was pushed aside. In the next instant, Kudar's father came to stand over them.

Glowering down at the couple with incensed astonishment, Amir's mouth fell opened. "What the hell is going on here!" he roared.

Suddenly, the exuberant music came to a screeching halt. The dance performance came to an awkward standstill. All talking abruptly ceased and every pair of eyes turned to gawk at the flushed lovers in the back of the room.

Chapter Eight

Laila became aware of a dozen pair of eyes leering at them. She heard a collective gasp echo throughout the room when Kudar rolled off her. Quickly, she shoved her caftan down and watched Kudar turn to stare in astoundment at his father.

Time seemed to stand still while Amir glared at them. He looked so incensed, it seemed any moment hot flames would appear from his eyes and devour them both. Finally, with an infuriated huff, Amir shoved the curtain closed obscuring them from view.

"Oh my god!" Laila wailed when they were alone again. "Your father is so angry. He looked like he wanted to kill us."

"Damn it!" Kudar hissed after his trousers were securely in place. He turned to her. "I'm sorry you had to go through this. I'm sorry our first time was beside a table and exposed to prying eyes. You deserve better than this."

"What are we going to do?" Laila whispered anxiously.

"I'll tell you what we're going to do. We're going to leave this room the way we came."

"But, they'll see us."

"Then they see us. The damage has already been done." With that said, Kudar stood and slid the curtain aside.

Immediately, a hush fell over the conversations that had commenced in the room. Every pair of eyes turned once again to the lovers. With the inquisitive audience watching, Kudar bent down and scooped Laila into his arms. She gasped with surprise, her arms settling around his neck.

No one spoke as Kudar, with long steady strides, carried Laila across the room toward the door. When he passed the table where his mother sat, he could not bring himself to look in her direction. Once he neared his father, however, he could not help but notice the obvious indignation etched on the elder's face.

"Next time, tend to your own affair and leave me to do as I please!" Kudar barked.

Amir did not answer. He just scrutinized his son and Laila as they exited the room.

The moment Kudar stepped into the hallway, Laila let out a poignant wail. "I can't believe this!"

Kudar didn't answer. Instead, he carried her out of his father's house and across the courtyard to his home. He kicked the door to his room open with his foot and stepped inside. The bedroom was dark except for the bright moonlight that streamed through the open door of the balcony. Using the moonlight as a guide, he walked to his bed and dumped Laila in the middle of it.

She sank into the plush covers.

"Take your clothes off," he ordered and removed the tunic he wore.

Without hesitation, Laila did his bidding.

When he was naked, she said, "We shouldn't do this. Your father will be—"

"We will do what we want," Kudar interrupted, his gaze unapologetically scanning her body causing him to harden instantly. "Lay back," he ordered.

Laila followed his command.

He watched her inspect his nude form as he approached the bed. He climbed into bed next to her then slipped his arms around her slender waist and swept her into his captive embrace. As their flesh touched, a blistering heat scorched them both.

Kudar stretched over her length, burying her body beneath him. With narrowed eyes, he stared down at her naked splendor which was illuminated by moonlight. She had a beguiling allure which aroused his senses. He ran his fingers through her shimmering black hair with his left hand, and with his right, he cupped her breast. He teased her pert nipple between his fingers, then bent his head and kissed her passionately.

When Kudar's lips touched hers, Laila could no longer ignore the tantalizing ache between her legs. She clung helplessly to him as his fervid lips left hers to roam over her heated flesh. She let out a wanton cry when he hungrily flicked one of her nipples with his tongue.

"Never in my life have I wanted anyone as much as I want you now," Kudar declared. His powerful arms tightened around her, forcing her delicate frame more firmly against him. To taste more profoundly of the sweetness that bewitched him, his tongue parted her lips and found their way into her mouth.

She quivered.

"I want to bring you pleasure beyond your greatest fantasy..." he started to speak but his words drifted away when his fingers felt the dewy wetness that coated her intimate treasure. Pleased by the evidence of her desire, Kudar slipped his finger into her slick inner passage. Reverently, he traced his finger along the inside of her sensitive walls and she responded by churning her hips against him.

Surrendering to her enticement, Kudar impatiently nudged her knees apart. Planting little kisses over her breasts, he submerged himself between her thighs.

"I can't believe we are going to make love again," Laila muttered in amazement.

"Well, believe me, we are going to do it again," Kudar replied as he slid his pulsating member into her.

Laila stiffened as he engulfed her. After he filled her, she relaxed and slowly began to move her hips. Eager to drown in the pleasure of her young body, Kudar clutched her hips and imitated her pace, but soon, set a pace of his own. Laila's hips rose to meet his demands, shamelessly accepting his thrusts and succumbing to the unrestrained need that built in her loins and flared into an intoxicating flame.

In one quick motion, Kudar rolled onto his back.

Still connected, Laila eased lower on his tower. She pressed her hips into him, giving him access to plunge deep within her. He continued to drive his enslaved member into her depths, intensifying his strokes, rousing sensations she had never acknowledged before. Over and over again, he drove his manhood in her. Faster and faster, he thrust into her sheath. Vigorously, he seared her with his touch, creating an unbearable friction.

Her breathing quickened and an excited moan escaped her lips when his brawny hand smacked her round bottom. She tried to muffle a cry of unexpected ecstasy when he whispered her name.

"Kudar!" she cried out with a lusty whimper and fell back against his arms as he released molten nectar into her essence.

✂

Sunshine warmed the room when Laila opened her eyes. Images of the night she had spent with Kudar flooded back to her and danced in her memory. She turned and looked at him. He was staring at her with a mischievous grin on his face. Laila followed the trail of his gaze until she was reminded that she was unclothed. She started to pull the covers over her body but he stopped her.

"Don't cover yourself. I like seeing your naked goodness," he admitted.

Laila blushed slightly but did not move to cover herself again.

Kudar began to trace his finger down the outline of her slender leg.

"Your father...."

"...Is going to be spitting fire when I see him. I know." Kudar let his finger meander up her arm. "But, last night was worth it. You are amazing. Well worth the wait." He tapped his finger on her nose.

"What time is it? Isn't it late?" Laila inquired.

"Aye. I have missed half the meeting this morning. I should have been in my father's study hours ago." Kudar leaned over and softly kissed her on the lips. "I

103

hate to leave you, but I've got to get going. I have a lot to discuss with the men before we see the Sultan in a few days." With that said, Kudar rolled over and climbed out of bed. "You may stay in bed as long as you like," he added happily.

Laila sat up. "That's all right. I'll go back to my room," she replied before climbing out of bed also.

When she started to walk past Kudar, he reached out to her.

"Not so fast," he ordered. Placing a restraining hand on her arm, he turned her so her back was to him and pulled her to his chest. His hands cupped her breasts. He placed a light kiss on the top of her shoulder. "I think I can find time to make love to you again," he said merrily as his huge hand clasped the side of her hip.

"Oh Kudar," Laila sighed as he began to enter her.

✂

When Laila made her way back to the harem, she walked to the area where she slept for a washcloth and a change of clothes so she could take a bath. But her belongings were gone. When she walked out of the room she heard someone call her name. She looked across the living area and saw Kudar's mother, Irene. The older woman looked very stately as she stood outside one of the bedrooms. Her gold hair, streaked with gray, was tied in a bun at the nape of her neck. She motioned for Laila to come to her before she disappeared inside the room.

"I came over this morning because I wanted to see you," Irene said when Laila stepped into the bedroom.

"What is this about?" Laila inquired quickly, noting the contents in the room had changed. Fresh linens covered the bed and the vanity table was clutter free.

"I came over to see my son. When I arrived, I was told you were still with him. And, I was informed my son ordered a room prepared for you."

"A room prepared?"

"It appears my son wants you to have your own room. So this bedroom has been given to you. You are now his favorite."

"But this was Vashti's room," Laila started to protest.

"She has been moved to another space. She will be fine. It is usual for the woman who is the *ikbal* to have a nice room to herself. It is what my son wants, so it will be done," Irene explained resolutely.

"I don't know what to say... I never expected this."

"Kudar seems to really be taken with you. Therefore, I want to get to know you."

"Really?"

"Yes, my dear."

"I must say, I'm really sorry about what happened at dinner last night," Laila began to apologize.

Irene waved her hand in dismissal. "Let's not speak of it."

※

Vashti slammed her fist into the palm of her hand. From the beginning, she had told herself that Kudar's infatuation with Laila was only temporary and one day he would return to his old self and to her. She had spent nights in reverie of the day it would happen... of the day she would be back in Kudar's bed. From the very first time she lay with Kudar, she had worshipped him with her body. She had given him her all. But now, the nights she once shared with Kudar seemed a distant memory to him because he spent practically every day with the former slave girl.

"You manipulative *houri*! Who do you think you are?" Vashti hissed when she walked into her old bedroom to confront Laila after Irene departed.

Laila turned to face the redhead. "Vashti?"

"You know I love Kudar. Yet, you wormed your way into his life and made sure I was pushed out!"

"Vashti, it wasn't like that. I never meant–"

"Save it, you little backstabbing whore!" Vashti's eyes narrowed as she glared at Laila. "When you first came to the harem you pretended to be nice and innocent, and I tried to be a friend to you. Now, this is how you choose to repay me? You force me out of my own bedroom and you make sure Kudar never calls me to his couch. How could you treat a friend in such a way? You've been with Kudar everyday for months…prancing around town…rubbing it in our faces. You have no shame."

"Vashti, I never meant for any of this to happen. I've never wanted to hurt you."

"I told you the very first day I met you that I cared for Kudar. You took that knowledge and used it against me."

"Vashti, that is not true."

"I heard about your shameless actions at dinner last night. You showed your true colors. Last night you made it with him in front of the guests. How could you do something so filthy? So–"

"It wasn't like that," Laila protested. "What we did was beautiful and right. There was nothing filthy about it."

"You think not? Well, you've managed to alienate all of the women in the harem. You have no friends at all. But, that's only the beginning of your problems since you are now alienating Kudar from his father."

"I'm not–"

"This victory you've won is only temporary. Rest assured, the rest of us are not going anywhere. You cannot stay the only woman in Kudar's life forever. Kudar will come back to me one day. I know he will. One day he'll tire of you and I'll be there to pick up the pieces. You think what you shared with Kudar last night was special. Well, darling, let me remind you, it isn't anything he hasn't done with the rest of us."

Vashti's words stung Laila's heart. Laila squared her shoulders and lifted her chin, refusing to show Vashti any sign of weakness.

"I'm warning you," Vashti hissed bitterly. "I will get Kudar back in my bed and I will be sure to make you very sorry you crossed me."

✄

When Kudar finally made it to his father's house for the meeting that morning, the men in attendance stopped to pat him on the back and jest with him about the scene at dinner. Unimpressed, Amir stood from his place at the table and nodded for Kudar to follow him out of the room. Kudar excused himself and met his father in the hallway.

"I can't believe your shameless behavior last night. Have you lost your wits?" Amir scowled with a fractious tone.

"It doesn't look like it bothered anyone. You saw them. They were practically congratulating me," Kudar explained with an insouciant air.

"That's because they've been away from their wives for too long. The facts don't change. You should not have screwed your whore in the dinning room."

"Laila is not a whore! Besides, no one would have seen us if you had just paid attention to your own goddamned affair," Kudar contended, raising his voice slightly.

"You *are* my affair, son. And if Laila is not a whore then what is she? A witch?" Amir countered, rubbing his beard as if he were trying to guess the answer. "That girl has gotten you to let go of your senses. The Sultan has asked us to prepare for war and all you can think about is fucking that infidel."

"Father, I apologize for embarrassing you in front of your friends. That should not have happened. But, you will not speak of Laila in such a way."

"Oh yes. Your precious Laila. Your mind should be on the assignment the Sultan has given you. The Sultan was pleased with your work on Rumeli Hisari and has asked you to prepare several new designs to

107

be used after the war. He could have given that task to anyone, but he gave it to you. Yet you aren't even thinking about it."

"I know what the Sultan has asked. Do you really think we will win the war? Turks already tried to capture Constantinople thirty years ago. That assault failed. Since then, the walls around the city have been strengthened. Besides, there are promises that if there is a war, Christian Europe will rally to the defense of the city."

"Look. It took Osman ten years to take Bursa, but in the end, he won. Mehmed says Turks never concede defeat. He is determined to capture Constantinople, and when he does, it will be an incredible victory. That is why you need to have your head on straight. Not up some vixen's skirt." Amir wagged his finger. "There hasn't been anything or anyone on your mind but Laila. Word gets back to me, you know? I know you call for her night after night like some lovesick shepherd boy. The women in your harem hate her for it, but you are too distracted to even realize it."

"Father, why should I live my life by some silly rules if they don't make me happy?" Kudar hedged.

Amir sighed and shook his head. "Spending time with that girl has warped your mind. It's a good thing you have to leave to see the Sultan soon. Once you're gone, you will be away from her for a long time. Maybe then you will have time to think of what you've done and come to your senses."

After the encounter with his father, Kudar engrossed himself in his work. Unnerved, he decided he should completely focus on the task ahead of him. Working late into the night, he scoured over design after design, reworking sketches as needed. That night he did not call for Laila. Nor did he call for her the following night. The day before he and the men were to meet the Sultan again, he contemplated seeing Laila before he left. After all, he wanted to see her because once the war started he did not know how long he would be gone. However, his father's unhappiness still weighed heavily on his mind. His father's anger was a disappointment that was not easy to swallow.

Meanwhile, the high Laila had from her night of making love with Kudar began to quickly fade when he did not call for her or send a note of explanation about his silence. Laila began to wonder if it had been a mistake to give herself to him. Self-doubt and despondency started to creep into her thoughts. She contemplated marching over to Kudar's quarters and demanding an explanation. But, she held back as one day slowly turned into another. The third night, Laila could not stand it any longer. Overwhelmed by suspicion and curiosity, she left the harem and made her way to Kudar's room. The lights were already out when she entered his room, but she could see his form lying on the bed. She stepped forward and saw that he was laying on his back staring up at the ceiling.

"Kudar," she whispered before she slid into the bed next to him.

"Laila!" Kudar exclaimed, rolling onto his side to face her. "What are you doing here?"

"I'm afraid," she admitted, looking at him through the dark.

"Afraid of what?"

"You haven't called for me since we made love. You're leaving tomorrow and you didn't say goodbye. If you regret making love to me or if you're tired of me…just tell me. I guess I knew what we had was too good to last."

Kudar moved closer to Laila and wrapped his arms around her. She lay her head on his shoulder.

"Oh Laila, it's not you. It's me. I was laying here thinking about something my father said to me. I've never seen him so angry at me. I must admit it does not feel good."

"Your father wishes you would never call for me again?"

"Something like that. He thinks I spend too much time with you."

"So what we have is over? I know you respect your father. I don't want to come between you two."

"I am not a child. I do as I please. I always have. I just wish my father would go back to being as indulgent and permissive as he used to be."

"Did you see the look on his face when he saw us?" Laila shivered as she thought about it and moved even closer to Kudar as if for protection.

"God! I don't want to think about it." Kudar shook his head as if to clear it. "Look, my love, I leave early tomorrow morning so let's not spend the rest of the night talking," he requested, placing a soft kiss on her lips.

✄

"You will have to accept my apologies for my son's indiscretion at dinner the other night," Amir said, attempting to raise his voice above the noise of the crowd.

"No need to apologize again," Ibrahim responded, keeping his eyes on the oil wrestlers in the circle in front of them.

"His actions were indefensible. Something I cannot explain. Ever since he met that girl he has not been himself," Amir protested.

A cheer from the spectators went up as one of the wrestlers was slammed to the ground. The noise quieted some.

"Don't be so hard on him. Kalilah is a very beautiful girl," Ibrahim said.

"Kalilah? Her real name is Laila."

"Laila? Huh? I didn't know that. What I do know is I would not have acted any differently than your son if she had stayed with me and I had her to warm my bed," Ibrahim confessed.

"Stayed with you? What do you mean?" Amir inquired.

"I purchased Kalilah...Laila at the auction house in Constantinople the last time my daughter and I came to visit your home."

"That's right."

"We found out she stole Kudar's ring so we could not take her to Karamania with us. She stayed behind so she could be punished. After that incident, I thought we would never be invited back to your home. But, I see your son has long since forgotten the incident and has put her talents to better use."

"She should have never been brought back to my home. She has been nothing but a thorn in my side. I have to get her away from my son."

"I'd be happy to take her off your hands," Ibrahim chuckled.

Cheers of delight rose from the crowd as the wrestler was pinned to the ground once again.

"You should have had her all long. The other men are planning on returning to the Sultan. You on the other hand are planning on returning to Karamania in a few days, right?"

"That is correct," Ibrahim affirmed. "I will no longer be a party to planning a foolish war."

"The men will be with the Sultan for several weeks until the war starts which means things will work out perfectly."

"What are you saying?"

"Kudar and the other men will return to the Sultan. Since you are not returning as planned, we can make things work out for the both of us. After the men leave you will return to your home. But, you will not be alone."

"Not be alone?"

Amir nodded. "You will take the handmaid with you."

"Tell me my friend, why would you consent to this?"

"My son has to get on with his life," Amir stated, then said, "Here is what you must do…"

Chapter Nine

Many miles of lush valleys and seemingly desert plains passed under the camel's feet.

Laila wished she could stop time. If she could she would not have gone willingly with Ibrahim and his small entourage. When they arrived in the city Ibrahim had her arms bound and he told her he was not taking her to Kudar as he promised. Instead, he revealed, he was taking her with him to Karamania.

At the realization, dread mushroomed in Laila. Her time with Kudar had been beautiful. Her heart was filled with love for him and she wanted to be by his side. Now she was not sure she would ever see him again.

A few hours after they left town, the travelers stopped for a short respite and to water the animals. It was then Ibrahim ordered one of the servants to untie the rope around her wrists.

The servant walked to Laila and began to do as requested.

"Here, let me help you with that."

At the sound of Ibrahim's voice, Laila looked up and saw he had walked to her and now towered over her. His voice was low and his eyes held a glint she could not read.

"There now." He placed his hand on the rope.

The servant took a quick look at his owner, then scurried away.

Ibrahim unraveled the rope. "I bet that feels better," he said.

Laila glared at Ibrahim and rubbing her wrists said, "You lied to me and told me you were going to take me to Kudar."

Ibrahim placed a heavy hand on her shoulder. "There is no need for you to be angry with me, Laila. Things have worked out for the best. After all, you are very pleasing to the eyes."

"What…what are you saying?" Laila leaned away from Ibrahim's touch.

He frowned. "Don't act shy with me, girl. I can be a very generous man if persuaded. I'm sure we can come to some kind of arrangement."

Unwilling to hear the rest of his words, Laila turned and hurriedly walked away.

✦

The small group arrived in Karamania early one morning. The Turkish town had not yet awakened. However, the smell of fresh bread filled the air. Shopkeepers were making their way to stands where brightly colored cloaks hung on display. A couple of stray dogs, with their noses low to the ground, scampered off in the distance.

About half a day elapsed before a large stone house in the middle of a field came into view.

When the procession stopped, Ibrahim disappeared inside. Moments later, Jamal exited the house and instructed some of the male servants to take the camels to their corral.

"Kalilah!" his voice was filled with happiness as he hugged her. "I guess I should call you Laila. Master Ibrahim just told me you were here. When he did he called you by your given name. Is that what we should start calling you?"

Laila nodded.

"All right then we shall. Now tell me Laila, what are you doing here?"

"I was tricked. I thought the Emir was taking me to see Kudar but instead he brought me here."

"Kudar? You call him by his given name?"

"I love him, Jamal. I miss him so much. We should be together."

"Little one, you reach too high. As a slave…" Jamal let his words trail off after seeing the pain in Laila's eyes.

"So Kudar doesn't know you're here?"

"No. He does not."

"Kalilah…Laila I told you I would look after you and I will. I hope that brings you some comfort."

Laila lowered her eyes.

"This is your new home." Jamal swept his arms about.

Laila raised her head to look around the premises.

The property was vast. The main residence was a capacious structure beautifully designed with unique architectural accents. Away from the main house, in the valley, animals grazed in fields covered with patches of green grass and in the distance there was a small pond. Scenic mountains rose up along the horizon.

"Laila, follow me," Jamal ordered.

Laila followed him to the rear of the house. They entered through the back door and Jamal led her to the cooking area filled with servants. The separate conversations in the room caused a murmur which sounded like a harmonious buzz. One of the servants looked up, and seeing Jamal, she walked to him, clasped his hands and kissed him on both cheeks. The woman turned to look at Laila before whispering something in Jamal's ear. Jamal nodded and a look of pity crossed her face.

"What did she say?" Laila asked Jamal when they left the room.

"She said, may Allah be merciful to you 'cause she thinks you will need his mercy if you stay here. Come," Jamal instructed. "I will take you to Zora's quarters."

A feeling of apprehension enveloped Laila as Jamal led her out of the cooking area and down the hallway.

They came to a bedroom and Jamal called out, "Mistress Zora!"

There was no answer. He stepped into the room and Laila followed. The luxurious chamber consisted of grandiose furnishings covered with piles of lavish clothing. There were beautiful tapestries on the walls and a small antechamber on one side of the room.

115

"Mistress Zora is not here. But this is her room," Jamal explained. "You will sleep in the antechamber. Get settled in. I will be back with some fresh clothes for you," he said and left the room.

Laila walked to the antechamber, sat on the bed and covered her face with her hands.

�֎

Zora tapped her feet as she waited impatiently on a bench outside her father's study. She looked at Laila who approached with a tray of afternoon tea. Laila always buzzed about like a docile bee doing her chores. But underneath the girl's placid exterior, Zora guessed she still dreamt of her homeland and of one day being free.

Zora remembered the first day she met her handmaid. The girl had looked her straight in the eye and demanded she be free to return to her home. It had been at that moment Zora decided she would never let Laila forget her place as a handmaid...a slave.

The door to the study opened interrupting Zora's thoughts. Two *gazi* warriors exited the room. Zora stood, straightening her clothing as she did so. The men acknowledged her then made their way out of the house.

"Can I come in?" Zora asked, walking leisurely into her father's office. "Did your meeting go well?" she inquired, aimlessly picking items up off the shelves and haphazardly replacing them where she pleased.

Laila followed behind her and carried the tray of hot liquid to a small table in the corner of the room.

"The meeting went well, daughter of mine," Ibrahim replied from his place behind the layer of maps on his desk. "Now, why did you want to see me? What was so important?"

"You've been in meetings all day, everyday," Zora commented. "You need a rest."

"You're so thoughtful but I am so very busy."

"So very busy," Zora mimicked sarcastically. "All you do is have silly meetings consulting with officials and those grumpy warriors. You never spend any time with me."

Ibrahim looked at his daughter wearily. "When will you get it, Zora? These silly meetings are my job. I am the Emir after all, and I have to do what I feel is best for my country."

Zora walked to her father's desk and picked up a sapphire colored stone that had an eye painted on it. She looked at the stone, which was seen as a symbol of good luck to ward off evil, and studied it for a few seconds. After which, she moved it to the shelf directly behind her father's desk. "Your meetings are still silly and you are boring, Father," Zora grumbled with a pout before gliding from the desk to the window where she pulled back the curtain and looked outside.

Laila passed Ibrahim's desk and picked up the stone.

Ibrahim glanced at Laila then at his daughter who had her back to him. "I'm only boring to you, daughter. There are many beautiful females who find me very exciting."

With that said, Ibrahim reached out his hand to his intended target.

As Laila bent over to replace the good luck symbol on Ibrahim's desk, she felt his huge hand grab her bottom then pinch it. Startled, she let out a boisterous gasp and dropped the stone, which fell to the floor with a blusterous crash.

Ibrahim began to laugh heartily at Laila's reaction.

Abruptly, Zora turned her attention back into the room. "Laila, what the hell is your problem?" she demanded. "You are so clumsy."

"There now, daughter," Ibrahim chuckled. "Don't be so hard on the girl. She's just a little skittish," he noted. Then, he reached out and pinched Laila's bottom again.

Zora's eyebrows narrowed as she noticed the way her father looked at Laila. Her lips twitched. "Father!" she fumed, before turning her wrath to Laila. "If you think you can seduce my father you are wrong!"

"I...I..." Laila was too flabbergasted to find any words of defense.

"Get out of my sight you sneak!" Zora seethed.

Laila rushed from the room with the sound of Ibrahim's heavy laugh following her.

✂

A few days later, Laila walked to the well, located a short distance from the house. As she did, she thought about how miserable she'd been since the day she arrived at Ibrahim and Zora's home. The bright blessing in her life was the fact she now spoke Turkish and could communicate with the servants who treated her kindly.

She could also understand a little Greek, which meant she understood most of the important visitors who came to see Ibrahim. Many of his guests were government and military officials, as well as *gazi* warriors, who were highly skilled men that fought to spread Islam and acquire land and riches in the process. Ibrahim and the men were always behind closed doors in meetings. On the occasions Laila was able to hear them talking, it became apparent that the group had a grievance against their Turkish Sultan, Mehmed II. From what Laila gathered, the men believed the Sultan was too young to run an empire effectively. They also said he was not waging the correct kinds of military campaigns.

Once at the stone structure, Laila lowered a clay jar into the well. Her thoughts drifted to Kudar and the fact she missed him terribly. There seemed to be a crater-sized hole in her heart that could not be filled. Her days where spent thinking of him and her nights were spent dreaming of him. She thought about his amber colored eyes, his audacious smile and the low timbre of his voice. Instead of waking up in his arms, her days were now spent in Zora's shadow, jumping to obey any orders that were meted out.

Laila paused for a moment and looked in the distance at the scenic mountains. Her gaze slowly moved to the pond, which reflected the light from the sun. As she looked at the pond, she thought about Kudar and the time they spent enjoying themselves in the waters of the sea. She wondered where he was and what he was doing at that very moment.

Lost in thought and bathed by the cool breeze, Laila raised her hand to her forehead. As she wiped her brow with the back of her hand, she cast a glance toward the house. When she did, she saw Ibrahim sitting on the veranda leisurely ogling her as he finished his morning coffee.

Immediately, the hairs on the back of Laila's neck stood on end and a sickening revulsion crept through her body at the realization he had been watching her.

At that moment, Jamal rounded the corner of the house. Laila looked at him, unable to hide the anxiety in her eyes.

Jamal's gaze shifted to Ibrahim then back at Laila. Hurriedly, he walked to her. "Little one, I see the way Ibrahim looks at you. He has noticed how beautiful you are. Beauty is a curse for a slave girl. If you stay here..."

"Please help me," Laila pleaded. "I need to be with Kudar."

"This house is not a safe place for you. I will think of a way to save you," Jamal promised.

✂

After dinner that evening, Laila served evening tea and *baklava* to Zora and Ibrahim on the veranda. As she did, she apprehensively thought about Ibrahim. She realized she had not wanted to see the lust that had been slowly developing in his stares. But the look he had given her that morning left no doubt of the salacious intent behind his gaze.

Night fell and Zora, complaining about the cool night air, excused herself, stating she was ready to go to bed.

"Laila, clean away the dishes," Zora ordered, before she made her exit.

As directed, Laila collected the teacups and platter of the remaining syrup and pastries. After she had gathered the dishes, and as she started to walk inside the house, Ibrahim's voice stopped her.

"It's such a nice night tonight. But it's a little chilly." He turned to look at her. "Go get the brown wool blanket that's in the bottom of my closet."

Laila took the dishes to the cooking area, then she walked to Ibrahim's sleeping chambers. An uneasy feeling overcame her as she stepped into the baleful room. The room was dark except for the light of one candle whose dim flame flicked shadows on the wall. Quickly, Laila walked to the narrow aphotic closet, stepped into the small space, then knelt on her hands and knees and began to feel around for the coverlet. She felt several objects but none were the blanket. Turning her back to the closet door, she leaned forward in an attempt to feel the recessed corners of the storage area.

"I believe this is what you are looking for," Ibrahim's deep voice sounded.

Laila gasped and turned in time to see him lifting a blanket from the top shelf. She quickly stood to her feet and found herself standing perilously close to him.

"Ah...you told me it was in the bottom of the closet," Laila challenged.

"You're right." Ibrahim grinned as if pleased with himself.

Laila waited a moment, hoping Ibrahim would step out off the closet. But, he did not. Clearing her throat, she stepped to the right in an attempt to pass him. Unexpectedly, Ibrahim shifted his body to the right blocking her exit. Laila quickly moved to the left. Hastily, Ibrahim shifted his body to the left.

"Not so fast, Laila. I want to talk to you," he said.

Apprehensively, Laila looked up at him.

"By now, you probably guessed what I want."

"I don't know what you mean."

"Of course you do. You're a very beautiful girl, Laila. I cannot forget the sight of your lovely body exposed on that auction block, no matter how hard I try."

"I don't want to hear this!" Laila objected.

"You're frightened, I know. But don't be. I'm not a monster. Just a man."

"Please move," Laila requested, trying to push past him.

Ibrahim grabbed her shoulders and precipitously pulled her against his bulging belly. Laila tried to extract herself from his grasp, but he held her firmly against his torso. Ibrahim shifted his feet in an attempt to steady himself and inadvertently kicked something with his foot. The item fell to the closet floor with a loud clang.

"Let me go!" Laila demanded.

"I could make you very happy if you'd let me."

"Let me go!" she insisted again.

"If you relax you will like it."

"Never!"

"You will do what I want!" Ibrahim instructed, suddenly angry.

"No! No! I won't!" Laila shook her head.

"I'm your master! Someone in your position cannot say no to me!" he replied.

A sob caught in Laila's throat and she lowered her face toward the ground.

"What was that noise? What's going on here?"

Startled, both Ibrahim and Laila looked up at the sound of Zora's voice.

Zora stood in the middle of her father's room glaring at the entanglement before her. "Father!" she shrieked. Suddenly, her shock turned to outrage. "Laila!"

Instantly, Ibrahim released Laila. "Daughter, it's not what it seems. I asked Laila to get a blanket for me. She almost lost her balance. I was just steadying her."

Zora stared at them skeptically.

Upon observing this, Ibrahim added, "Isn't that right, Laila?"

Seeing the disgust in Zora's eyes, Laila nodded.

"I found the blanket though, so all is well," Ibrahim said, before adding, "Gratitude for your help, Laila. You may retire for the night."

Laila hastily exited the room, leaving Zora and her father quarreling in hushed angry tones.

�֎

A few weeks later, Laila's eyes fluttered open, interrupting a dream of Kudar. She looked into the dark, unsure what had awakened her. Groggy and indolent from sleep, she noticed a shadowy figure standing at the foot of her bed. As her eyes adjusted to the darkness of the antechamber, she stared at the figure until she realized it was Ibrahim who stood at her feet.

"You awake?" he murmured and stepped forward.

Laila's heartbeat quickened as she watched him advance and sit on the bed next her. She started to raise herself to a sitting position. Ibrahim gently nudged her back onto the bedding and gathered her wrists in his hands.

"Get your hands off of me! Don't touch me!" Laila ordered.

"You don't have to be so disagreeable," he chided.

"Why are you doing this?" she questioned.

"Isn't it clear? Besides, you should be flattered to have someone in my position desire you. I can take care of you. Make your life easy," he whispered leaning toward her.

"Let me go!" Laila objected nervously.

"Don't fight me."

"Let me go!"

"Kiss me and I'll let you go," Ibrahim countered.

"No!"

"Obey what I tell you, Laila." Ibrahim's voice became stern. Moments later, it softened. "Kiss me or would you rather undress for me instead?"

"Oh God! This isn't happening! Please God! I won't kiss you! Now, get off of me you swine!" Laila squirmed underneath him.

"Don't try to escape. It will do you no good. There's no one here to help you," Ibrahim proclaimed and lowered his lips towards hers.

Laila impulsively turned her head. His lips crushed against her cheek.

"Kiss me and I'll let you go," Ibrahim countered again, his warm breath brushed her smooth skin.

She shook her head.

"Don't act innocent. I saw you sprawled underneath Amir's son, remember?"

"If Kudar knew I was here, he would come for me. If he knew you were doing this, he would make you sorry."

Ibrahim laughed lightly. "Amir's son can no longer enjoy the pleasure of your body but his loss is my gain. What you did for him, you can do for me," he affirmed.

"You're disgusting!" Laila hissed.

"It is not a request."

"Your daughter is on the other side of that door! She–"

Ibrahim managed to press his cold lips against her soft ones, cutting off any words.

When he removed his lips from hers, he said, "She's sound asleep."

"You let me go now! Or, I'll scream for your daughter, and she'll see what kind of man you really are!"

At her words, Ibrahim recoiled slightly.

Emboldened, Laila quickly continued in a scathing tone. "Take your hands off of me or I'll make sure Zora knows that her suspicions are true! She would never forgive you for being with a slave! You know that what I say is true!"

"You leave my daughter out of this!"

"You leave me alone!"

"I paid the price for you when you were on that block! I intend to get my money's worth!" Ibrahim declared staunchly as his hands slid over the sheet to her breasts.

Desperate, Laila cried into the darkness, "Zora!"

Immediately, Ibrahim released her.

Seconds later, like a ghost in the wind, he was gone.

Laila sat up in bed. Her heart pulsed rigorously in her chest as she peered into the dark for the remainder of the night. She couldn't sleep…didn't want to sleep less Ibrahim should return.

But he did not.

※

The next morning after a sleepless night, Laila worried anxiously about the consequence, if any, she faced because of the previous night. She managed to avoid Ibrahim and Zora until dinner. After father and daughter finished their meal, she carried cups brimming with tea to them as they sat on the veranda talking. As she placed the cups on the table, she glanced nervously at Ibrahim. When she did, one of the cups slid precariously in her fingers. Reacting quickly, Laila was able to stabilize the cup and sit it on the table without spilling its contents.

"Clumsy fool! You almost dropped that on me!" Zora screeched. "You did that deliberately!" she accused.

"No. I didn't!" Laila protested.

"You ingrate! Don't talk back to me!" Zora shouted, before picking up the cup from the table and splashing the hot liquid down the front of Laila's caftan. Laila shrieked with horror as the scorching liquid soaked her clothing. "That should teach you to pay more attention, you clumsy whore!" Zora yelled caustically.

A sob caught in Laila's throat. It took every ounce of her pride not to shed a tear in front of Zora. Hastily, she turned from Zora and fled from the veranda.

As Laila ran, her soaked caftan clung to her legs. She stopped running when she came to the small pond. She looked back toward the house and saw that Ibrahim and Zora had disappeared inside. Kneeling near the edge of the pond, she began to splash cold water on her caftan and legs.

She rubbed the material of her caftan together in an attempt to scrub away the dark stain. While she scrubbed, tears escaped from their hiding place followed by a sob. Laila scrubbed harder and willed herself not to cry. Unable to hold back emotion any longer, she fell forward. Her knees sank into the cool wet mud as she buried her face in her hands and wept.

All of the heartache and pain that had been mounting over the past weeks overcame her, and she began to cry uncontrollably. She wanted to be away from the hellhole she was living in. She wanted Kudar. She wanted to be in his arms where she could be safe; secure from the insults, harassment and constant abuse.

Laila cried until she could cry no more. She did not know how long she cried. When her tears finally stopped, the sun had set behind morose clouds and endless darkness surrounded her. A cold breeze chilled Laila as her wet clothing clung to her body. She wiped her face then took off the sticky caftan. Her arms, legs and feet were caked with mud. She waded into the cold water and began to wash herself. As she quickly cleaned her body, she thought about how much she dreaded the idea of returning to the house and contemplated staying out all night in the elements.

Laila noticed undulating ripples in the water before she heard a splash. Startled, she turned around. Fear paralyzed her when she saw Ibrahim's naked body disappear under the water. Seconds later, Ibrahim broke the surface of the water not far from her. Their eyes locked at the same moment a raindrop splashed onto her shoulder.

"Tonight is the night all of the games end, Laila," he said. "I didn't push the issue more forcefully last night because of my daughter. I've made sure she won't be disturbing us tonight," he confided. "Don't look at me that way. I am only a man…only human after all. I've waited long enough to have my due. The time has come. I will have you right here, right now. Come to me," he instructed softly.

The sound of Ibrahim's voice brought speed to Laila's feet. She started to wade frantically toward the bank. However, the resistance of the water slowed her escape. Desperate, she pushed out her hands in an attempt to move more expeditiously to the shore.

Nimble for a man his age, Ibrahim swam to her and caught her in just a few strokes. He grabbed her waist.

"No!" Laila screamed as he spun her around to face him. She slammed into his chest despite the impeding water. At the same moment, the heavens opened up and a thick sheet of rain spilled to the earth.

Ibrahim's dark eyes and red lips glistened with raindrops that cascaded from the hair plastered on his head as he used brute force to pin Laila firmly against his pulsing manhood. Raising one of his hands to her chin, he forced her face toward his and he leaned into her.

Laila recoiled, closed her eyes, and clasped her hands around her body. "Please! I beg you! Don't do this! Leave me alone!" Her eyes darted from side to side as she searched for an escape.

Ibrahim's response was a laugh.

Mortified, Laila opened her mouth and let out a scream.

Ibrahim laughed again when her terrified scream was swallowed up by the wind. "No one can hear you. Not in this rain. You are all mine," he scoffed with a smirk.

At his words, Laila trembled and whimpered. "Please! Let me be! I am but a worthless slave to you! Please, let me keep my virtue!"

"Girl, virtue is but wasted on a slave," he replied before he burrowed his lips into hers and fondled her breasts.

Laila struggled against his touch and punched his chest.

When he lifted his head, Laila's response was to slap his wet face hard.

Ibrahim's eyes became tiny slits as he gritted his teeth against the unexpected sting. His grip tightened around her waist then he shoved her down into the atramentous water.

As the piceous water filled her mouth, ears and covered her head, desperation enveloped Laila. Panic exploded in her chest, its tentacles threatening to suffocate her. Her arms flayed about in a frenzied attempt to rise to the surface. She scratched at the hand that held her under. Finally, she was pulled to the surface. She spat out water and inhaled deeply. Choking on air and water, she broke into a coughing frenzy. When Laila recovered a little, she spat in Ibrahim's face. He wiped his face angrily, anchored his large hand in her hair and plunged her into the water again.

Laila thrashed franticly about, jerking her body in all directions. As her need for air increased, the pounding of her heart echoed in her ears. Just when she thought she could not hold her breath any longer, Ibrahim allowed her to rise to the surface once more. She coughed and sputtered. Breathing in deeply, she tried anew to fill her starved lungs with air.

"Settle down and this will go a lot smoother for you. We could go on like this all night. Or, you could stop fighting me." Ibrahim yanked her hair at the roots until she shrieked in pain. "Now, let me kiss you or I will push you back under the water. Next time, I will not let you come up for air!" he hissed rancorously. Once more, despite the cold water, he pressed his feverish body against hers. This time when he leaned toward his prey, Laila lay rigid as if she had been dead for a week.

Knowing he could force her at any moment, Ibrahim relaxed and with his lips slowly trailed the outline of her neck. "I want this to last. Let's get out of the water," he said impudently and still holding her sagging body, he swam to the bank.

As they exited the water, Laila's tawny form became exposed to his view. Her nipples were pert and erect in opposition to the cold.

Never taking his eyes off her naked figure, Ibrahim groaned and let his hands roam her breasts. He ground his mouth into her lips. Still, she lay lifeless in his arms, her face tilted toward the darkened sky, her lips like a pillar of ice – cold and unresponsive. Ibrahim relaxed his hold on her and cursed.

Laila came alive then. She broke free of his clutch.

Ibrahim reached out to seize her arm, but her wet limb slipped through his grip. Recovering quickly, Ibrahim lunged at her again. This time, he managed to capture a fist full of her hair. With a fierce grunt, he forcibly yanked her tresses causing her to be propelled back to him. Her body collided into his with such force he lost his footing. Both bodies broke free of the other and hurled toward the ground.

Ibrahim landed on his side. Laila fell on her hands and knees with an anguished cry. Blinded by rain and tears, she pushed her hair away from her face and began to crawl away from the bondman. Ibrahim reached out, gripped her ankle and with a brutal tug, he yanked her back toward him.

Laila's arms gave way beneath her causing her head to slam into a rock that jutted out of the ground. There was a cracking sound and in the next instant, blood squirted from Laila's head. She whimpered and placed her hand over the wound. Ruby red blood began to slowly ooze between her fingers.

"Damn it!" Ibrahim exclaimed, releasing her he quickly rose to his feet.

Laila wiped the blood away from her eyes in time to see Ibrahim gather his clothes and scurry away. She collapsed on the wet ground with a plaintive wail while tears flowed unchecked down her cheeks. Cold rain pelted against her frame and uncontrolled shivers consumed her body.

The rain slackened slightly just as the sound of footsteps reached her ears. Fearing Ibrahim's return, Laila scrambled to her feet and peered into the thick mist of rain.

"Laila!" A strong voice called her name from a distance.

Laila's heart thumped in her chest. Her legs suddenly felt weak when she saw a form rising out of the darkness. Her eyes darted around in search for a place to escape. But there was no time to evade the advancing intruder.

"Laila? My god! Are you all right?" came the question as the male form hastened toward her. The intruder neared and his identity suddenly became clear.

Laila gasped in astonishment just before her legs gave way under her.

Instantly, strong arms encircled her stopping her descent to the ground. Raising her eyes, her voice croaked, "Kudar?" and then she lost consciousness.

Chapter Ten

"Laila. How do you feel?"

"Kudar?" Laila questioned.

"Yes, sweet one."

Laila raised herself to a sitting position and saw Kudar sitting beside her bathe in light from the oil lamp. "You came for me?"

"Of course," he answered. "The physician says you will be all right. Don't try to speak." His voice was gentle as he nudged her downward. "Rest, my love. We will talk later."

✂

"You awake?" Kudar asked as he walked into the confines of the tent with a bowl in his hand. "How are you feeling?"

"I'm fine," Laila replied.

"I hope your first day on the trail wasn't too grueling," Kudar revealed. "I know we left in quite a rush. Jamal insisted we leave Karamania immediately after the physician said your wound was a small cut which should heal quickly. Here, try this," Kudar lifted warm broth to her lips. "We will take it slow and stop at sunset every night to make sure you are able to rest," he said after she had partaken of the broth.

"I want to get home as soon as possible."

"Me too."

"How did you find me?" Laila wanted to know.

"The servant, Jamal, sent a messenger who found me and let me know where you were. I had no idea Ibrahim had taken you. I came with much haste to get you."

"Ibrahim—"

"You don't have to worry about him or my father. Ibrahim confessed that he and my father devised a plan to separate the two of us. Believe me, after I finished with him, he won't try that again. I will deal with my father when we get home and he won't try that again either."

"Did Ibrahim tell you what happened by the pond?"

"When I arrived there, he told me you were bathing. It appears you slipped and hit your head."

Laila lowered her eyes. "Is that all he said?"

"Yes. What is it, sweet one?"

"Nothing," Laila answered, trying to decide if she should tell him the truth.

Suddenly, she began to cry.

Kudar immediately gathered her into his arms and held her as her body shook with sorrow.

"It's over. The nightmare is over. We're together again. That's all that matters," he whispered in her ear.

When her tears subsided, she lifted her face to Kudar and unable to speak she placed her hand on his cheek. He responded by leaning down and kissing her neck. As he did so, Ibrahim's face flickered in Laila's mind.

Kudar's lips trailed up her neck before his lips touched hers. In that moment, a haunting image of Ibrahim pressing his cold lips on hers invaded Laila's thoughts.

She recoiled and turned her face from Kudar.

"I can't..." she murmured.

"Laila, what is it?" Kudar wanted to know.

"I...I can't go any further tonight. I am really tired. Please understand."

"Certainly my love," Kudar replied gently.

Laila responded by closing her eyes. "Just hold me close," she pleaded and lay her head on his chest.

�֍

"May I come in?" Kudar asked then stepped into the tent before Laila could answer.

The light from the lamp revealed Laila was already lying down on a pallet. The top of her caftan was pushed down below her shoulders and the bottom half was pushed up to her thighs. Kudar thought she looked like a half-dressed goddess in her efforts to catch the cool night breeze.

He smiled, lowered himself to the ground then folded his legs. "I was hoping you weren't sleep yet. It took longer than I thought to water the camels. They are restless. I think it is because they can sense we are close to Constantinople."

"How much longer will it take?"

"We should reach the palace tomorrow."

"That is good news."

"Unfortunately, I will only be home long enough to drop you off and get you settled. After which, I have to meet back up with the Sultan. The war is going to start any day now. I don't want to worry you. Just came in to tell you good night. I will leave you to get some sleep." Kudar started to rise to his feet.

"You don't have to go," Laila's voice sounded through the faint light. "You can stay if you want."

"I've wanted to stay with you every night since our journey began. But each night you sent me away. Is tonight going to be different?" Kudar inquired.

Laila's response was to reach up and pull him toward her.

Kudar stretched out alongside her.

They lay in silence for several minutes. Suddenly, Laila rose upon her elbow and looked down at him. Without speaking, she leaned down and let her lips graze his. He lifted his hand to her shoulder. She intertwined her fingers in his and pulled his arms securely around her.

"You are the best thing that ever happened to me," she confessed.

Kudar's response was to pull her snugly against him.

❁

Laila breathed a sigh of relief when she saw the palace appear on the horizon. After they walked into the courtyard, Kudar took her hand and led her to his father's house.

When Amir saw the two of them, a look of astonishment crossed his face.

"Your plan failed, Father!" Kudar declared sternly.

"I–"

"Think carefully before you speak, dear Father! The next words you say could be the last we ever speak to one another!"

Amir was silent for a while. At last, he spoke. "I apologize for my actions," he said somberly.

"Laila is a part of my life! There is nothing you can do about that!"

"I did what I thought was best."

"Father, if you ever force Laila to leave this palace again, you will be sorry!"

"Son–"

"No, Father! You better promise me you will never ever force Laila to leave my home again!"

"You want me to promise not to force this girl to leave the palace?"

"You heard me!"

"Son, think about your future–"

"Father!"

"All right! All right! I won't force her to leave again."

"Swear it!"

"Why must I swear it?"

"I am returning to meet the Sultan tomorrow. I want to know Laila will be safe if I leave her here. So, promise me. You have never broken a promise to me."

Amir looked at Laila then back to his son. After many moments, he said sullenly, "Fine. I swear to you. I will never force Laila to leave our home again."

❁

Kudar was up early the next morning making finishing preparations for the journey. He left Laila fast asleep in his bed. When he walked outside he saw his father waiting for breakfast to be served on the courtyard. His father invited him to sit so he did. The morning sun began to rise as the men started to eat.

The conversation turned to the journey ahead of Kudar, as well as to predictions on the outcome of the war. Heavy footsteps hurrying across the cobblestone toward the men caused the conversation to stop. The men turned in unison to see who approached with such haste.

"Master Kudar." One of the stable hands appeared and rushed to Kudar bowing hastily.

"Yes, what is it?" Kudar answered.

"There is a visitor at the gate. She says it's important," the stable hand panted.

"She?" Kudar questioned. "Who's there?"

"The lady said her name is Mistress Zora of Karamania. She asked to see you immediately. She says it can't wait."

Kudar's brow wrinkled at the mention of Zora's name. *What was Zora doing here?* He excused himself from the table and followed the servant across the courtyard. He saw Zora standing near the gate dressed in riding gear layered with trail dust. Her hair was wind blown and she had a worried look on her face.

"Kudar!" Zora rushed to him when she saw him.

"Zora? What are you doing here?" he questioned barely concealing his surprise. "Where is your father?" Kudar inquired as they quickly embraced. He pulled away from her and looked about for Ibrahim.

"My father is not here," Zora replied.

"You came here alone?" Kudar questioned bewilderedly.

"I had to," she explained solicitously.

Kudar noticed her hands were trembling. "Come with me." He led her to a bench that was placed against the wall of his home. "Here, sit," he instructed.

Zora sat, then said, "I wouldn't have come except you are my last hope." Her voice was shaking now.

"What do you mean?" Kudar asked sitting next to her.

"It's my father!"

"Ibrahim? What about him?"

"He did not agree with the upcoming war and was planning to lead a revolt against Sultan Mehmed II. But, right after you came for Laila, the Sultan's men led a surprise attack against him and his *gazi* warriors. Our home was invaded and everything was ransacked. Our house was burned to the ground and all of the servants fled. Father was taken prisoner. I'm afraid of what the Sultan will do to him." Zora's words caught in a sob. She wrung her fingers together as a tear rolled down her dust-stained cheek.

Unnerved by her display of emotion, Kudar reached out and put his arms around her shoulders. "It's going to be fine," he assured calmly.

"Kudar, I came here because you are my only hope." She started to cry.

"Me? How can that be?" he wanted to know.

Zora turned to him. "You know the Sultan. You work for him. You could talk to him and ask him to release my father."

"Zora, your father has been against the Sultan for a long time. He actively tried to turn people against the Sultan, including me and my father. Now you tell me he plotted a revolt and was captured. Frankly, I don't think there is much I can do." Kudar rose to his feet and took a few steps forward.

"Oh please! You've got to do something!" Zora stood. "I can't give up on my father! Please! Please, I beg you!"

The look of pure desperation in Zora's puffy brown eyes was unsettling to Kudar. He had never seen her this unraveled before. "Zora, I want to help you. Really I do. But honestly, I don't know if I should. I don't think anything I say will help."

"Please!"

Kudar was silent for a moment as he ran his fingers through his hair. He motioned to the stable hand who stood nearby. The man approached and Kudar whispered something in the servant's ear. When the servant scurried away to do his bidding, Kudar turned his attention back to Zora and spoke. "I have to be honest with you, Zora. I don't feel comfortable with this. I don't feel there is anything I can say to the Sultan that would help."

"Kudar, you must understand. I wouldn't request this of you if there was any other option. The Sultan respects you. If you speak to him it could mean the difference between life and death."

"Frankly, I shouldn't be the one to decide whether I talk to the Sultan about this matter. There's someone else who should make the decision."

"Who?" Zora asked impatiently.

As if on queue, the door to the palace opened. Zora turned and looked at the doorway.

Laila appeared dressed in one of Kudar's robes. She stepped into the courtyard closely followed by Omar. When Zora saw Laila, her eyes widened.

When Laila saw Zora, her heart began to pound rapidly in her chest then it slowed when Kudar smiled and stretched out his hand to her. "Laila, sweet one." He took one of her hands into his. "Zora is here because she needs something. Her father planned to lead a revolt against the Sultan. It failed and he was taken prisoner. Zora wants me to try and help her by speaking to the Sultan on her father's behalf."

Laila glanced at Zora, then inquired, "Are you going to speak to the Sultan?"

"That's what I was trying to decide. However, I asked myself. Why should I decide when you're here?"

"Me?" Laila looked at Kudar inquisitively.

"Yes. You had to live with Zora and Ibrahim and were able to see them for the people they really are. So Zora and her father's fate are in your hands. Now, tell me, should I speak to the Sultan about them or not?"

Astounded by Kudar's question, Laila let her eyes shift back to Zora. For the first time, Laila saw fear in Zora's eyes. She had never once seen Zora look anything but confident and proud. Now Zora evaded her gaze and looked toward the ground.

"Well?" Kudar prodded gently. "What's your decision?"

Laila thought about all of the times Zora had treated her harshly. She remembered the times Zora slapped her and she definitely could not forget the beating she received at Zora's hand. She had been at Zora's mercy then. Now, she held the position of power and it was Zora and Ibrahim who were at her mercy.

"Zora," she began. "I hoped to never see you again. It will be hard for me to forget the way you and your father treated me."

A look of guilt settled on Zora's face and she appeared to be remembering the past as well. She continued to evade Laila's stare and did not say a word.

Laila continued, "You never cared about me or my feelings. All you wanted to do was hurt and humiliate me. Well, those days are over. I am back with Kudar and I am no longer your slave. I will never again have to work or serve your whims. You can no longer force me to do your bidding.

I remember how you beat me because you thought I stole a ring. You refused to listen to me when I tried to explain my innocence. So why should I listen to you now?"

When Zora still did not speak, Laila started to turn her back on the woman.

Suddenly, Zora reached out and clasped her cold hand over Laila's warm one. "Please!" she whimpered. "Please, help my father!" Her words were cut off by a sob and a fresh batch of tears crowded into her eyes.

Laila was silent for a long moment as she contemplated her decision. She thought about Ibrahim. He had tried to rape her. It was due to pure luck that he had not succeeded. Now, she had the power to make him suffer for the assault. She now had the power to make them both pay for the pain and suffering they had caused her. At this moment, they were both at her mercy. Revenge. If she wanted it, she could have it now.

She never told Kudar about Ibrahim's assault against her. She knew if she had, there would be no question as to what decision he would have made about Ibrahim's fate. She hadn't told Kudar about the attack because it had been such an ugly thing and what she had with him was beautiful. It was because of Kudar, she was happier than she ever thought possible. It was because Zora had not set her free that she had eventually met Kudar. Kudar had been the one saving grace in all of it.

The facts were, because of Kudar, Ibrahim and Zora could no longer hurt her again. At the moment, all of the unhappiness she endured in Ibrahim's household seemed a distant memory. Even so, could she really let go of the past?

"You and your father are both suffering as a result of your own destructive actions. It seems to me, you are both getting your due," she spat grudgingly. "You hurt me and I have not forgotten it. You made life miserable. But because of Kudar, I must admit, my life changed…for the better. I know that is something you didn't want."

"So, you don't want me to help Zora?" Kudar asked.

Laila was silent for a moment. She glanced at Kudar.

He smiled encouragingly and nodded his head. "Just say what you want and it will be done," he declared.

Laila took a moment to search her heart. Finally, she spoke. "Zora, despite you and your hate, I found peace. I've found acceptance. I found heaven on earth. My life is so beautiful. I don't want to cloud it with resentment and hate. I no longer wish to hold a grudge.

Kudar, it's all right with me if you speak with the Sultan on Zora's behalf," she announced.

Zora let out a loud sigh of relief and fell to her knees. She brought Laila's hand to her lips and placed a kiss on her knuckles. "Many thanks! Many thanks! I am so very sorry for the way I treated you. You did not deserve it. I should have freed you when you asked."

Zora's display of appreciation was unnerving. Laila was glad when the woman released her hand and stood.

"Now that that's settled, I must be leaving," Kudar said.

"Kudar, please take me with you. I want to see my father," Zora sighed wearily.

Kudar nodded his approval then instructed Omar to see to it that Zora was refreshed and made ready for the journey. Omar bowed to Kudar then led Zora inside the palace.

"I'm proud of you," Kudar told Laila when they were alone in the courtyard. He took her into his arms.

"It's hard to release all of the anger I have inside me toward Zora and her father. But, I don't want to hold on to it any longer. I want to let it go and it's all because of you."

"I'm glad you are able to say these things. I just want you to be happy."

"I would be happier if you were staying here. Since you're not, I wish I could go with you," Laila admitted.

"Oh no. It's too dangerous. The battle is going to start. I am not a soldier but I am sure to be in the thick of things since I will be near the Sultan. I definitely don't want you getting near any danger."

Now finished with his breakfast, Amir strolled into the courtyard. He took a quick look at Laila, then said, "Are you leaving, son?"

Kudar nodded his head. Amir turned and walked away.

"Looks like that's my sign to leave. Once Zora is ready we will be on our way," Kudar explained before kissing Laila on the forehead.

"How long will you be gone?"

"I will be away until the war is over. But I will be back. I promise. I will miss you terribly. Goodbye, my love." Kudar kissed her briefly on the lips before leaving the courtyard.

Laila watched Kudar walk away before she returned to the house. As she walked back to the harem, she decided she could not stand being separated from Kudar indefinitely. She had already been separated from him for far too long. Also, she feared for his safety and imagined him getting hurt and having no one to look after him. She made up her mind to go with him.

Laila took a quick bath, dressed in traveling clothes then quickly packed a travel bag. As she made her way to the stables, she saw Kudar and Zora riding away from the palace. She picked out a mare and led the animal to the side of the palace. She saw Kudar and Zora about to disappear in the distance. Throwing her travel bag over the steed, Laila climbed on the horse and prompted the animal forward.

She would have to hurry if she did not want to lose sight of them.

❃

Laila rode her horse a safe distance behind Kudar and Zora so she would not be spotted. She followed the riders until they neared the Golden Horn. She saw that a great iron chain supported on floating pontoons now sealed off the port. Laila watched as a section of the iron chain was lowered to allow a Christian ship to move freely through the water.

The travelers finally arrived at the Ottoman army encampment made up of thousands of soldiers. A quick overview of the camp revealed the bulk of the army was made up of feudal levies, mostly horsemen called *sipahis*. A fifth of the men appeared to be irregulars known as *bashi-bazouks*.

There were members of the army who were not Turks called *janissaries*. *Janissaries* were individuals who had been taken from their Christian parents as children and trained to serve as the Sultan's foot soldiers. Seeing all of the soldiers as well as the artillery was an intimidating sight. The artillery included the biggest cannon ever built which had a barrel over twenty-five feet long. Laila would later learn that the cannon had been made by the same man who had cast the cannon for the fortress Rumeli Hisari.

To the north, in front of the Turkish encampment, were the main walls of the city. There were soldiers from Venice and Genoa who moved constantly along the Great Wall surrounding Constantinople. A deep foss had been dug in front of the outer wall. Across the foss, there was a stone rampart which towered more than twenty feet above the bottom of the pit. Cannons were installed near the Military Gate of St. Romanus.

Kudar and Zora finally stopped near the back of the Ottoman camp. They dismounted. Laila watched from a distance as Kudar's tent was erected. She heard someone tell Kudar that the Sultan's tent was north of the Civil Gate of St. Romanus. She watched as he and Zora headed off in that direction before disappearing in the crowd of men and tents. Laila tethered her horse then slipped inside Kudar's tent to wait. She waited for hours until he finally returned.

"Laila? What are you doing here?" Kudar questioned when he stepped into his tent and saw her.

"I followed you," she revealed.

"What? You shouldn't have done that! You shouldn't be here! It's too dangerous! You must go back home now!"

"Zora's here."

"I took Zora to the Sultan's tent. She will be safe there. But, you—"

"I had to be with you," Laila admitted. "I can't bear the thought of being apart from you again."

"There is going to be a war. People are going to get hurt and people are going to die. You shouldn't have followed me here."

"It's just–"

"Laila, this is not a game. Not only has Mehmed amassed troops, but he has approximately two hundred ships that have sealed the capital from the sea. He has placed the Bulgarian renegade, Suleiman Baltoghlu, as his Admiral. Baltoghlu is a worthy adversary who has an exceptional military record."

"Please, don't make me go home. If you're here I want to be here."

"I can't allow it. It's just not safe."

"I will stay out of the way. I promise."

Kudar was unimpressed. "Even as we speak, the Sultan has already made the final step toward war. He has sent a flag of truce to the Emperor, which is required by Islamic law. If the Emperor and his subjects do not surrender, they will not be spared nor given quarter once the attack begins."

"It all sounds ominous. But, I don't want to return home."

"I should put you over my knee and paddle you for defying me."

"Paddle me if you must. Just, please don't make me leave you," Laila replied.

"Damn it, Laila," Kudar sighed pulling her snugly to his chest.

"What happens now?" she inquired.

"Now, we wait."

Chapter Eleven

Anger and resentment scratched at Vashti's heart. She sank down on a nearby bench and buried her face in the palm of her hands as unchecked tears streamed down her face. Kudar and Laila were gone. The moment she realized that, it was as if reality hit her. The pair could be gone months, enjoying the time they shared on their adventure. Meanwhile, she would be wasting away in the harem. It was not fair that she had been pushed aside. She was tired of being forgotten. She had to do something about it. But what?

"What is it, my dear?" a voice with deep timbre asked.

Vashti looked up through sorrowful eyes and saw Kudar's father standing over her. He looked very much like Kudar, except for the beard, salt and pepper hair and the few extra lines that creased his face. He sat down beside her and put his arm around her in a benevolent gesture.

"A face as beautiful as yours should never be soured by tears. What is the problem?" he probed.

"It…it's nothing," Vashti answered carefully, wiping away warm tears with her fingers.

"You were crying for a reason. Tell me why," Amir instructed gently.

Vashti hesitated for a moment. She didn't know if she could trust her voice. Finally, she spoke. "It's Kudar."

"Kudar?" Amir's eyebrows crinkled with concern when he heard his son's name. "What about my son?"

"I love…love him so much…but he has forgotten me," Vashti whined.

"Oh, I'm sure there is no way he could really forget such a beauty as you."

"Then why did he take *her*?" Vashti goaded.

"What do you mean?"

"He took her with him." Vashti folded her arms in opposition.

"He took who, my dear?" Amir wanted to know.

"He took Laila with him on his trip," she revealed sourly.

"He did what?" Amir rose to his feet.

"He would never take one of us girls with him on such a trip. Yet, he takes Laila with him. It's just not fair."

"Damn it!" Amir roared. "There is going to be a war! He's supposed to be with the Sultan and he took *her*! He just won't listen to me! He refuses to understand what I have been telling him!"

"He hasn't been the same since she came into our lives," Vashti lamented.

"I tried once to make his concubine disappear. He made me swear an oath not to do it again. So, my hands are tied. But, something has to be done," Amir snarled.

"Yes," Vashti concurred. "Something has to be done."

"This madness has to end," Amir fumed. "There has to be a way."

As Amir talked, Vashti's mind raced. She wiped the remainder of her tears from her eyes with the back of her hand. There was a way to push Laila out of Kudar's life and reestablish herself in Kudar's heart. If her plan worked, she would be the one who not only ruled Kudar's heart, but his household as well. The truth was, if she wanted to get back into Kudar's life, she would have to have his child. She chided herself for not thinking of it sooner. As the mother of Kudar's child, she would be afforded the title of *kadin*. Her place in Kudar's harem and life would be assured. She had to make it happen. It was the answer to all of her problems. She had to conceive Kudar's child, and every day as her stomach grew bigger, Laila's hold on him would weaken.

There was only one way she would have a chance to conceive. She would have to find a way to stop

144

taking the daily capsule that had the anti-fertility potion in it. Instead, she would search for a medicine man to give her a fertility elixir to take instead. Once Kudar returned, she would find a way to bed him. When they finally made love, she was sure the natural result would be Kudar's seed growing inside her belly.

"I can help you, my lord," Vashti interrupted Amir's banter. "I may be able to rid us of our problem."

"That would be nice," Amir said.

"Your son has pushed me aside once too often. As a woman in the harem, he owes me my due. If he spends a night with me, Laila will not be happy. It will cause problems between the two."

"You think so?"

"Yes. I need one night with Kudar when he returns. I will make him realize what a mistake he is making. And, it will make Laila realize she is not as special to him as she thinks."

"Maybe you are the solution," Amir acceded.

"Just one night. Do you think you can get it for me, my lord?" Vashti batted her eyelashes at the older version of her former lover.

"A night with my son? That sounds very reasonable to me. Maybe that is what it will take to free my son from Laila's clutches," Amir surmised.

✄

Laila did not feel at ease in the encampment surrounded by battle hungry warriors. She stayed in the tent most of the time. But she did get a glimpse of the Sultan riding his horse as he surveyed the walls along the city. He looked younger than she expected. He wore a turban with a *mucevveze*, had a pair of vengeful eyes and a slim nose that curved at the tip.

The next morning, a loud explosion caused the ground to shake. Laila shot straight up in her bedroll. Instantly, she was awake though it took a second for her to realize the noise was cannon fire. She scrambled out of her bedroll and stumbled out of the tent.

The purple and pink light of dawn breaking over the horizon revealed a massive display of Ottoman troops standing rank and file, surrounding the city by land, and Ottoman ships besieging the city by sea. Hurried movement atop the city walls drew Laila's attention as gunfire irrupted. In the next instant, the sound of thousands of guns being fired filled the air. Laila whimpered as she thought of Kudar and prayed that he was safe.

✂

Cannon fire exploded through the air and dispelled any peace that had been present in the predawn light. The ground shook. Kudar watched as troop leaders shouted to their men, barking orders to fill the trench around the city and mine weak sections of the city's wall. All day long, cannon bursts shook the earth around the huge outer wall, drowning out the shouts and cries of the men present. Soldiers defending the city along the top of the wall responded with their own fire. The blasts continued as the sun began to climb in the sky and persisted as it began a gradual descent that evening.

Slowly, the first day of fighting turned into another. Then another.

Day after day, the war raged on, creating a hailstorm of debris, smoke and cries of anger and pain. Day after day, the Ottomans shot at the fortress and everyday they were answered with return blasts from the defenders. Small pieces of the wall began to crumble to the ground. Finally, after a week of constant assault, the outer wall and two of the towers facing the valley of the Lycus were severally battered. However, the Christians used hastily yet solidly built stockades to foil the Turkish advancement.

Nearing the start of the second week, Mehmed ordered a full-scale assault on all the weak points of the remaining wall. On command, the Turkish soldiers once again filed into long straight rows in front of the wall. From somewhere in the middle of the rows, a loud battle cry went out and swelled through the ranks. Soldiers began beating their swords against their mammoth shields. Others began to beat their chests.

On queue, the horde of warriors advanced toward the city. However, the soldiers atop the outer wall were waiting for them. As the first line of fierce fighters edged forward, a shower of arrows and gunfire rained down on them – a warning to the others not to advance any closer to the city. The warning was heeded and the advance was aborted.

Mehmed called a meeting early one morning and announced that a secret attempt to break the iron chain had failed. Kudar listened as the Sultan addressed the soldiers. "My fleet of ships will not give up. We will break the iron chain in the sea. My ships will be used to bring this city to its knees. We must win this war. Defeat is not an option."

As the Sultan spoke, a commotion grew from the edge of the encamped troops and spread to the center of the mass. A flurry of conversation around the Sultan began and became more frenzied.

Suddenly, someone shouted, "Look! There are foreign ships in the sea!"

All eyes, including Kudar's, turned to look out over the Sea of Marmara. Four large vessels were bobbing in the green seawater. All of the ships' sails had Christian crosses emblazoned on them. The additional markings on three of the sails revealed the ships were Genoese, while the largest vessel was a Greek transport.

"Those ships contain provisions to replenish the city! There is no way they can be allowed to enter the city!" Mehmed shouted when he saw the boats. He turned to his admiral, Suleiman Baltoghlu. Staring him straight in the eyes, he shouted, "Stop the ships at all cost!"

Immediately, Admiral Baltoghlu barked orders dispatching the Turkish fleet to attack and capture the foreign ships. Men rushed to relay and obey orders. The mass of soldiers that remained on land began making their way to the water's edge. Mehmed ordered his horse brought to him. His army parted to make way for him when he rode his horse to the edge of the sea. Then, the soldiers closed ranks behind him.

Soon, Ottoman ships began to dot the water and surround the foreign transports. The Ottoman ships were not large and looked like logs floating beside the huge transports. The smaller Ottoman vessels opened fire on the larger ones causing smoke to bellow in the air. The air quickly filled with the smell of burnt wood as ammunition splashed into the water. The Sultan began shouting at the ships in the water and his army joined in with him as the battle raged on.

Without warning, the wind picked up and began pushing the foreign transports closer to the city. The larger ships rammed into the smaller Ottoman ones and nudged them aside as if they were toys. Upon seeing this, cheers irrupted from the spectators crowded along the walls. In response, the Turkish soldiers began to yell disapproving protests. The Sultan cursed in frustration at the sight before him. He yanked on his horse's reins causing the animal to stomp its hooves and bay. Unmoved, Mehmed prodded the horse into the shallow water along the bank. As the wind continued to drive the foreign carriers closer to the city, he screamed furiously and rode the beast in circles, causing water to splash up around him and soak his robes. Along the crowded walls, the ovation transformed into taunts and insults directed toward the angry Sultan and his soldiers.

As suddenly as the wind arose, it died down. However, a strong underlying current continued to push the transports onward until the ships came precariously close to shore. The sailors on the boats began hurling projectiles at the Sultan and his troops. The men near the edge of the water began to move back as a torrent of javelins and stones landed around them. With a curse, the Sultan guided his horse out of the water and back onto shore. Kudar, who stood near the embankment, felt a sharp pain on the upper part of his right arm. He clutched his arm and realized he had been hit when bright red blood began to soak through the cloth of the tunic he wore. He backed away from the fray, ripped the end of his tunic then tied it around his wound.

The wind rose again and the huge sails on the transports were unfurled. The huge enemy carriers once again shoved their way through the mass of Turkish ships. People along the wall jumped up and down for joy and their voices combined in a loud cheer as the transports finally entered the waters of the Golden Horn.

"Those ships were not to get through! Now the city has been resupplied! I want all of my Advisors and Generals at my tent! Now!" the Sultan bellowed as his horse kicked up dust and galloped back toward the encampment.

Kudar was busy tending to his wound when the Sultan's request was relayed to him. Slowly, he made his way toward the crowd assembled outside the Sultan's tent. When he walked near the front of the encircled crowd, he saw the Sultan standing with his arms folded staring toward the middle of the circle. Kudar followed Mehmed's gaze and saw that Admiral Suleiman Baltoghlu knelt with his head bowed. Over the Admiral stood a hooded man dressed in all black with a sword drawn above his head.

"Off with his head!" the Sultan commanded.

In one curt motion, the hooded man brought his sword down, and in a flash Baltoghlu's head separated from its body. An audible groan went through the onlookers as blood squirted everywhere and the Admiral's head rolled along the ground. Kudar turned away in astonishment and disgust.

When Kudar returned to his tent that night and saw Laila, he wrapped his arms securely around her.

"What is it? What happened to your arm?" she inquired when she saw his makeshift bandage.

Kudar brushed her hands away from his arm. "We'll deal with it later. All I want to do right now is forget the horrors of war," he murmured and hugged her close.

✂

After the beheading, the Sultan went into seclusion.

Several days went by before he finally emerged. When he did, he called his men before him. In a loud voice, he said, "There is a road that runs from the Bosphorus to a place called the Valley of the Springs on the shore of the Golden Horn. I have decided a slipway will be built. It will start at the Bosphorus and run up over the heights of Galata to the Golden Horn. Our ships will then be put on cradles and moved along the slipway to the waters of the Golden Horn. After which, we Turks will be able to attack the city from every side."

The men present looked at each other. Could ships really be moved over land? Slowly, smiles curled on the men's faces as they realized the plan was ingenious.

Work began soon afterwards. Carpenters labored to construct wooden platforms into cradles that could support the keel of a ship. Planks and tree trunks were laid together, tied with rope, then greased with sheep fat and oil. Next, ropes were attached to the forward corners of the ships. One by one, Ottoman ships were hauled out of the water and oxen were used to drag the boats to the slipway and place them on the oiled cradles. Once on the cradles, men were placed behind the oars and the ships' sails were unfurled. A team of troop leaders bellowed instructions for the men to start rowing and lashed their whips across the backs of the oxen in order to get the animals moving.

Slowly, the ships lurched forward. Minutes turned into hours and as the hours dragged by, the ships inched up the side of the hill. Finally, the vessels made it to the summit. After a brief respite, the boats slid to the foot of the hill before splashing into the waters of the Golden Horn.

Once eighty ships were floating in the Golden Horn, fighting commenced. Gun blasts pounded the wall along the sea as the ships from opposing sides skirmished to a stalemate. The Sultan, angered by the lack of a quick victory, ordered captured enemy sailors impaled in front of the city's walls. The men screamed and begged for their lives but to no avail. They were led to their deaths. In response to the executions, Turkish captives were killed and swung from the Christians fortifications.

Over the days that followed, hundreds of dead bodies baked in the hot sun. Soon, the stench of rotting flesh saturated Constantinople and the Turkish camp.

The fetid smell of rotting flesh made Laila's stomach turn violently. Her only relief was sleep. She wished Kudar was beside her, but over the past few days, he had not come to the tent much. She hoped the battle would be over soon so things could return to the way they were.

But the battle drew on.

By the time April finally turned into May, the Turks were feeling the affects of the prolonged war. Fourteen attempts had been made to mine underneath the massive walls surrounding the city. However, each attempt had been thwarted and supplies were running low. A beam of sunlight shrouded the church of St.

Sophia with a burnished glow. The mysterious light was interpreted as a sign of divine intervention for the city. Soon, rumors spread that the wealthy families of Anatolia did not believe the Sultan could capture Constantinople, had started to openly oppose him, and were considering having him deposed.

Refusing to give up, the Sultan called a meeting of the council.

"The time for a final assault on the city has arrived," he announced. "Preparation for the final assault must begin. The trenches facing the collapsed ramparts are to be filled. We will then make our advance, scale the walls and enter the city. We will win this battle."

Preparations for the final assault began immediately. Once completed, the Sultan rode along the city's walls attentively examining them for new signs of weakness. Bells from the churches began to ring mournfully when the Sultan called his army before him.

"My brave valiant troops," he began as he rode before his men. "Our success in this campaign is near. We are warriors and we fight for victory. The riches of this city are immense and laid out for you. All you have to do is enter the city and take them. According to tradition, you are free to loot and sack the city for three days. The treasures of the city will be distributed fairly. Our assault will be fierce throughout the line of the walls on land and in port areas. The *bashi-bazouks* will go first and they will be followed by the Anatolian feudal levies who will attack the southern sector of the land walls. The *janissaries* will wait opposite the weakest section of the fortifications. Our fleet will renew its offensive on the walls along the sea. We will be victorious. Victory will be ours, for Allah is with us. We are on the verge of conquering a new capital for the Ottoman Empire."

The meeting ended near sundown. As it did, an eerie silence saturated the Turkish camp, which was briefly interrupted by the sound of evening prayers.

During the deepest part of the night, the Sultan ordered his war banner unfurled. When he did, somewhere in the darkness, the sound of a drum began to beat. *Fifes* sounded, cymbals clattered together and cries of "Allah! Allah!" filled the air. The warriors began to gather together like a growing storm. Behind the Great Wall, the church bells started to ring erratically. From somewhere in the camp, flares were shot into the sky. As darkness illuminated with light, a legion of defender soldiers standing atop the remaining outer wall could be seen, their swords and guns drawn, ready for battle.

Upon seeing this, the *bashi-bazouks* drew their swords and surged forward in a fierce mass. Swords clanked against the rampart. The men on the wall, daunted by the sight beneath them, began to fire frenziedly down on the invading irregulars. There were cries of pain and death as ammunition contacted human flesh. Arrows also pelted the mass of attackers, hitting one soldier after another, causing numerous soldiers to fall back.

Countless others crashed forward. Within a short while, mounds of dead and wounded soldiers littered the ground as the advancing warriors carved a pathway to the foot of the huge wall. For a moment, it seemed the invading horde would enter the city. However, the torrent of gunfire unleashed from atop the wall eventually drove the progressing soldiers back.

Denying defeat, the *janissaries* tromped over the bodies of the wounded and dead *bashi-bazouks* in a daunting formation. When one fighter succumbed to enemy fire, another warrior surfaced to take his place. Several scaling ladders appeared and were placed against the stronghold. A few men climbed them and were able to reach the top of the wall. However, they were vanquished in seconds and the rest of their comrades were held at bay.

Just before dawn, the Sultan cursed, then yelled, "I've seen enough! Tell the troops to withdraw!"

The command for the Ottomans to withdraw slowly filtered through the ranks of fighting men and the *janissaries* began to retreat.

However, at the northern end of the wall, close to the Golden Horn and the Imperial Palace, a few Turkish soldiers noticed that a sally-port, called the Kerkoprota, was unlocked. The soldiers opened the gate, ran into the city and climbed to the top of the towers. The men began to pull down the Christian flags and replace them with Turkish flags. Upon seeing Turkish flags flying over the city, fighting by the Christian defenders subsided around the stockade.

The Sultan, close to the heaviest fighting of the battle, noticed this, reversed his previous announcement and bellowed, "Riches shall go to the first man to enter the city!" before he plunged his sword into the body of an enemy soldier who charged at him.

A tall stocky *janissary* dashed to bid the command. He scaled up the stockade and managed to challenge several defenders. Other *janissaries* quickly joined him and soon they had secured a foothold on the outer wall. Turkish soldiers rushed over the wall and trotted across the hard earth.

Once at the Great Wall, they scaled the ladders and charged into the city. Inside, the Military Gate at St. Romanus was forced opened and masses of highly trained *janissaries* stormed into Constantinople. The Turks breached the walls in two additional locations and they surged into the city like a tidal wave. One by one, the other gates of the city were opened and thousands of Ottoman soldiers swarmed upon the defenseless citizens.

Untamed warriors smashed down doors, stabbed and strangled their enemies. Shops and homes were looted and set a blaze. Young children, who had little value in the slave market, were killed immediately, while the men and women were shackled into groups bound for the slave market. At St. Sophia, the door of the church was kicked open to the fearful screams and sobs of the worshipers inside. The soldiers began to shout at the people, overturning statues, and cutting and tearing holy books in half.

Kudar and the other nonmilitary men followed the soldiers into the city and were witness to the victors' depredation. When Kudar saw the church being pillaged, he left the carnage and returned to the tent. "The Turks have entered the city!" he told Laila.

She sighed with relief. The war was over.

Kudar continued, "The Sultan has called for his top architects and advisors who are in charge of rebuilding the city. I have to rejoin the group. I want you to come with me."

Laila agreed and walked next to Kudar as they entered the city behind a small group of men and the Sultan, who rode a horse. The group toured the ruins. Ottoman flags were now draped over walls and towers and on the palace at Blachernae. Fires were burning, buildings lay in ruin and hundreds of dead bodies polluted the streets. The town looked nothing like the magnificent city it had once been. Overwhelmed by the destruction about her, Laila lowered her eyes.

The entourage stopped in front of St. Sophia and Mehmed dismounted. A soldier ran out of the church dragging a half-dressed nun and disappeared down the street. The Sultan frowned and in a gesture of humility, stooped, picked up a handful of dirt and sprinkled it over his turban. He then stood and walked inside the church, most of the men followed him. Laila did not go in. She did not think she could handle the sight of what lay just beyond the church doors.

When the men came out of the church they trailed the Sultan as he walked across the town's square. Laila followed behind the men and listened as the Sultan mused. "What a city we have given over to plunder and destruction. Let there now be an end to this death and destruction. I want the church of Holy Wisdom converted into the chief mosque of the city. The former capital of the Christian Roman Empire, the city of Constantine, is no more. We have now removed the last major barrier toward expansion into Northern

Anatolia. The Ottomans will now dominate the Straits and the southern shore of the Black Sea."

They stopped at the Palace of the Emperors, which had been founded by Constantine the Great, eleven and a half centuries before. The Sultan entered the ransacked palace followed by his small entourage. The dust on the floor mosaics swirled around their feet.

"We will build and rebuild," Mehmed announced. "Mosques, mausoleums, *madrasahs* as well as a *kulliye* will be built containing *tekkes* for our dervishes and holy men. Pavilions, halls, fountains must all be rebuilt. We will leave our mark yet respect the past. Kudar al Numan, what are your plans?"

Kudar stepped forward. "According to my designs, all of the mosques, mausoleums and *madrasahs* will be built with a domed construction, as is our tradition. However, as you suggest, we will respect the Byzantine tradition and take some inspiration from Christian art and architecture. We will combine both Islamic and European artistic tradition."

"Where would you start?" Mehmed wanted to know.

"St. Sophia is respected as a place of faith. I think we should start there. I would like to add four minarets to the church."

Mehmed nodded his head in approval. "Very well," the Sultan acceded. "Your designs will be reviewed and then construction will commence."

❀

That night as they settled in their tent, Kudar and Laila held each other close glad that the war was finally over. Kudar was excited that his plans were going to be used to rebuild the city. Laila felt elated that she was with him and able to share in his happiness.

Several weeks later, with construction in the city well underway, Kudar announced he had some free time he would use to take her home.

"Good. I am ready to get out of here and get home. War is not for me," Laila assured.

The ride back home got off to a slow start. The day they were supposed to leave, they slept in late and found it hard to rise once they awoke. It was as if they both were trying to recover from the events they had just lived through. After a late lunch, the couple finally started their ride home. Slowly, the city began to fade from view.

"I know it was not safe for you to be with me. But I'm glad I had you to return to on the nights I could return to the tent," Kudar admitted as a drop of rain fell on his nose. He wiped it away as another drop fell, then another. "Let's make a shelter," he suggested.

The duo stopped the horses and Kudar quickly erected a tent. The two climbed inside the tent just as cold rain began to pour down in sheets.

"Your clothes are soaked," Kudar commented when he turned to her. "Take them off," he bade as he stepped out of his wet clothes.

Laila removed her garment. "I'm cold." She shivered.

"Let me warm you," Kudar suggested and he turned her so her back was against his chest. He encircled his arms around her covering them both with a blanket he held in his hands. He put his chin on top of her head then hugged her tightly. "I haven't been in the mood for lovin' lately," he disclosed. "Living through a war will do that to a man. But being so close to you now is bringing life back to my loins."

As he finished speaking, Laila felt the nudge of his manhood against her backside.

"Oh, Kudar…"

"Come on, give me some," Kudar chided playfully as he fondled her breasts with his fingers.

"Your wish is my command," was her reply.

"I am glad you are back home, son," Amir said.

Kudar looked at his father who sat across the dinner table from him. He took another bite of the savory meat on his plate, then sipped wine to wash it down before he responded. "Laila and I just returned home from our journey late this afternoon. Why did you insist I have dinner with you and Mother tonight?" he asked, noting the pompous expression on his father's face.

"I asked you to dine with us tonight because I have an announcement to make," Amir declared.

"Announcement? What announcement is so important it couldn't wait until morning?" Kudar asked cavalierly.

"You know you are important to me," Amir began. "So is your future. That's why I had to use my best judgment to help you. While you've been gone, I've been looking out for your future."

"What do you mean, Father?" Kudar questioned.

"What I am saying is I've found a bride for you...and I have arranged for you to be married," Amir proclaimed with a smile.

Kudar choked on the wine going down his throat. He coughed to clear his passageway. *"What?!"* he exclaimed.

Chapter Twelve

"I found the perfect bride for you and I've arranged for you to be married," Amir repeated, ignoring his son's grimace. "She's more perfect than I'd hoped. Not only is she Turkish, of our faith and comes with a very handsome dowry, she's of royal blood. I'm sure you will like her."

"Father! What are you talking about? What have you done? I'm not getting married!" Kudar slammed his cup on the table causing its contents to spill over the sides.

Amir's smile faded instantly and the hard line of a frown creased his lips. "I've left the decision in your hands long enough. I know now, if it is left up to you...you will never wed. You would go on with the way things are indefinitely. Well, I told you, this madness had to end. Look son, you've had plenty of time to sow your wild oats. Now, it's time for you to fulfill your duty."

"There's no way–"

"Things are going to work out even better for you than I'd hoped. Your bride's mother is the Sultan's fourth cousin. Her husband is the Governor of the Southern Province. This is a betrothal you cannot say no to. Everything has been finalized. Promises have already been made. You will meet your bride at her home in one month's time. After which, you will bring her back here to live with you as your wife."

"I won't let you coerce me into an arranged marriage!"

"You know this is our way...our culture. It's your duty. Our family name must be preserved. A union between you and a royal would cement our family as honored members of Turkish society. You want to turn your back on that?"

Kudar was silent.

Amir continued, "I'm beginning to wonder if you are the same son I've always been proud of. I am

159

beginning to wonder if you are still a man. After all, you ran to Karamania chasing that wench of yours like you were her shadow."

"Father!"

"It's true! You haven't been with any other woman since you met her! It's unnatural! You used to call Vashti a lot! You were happy with her! Now, you have your head so far up Laila's apron you can't think straight!"

"You leave Laila out of this!"

"How can I? Not only have you refused to satisfy any of the other women in your harem, you took your slut with you when you saw the Sultan! Have you lost your mind? No! I let you go on long enough! You will start acting like the heir of our family and accept your marriage! You will do your duty and produce an heir so our name can go on!"

"Father, you can't make me do this!"

"I am the head of this house! You are my son! You will honor me with this request! You have been turning your back on your responsibilities long enough!"

"I don't give a damned about any of that!" Kudar barked.

"That's obvious! That's why I had to take matters in my own hands! Starting now, things will go back to the way they were *before* you brought that whore back to our home! There's no more discussing the issue!" Amir pushed back from the table and stood up in a huff. He glared at his son, threw down the towel used to wipe his hands, then stormed from the room.

"Mother!" Kudar protested, turning to his mother who remained silent up until that point.

"You heard your father. The dowry has already been agreed upon. Your marriage is going to happen," Irene confirmed matter-of-factly.

"I don't want to marry a stranger," Kudar grumbled.

"There are hundreds of men in arranged marriages and they manage to survive."

"I thought you would understand how I feel and side with me."

160

"Son, you don't have to be in love to marry your betrothed. Just marry the girl and produce an heir. That's all that is asked."

"But–"

"I want you and Laila both to be happy. You can still have her as your *ikbal*. That does not have to change."

"Father is trying to control my life!"

"My son, don't fight your father on this, please. There's been enough unrest around here. You know he just wants what's best for you. This issue has continued to divide you and your father. Because of it, you are both unhappy. Don't you think it's time that you both stop being at odds with each other?"

Kudar angrily ran his fingers through his hair. He couldn't believe his father had gone behind his back and betroth him to a perfect stranger. Even if the girl was of royal blood, he did not want her. Now, however, he was duty-bound to marry a girl he didn't know or care for.

What had he expected? Had he really expected to live the rest of his life immersed in Laila? Had he really thought he could get away with shutting everyone else out? Had he really expected not to have to get married at some point?

'You will start acting like the heir of this family,' his father's voice echoed in his mind. *'You don't have to be in love to marry your betrothed.'* He couldn't forget his mother's words either. Her words repeated over and over in his mind for they were the truth. He didn't have to marry for love. Wasn't expected to. But if he was going to please his parents, he had to marry.

He had to admit, it felt very uncomfortable to be angry at his father and have his father angry at him. Over his lifetime, there had been very few times when he and his father disagreed on issues because his father had always been content with letting him have his way. Now, things were different. *'Don't fight your father on this, please,'* his mother had asked of him.

'It's your duty. Our family name has to be honored,' his father had said.

His father was right. The marriage would mean a lot for their family. It would, in fact, cement their family into Turkish society which was exactly what his father had spent his life hoping for.

How was he going to explain it all to Laila? She had requested that she be the only one in his heart. And in truth, she was. She had indeed captured his heart and no other woman could ever take her place. Could he make her accept the fact that although that was true, his father already made an agreement which he had to honor? Could he make her understand that for his family's sake he had to marry a woman of his own race?

❧

Kudar spent the night alone stewing over his father's mandate. Unable to sleep, he rose early the next morning and tried to spend time going over a few designs he wanted to show the Sultan. Too distracted to work, he decided to take an early morning run around the palace grounds with the hope it would help clear his mind.

When he stepped outside into the courtyard, his father waved him over. "I was just coming to see you," he stated after Kudar walked to him.

"What is it you want, Father?" Kudar asked flatly.

"I heard you are going to return to the city today."

"Yes, I am leaving the palace around noon today. Construction is well underway, so I have to get back to check the progress. I just came back to bring Laila home."

"Did the Sultan see her when you were in the city?"

"He did," Kudar answered.

"What the hell were you thinking?" Amir shook his head. "Your concubine should not be in the presence of the Sultan. If word gets back to your intended, there

162

could be problems. When are you going to grow up and start taking life seriously? You are being led by your cock, not your brain."

"Father! Don't start!"

"What kind of man gets led by a woman?"

"It's not like that!"

"No? That concubine of yours gets away with doing whatever she wants. She never participates in evening prayers. She doesn't celebrate Ramadan. She even has your mother remembering her Christian upbringing.

I thought our faith and tradition was important to you. Laila is not one of us. She is not part of our faith. I ask myself, why is she the only woman you have taken to your bed?" Amir wanted to know. "Before she came, you had a way with all females. You gave each of the women in your harem their due...especially that fiery redhead, Vashti. Now, I wonder if you are man enough to be with any other woman."

Kudar bristled at his father's words. He was so enraged by his father's insinuation he walked away without saying another word. Instead of going for a run, he stormed to his room, poured wine into a goblet and began drinking it.

Was his father right? Maybe he could never have a relationship with Laila outside of the harem. Did everyone think he was being cuckold by a woman? Maybe he did need to start living in reality and stop living in a dream world as his father suggested. He thought about the women in his harem. Bella, her sweet smile... Yasmine, her beautiful laugh... Vashti, fun and lighthearted... He used to like spending time with her... Her deep green eyes, cinnamon colored hair and curvaceous body... An image of her writhing underneath him flashed across his mind. She had always been willing and happy to please him. It had been many months since he had spent time with any of them. Maybe he should call for Vashti as his father suggested. If anyone could improve his mood, she could.

He thought about Laila and a frown creased his face. God knew he missed her. He hadn't called for her the previous night, and he knew she would worry. Truth be told, he didn't want to see the look in her eyes when he told her he was going to be married.

What was he thinking? His father was right. He was a man. He didn't have to explain himself to a woman.

"Omar!" Kudar called for the eunuch.

Omar appeared instantly.

"I want Vashti sent to me as soon as possible," he announced.

"As you wish," came the reply.

※

When Omar entered the harem and announced that Kudar wanted her, Vashti could not help the swell of excitement that rose in her chest. She stood and glided across the room, glancing quickly at Laila, who had an astonished look on her face.

"What? Master Kudar wants me?" she questioned breathlessly with a smile. "Tell him I will be there shortly to serve him as he pleases."

All of the women crowded around Vashti chatting excitedly, each trying to talk over the other.

"He must have gotten tired of having the same girl day after day," Vashti spoke louder than necessary. Her words were clearly meant for Laila. "I knew the feelings Master Kudar had for me would never die. I knew all along he would come back to me," she revealed triumphantly.

Vashti felt giddy about what was to take place. Soon, she would see Kudar and then she could put her plan into action. She had decided she was no longer going to play by the rules and had stopped taking the capsule which reduced fertility. Through the grapevine she had found a healer and asked for something that would ensure her fertility. The old woman had given her special herbs.

After that, she started to rise early for breakfast before the other women awoke. She would have her breakfast served on the patio. When she was given the capsule, she would drop it in her hot tea to dissolve it. Then, to dispose of the evidence, she would pour the tea into the pot of a green plant near the table. After which, she would mix the special herbs in her food and eat everything on her plate.

Eating breakfast became her favorite meal of the day. She would savor every bite knowing all that was needed was one more time with Kudar. One time and she would conceive. Of this she was certain. And now, finally, her dream was about to come true.

Laila felt curious eyes on her as Vashti prepared for her morning with Kudar. Some looks were hostile while some were sympathetic. Laila wanted to escape to her room but she refused. She did not want Vashti or anyone else to think that she was running and hiding.

Finally, Vashti left the harem and Laila was able to retreat to her room. She sat in front of the vanity table. Warm tears crowded into her eyes. She had known things had changed between her and Kudar the moment she stepped into the harem after returning from Constantinople. Vashti gladly revealed that Kudar was betrothed to a royal and would soon be married.

The news had astounded her.

"I can tell by the look on your face you didn't know," Vashti had sneered. "Well, get used to it because the days of you manipulating Kudar are over."

Vashti's words had wounded her deeply. But what hurt most of all was the fact Kudar had not been the one to tell her about his betrothal. *How soon was he to be married? Who was the girl?* Laila did not have answers because Kudar had given her none. It was as if overnight he forgot about her. This time, she had too much pride to run after him for an explanation.

Why had she fooled herself? There were three other women in Kudar's harem. She knew he would want to be with one of them at some point. But she wasn't the type of woman who wanted to share a man. She had told Kudar of her feelings before they ever made love. She had been sure he cared for her. But if he did, why didn't he at least have the common courtesy to tell her his feelings for her had changed?

He should have talked to her. He should have warned her he was going to call Vashti. At least then she wouldn't have been totally caught off guard and humiliated in front of everyone. Oh why had she ever cared for Kudar? Why had she allowed her heart to become involved? She wished she could dismiss the feelings of betrayal and jealousy in her heart. For some irrational reason she felt betrayed and abandoned, just like her mother had been. As she thought of it, tears overflowed and streamed down her face. She bent her head, covered her face with her hands and wept.

"Don't cry. Please don't cry," a soft voice pleaded.

When Laila heard the voice, she tried unsuccessfully to brush the tears from her face. She looked up through puffy red eyes and saw Kudar's mother. Irene looked tall and stately standing in the doorway.

Irene stepped forward gracefully. "You remind me of me," she said. "I had a good cry the day I learned Amir was bringing another woman into our home. I could ignore the women who were here before me. I told myself that Amir loved me and he would have no need for anyone new after me. But right after I gave birth to our son he brought another woman into our home for his harem. He said it was the way of his culture and he ignored my tears. However, it wasn't all bad."

Irene gently placed a thin alabaster hand on Laila's shoulder. "I was the only one of the women who sired him a son. Because of it, Amir listens to me and shows me honor and respect. I reminded him that doing so for the mother of the firstborn son is part of his culture

166

also." Irene patted Laila's shoulder and smiled weakly. "Don't worry. I know my son and he does love you."

"Love me? He doesn't love me. If he did, he would have told me about his upcoming wedding. I don't know why he bothered to rescue me from Ibrahim's house. And he's with Vashti as we speak. He could have at least warned me."

"It's his father. Amir sees Kudar as a better version of himself. He wants Kudar to be successful, admired and more importantly, to have status among the people. If Kudar doesn't do exactly as expected, my husband doesn't know how to deal with it. He thinks that our son being with you all the time is a sign of weakness. He encourages Kudar to pull away from you."

"And Kudar does it! It hurts so much!" Laila admitted.

"It hurts because you care. It will be fine. Sometimes men have to be with other women. Let's both hope the morning goes by quickly. My son does love you and I think that's wonderful. Though I must admit I am a little jealous of the two of you and your relationship. I've been watching you two. The way he looks at you...the way you touch him..."

Laila watched as a shadow came across Irene's face.

"You have been very kind to me," Laila acknowledged. "You remind me of my own mother." As she thought about her mother, a new stream of tears started down her face.

"Just let all the tears out. Don't try to hold them back," Irene coaxed as Laila's body shook with sobs.

※

The door opened. Omar brought Vashti in, bowed then made his exit.

Vashti created a breathtaking vision in the early morning light. Her red hair was styled attractively on her head. She was dressed in a sheer vestment. Her alabaster skin glowed beneath her garment. Her round breasts, with their rosy tips, strained against their confines. Her curvaceous hips topped long shapely legs and the short reddish curls between her legs had been shaved. She looked at Kudar, who sat on the edge of his bed and shimmied toward him.

"Kudar," she purred breathlessly and fell into his arms.

Her peach and mint scent filled his nose, bringing back memories of many pleasurable nights. Her soft skin melted at his touch. "I hate you for ignoring me for so long. I should be angry with you and refuse to speak to you. Fortunately for you, all I want to do is kiss you," Vashti whispered and pressed her lips to his. "Phew! You've been drinking," she noted. Wrinkling her nose, she wrapped her arms around his neck. "I missed you. Tell me that you missed me." Her words were a plea.

Kudar did not answer. Instead, he lowered his eyes.

"What does *she* have that I don't?" Vashti pouted. "What do you like so much about *her*? Does she touch you here?" Vashti's voice softened as she slid her hands slowly up his chest and slipped his *gomlek* off his shoulders. "Mmm!" Her words swallowed into a moan as her fingers traced the muscles that rippled over his tanned chest.

Her hands trailed lower until her fingers grazed the material in front of his trousers and briefly brushed over the bulge beneath it. Vashti untied his trousers at the waist and pulled them down slightly. She smiled triumphantly before she wrapped her fingers around his manhood and began to gently stroke it.

"I've missed this." Her words were barely a whisper.

After a moment, she stood up and wiggled her hips as she guided her raiment above her hips then pulled it over her head. Her creamy breasts popped free, bouncing slightly. After she tossed her garb to the floor, she moved her hands and cupped her breasts before shaking them invitingly. With a gleam in her eye, she licked one of her fingers then ran her thumb over one of her taut rosy nipples. She did the same to its twin before sliding her hand between her legs.

Kudar's arousal did not go unnoticed by Vashti. She walked to him and placed a soft kiss on his neck. She took his now hardened member in her hand. "I'm going to remind you how nice things were between us. I'll make this morning a morning you will never forget," she promised, then bent down and lowered her mouth to his member. She licked and sucked gladly, eager to feel him inside of her and conceive his child. She was so close to her goal. She had to make sure Kudar never forgot her again.

Impatiently, she straddled him and gently pushed his shoulders.

He fell back on the bed.

She smiled, raised herself a little, then slowly lowered herself onto his erect member.

Chapter Thirteen

Kudar looked up at Vashti when he heard a triumphant moan escape her lips and ran his fingers through his hair. She looked like she was really enjoying herself. He really should be enjoying himself too. Hadn't he always enjoyed it with Vashti? Yes, he had. So why wasn't he enjoying himself now? He didn't feel pleasure. He didn't feel anything. He just watched Vashti bounce up and down on him quickly losing interest.

"Oh no." Vashti clicked her tongue against the roof of her mouth and rose off of him. She looked at his softened member. "Did you drink too much alcohol?"

Kudar shrugged his shoulders.

Vashti refused to be defeated. She had waited months for this time with Kudar...had planned for this moment. She had to get him to release himself into her. That was all she needed.

It took several minutes, but soon she had his member rehardened slightly. She resumed her position over him and slid down on his tower. She moved her hips urgently. Her plan could not fail. "Come on, Kudar," she pleaded. "Let me have all of you."

Why, at this very moment, did he feel like a dirty dog? Kudar asked himself. However, he knew the answer before he asked himself the question.

What was wrong with him? No woman was his master. He was the man! He made the rules! Then why, at this very moment, did he feel like dirt? Why couldn't he enjoy the comforts of Vashti's body when he told himself it was what he wanted? Who was he fooling? The answer was painfully clear. There was one woman who had managed to conquer his heart and soul and that woman, no matter how he tried to ignore it, was not the one who rode him at this very moment. While thinking of it, he felt his member go flaccid again.

170

When Vashti felt it happen, she stopped moving and looked accusingly down at him. He pushed her off him. She landed with a thud on the pillow beside him. She rolled over and stared at him inquiringly.

Kudar sat up. "Leave me alone," he grumbled with annoyance.

"But Master…" Vashti started to protest.

"You heard me!" he snapped.

In an instant, Vashti's eyes became thin slits. She flew at him, her arms flailing wildly. "Do not send me away!" She punched at him. "I won't let you do this to me!" She scratched at his eyes.

Kudar managed to catch her flaying wrists after she delivered several punches. She tried to pull away from his grasp. They were a rough tousle of energy for a moment before Kudar shoved her out of bed. "Get out of here!" he yelled.

When Vashti's feet hit the ground, she stumbled slightly but managed to stay upright. She glared at him. "I hate you!" she hissed.

Kudar reached for her garment and threw it at her. "Don't make me tell you again!" he barked.

With an angry huff, Vashti stormed from his room.

As soon as Vashti left, Kudar reached for his drink near the bed and emptied the goblet. When it was empty, he hurled it across the room and it hit the wall. He reached beside his bed and picked up a jug of liquor he had sitting there. He turned the jug to his lips and began drinking straight from it.

He wanted to drink until the dirtiness he felt in his heart faded away.

"She said she was taken from her home…abducted and forced into slavery," Vashti spat. After Kudar had thrown her out, she had gone straight to Amir.

Amir listened quietly while Vashti told him the story of Laila's life. Laila, the woman had been a thorn in his side far too long. When Vashti finished her story, he asked, "Has she mentioned her home much?"

"She has repeatedly said she misses her home. When I first met her, she used to talk about it all the time."

Amir was quiet for a moment as he contemplated the best course of action.

Vashti sat and looked demurely at him.

Finally, he said, "She should be persuaded to return to her homeland."

"Homeland? What do you mean, my lord?" Vashti questioned.

"She should return to her family. I made a promise not to force her to leave. So, I cannot force her. However, if she decides on her own..."

"That's a marvelous idea. However, she won't do it without telling Kudar and Kudar will not let her leave."

"She will not be able to tell Kudar if he's gone. He's leaving today at noon to return and assist with new construction in the city."

"Once Kudar finds out she's gone, he will go after her."

"My son is scheduled to travel to his bride's house before he returns to the palace. By the time he returns home and finds out about Laila, it will be too late. He will have a new wife to worry about. He will have no time to go chasing an old lover."

"I think it is a great idea. I just hope it works," Vashti replied.

"It will work. It has to work this time. I will take care of the details myself," Amir said impudently.

"There is still one concern that lingers," Vashti admitted.

Arching his eyebrow, Amir asked, "What is that?"

"Your son can never find out I came to you."

"He won't, my dear. Besides, I would have come up with this solution sooner or later. It is what's best for my son. Soon you will be rid of your biggest competition. And I will have what I want."

"And what is it you want, my lord?" Vashti wondered out loud.

Suddenly, a shadow crossed Amir's face and hard lines creased his forehead. His voice was cold when he answered. "I want that wench away from my son. Once and for all."

❁

Laila was shocked when Omar told her Amir wanted to talk to her. Her heart started to pound in her chest because she knew Kudar's father did not like her. She squared her shoulders and followed Omar across the courtyard to Amir's home. They entered Amir's palace and passed the dining area where she and Kudar made love for the first time. Her cheeks felt warm as she remembered that dinner.

What had she been thinking? Her thoughts were interrupted when she looked down the hall and saw Kudar's father standing in a doorway. He stepped aside as Laila and Omar approached to let them pass him and enter the room. The room was a small sitting area with cozy looking seats. Omar backed away and stood in the corner.

Without speaking, Amir slowly circled Laila then stopped and stood in front of her. He took a moment to look her over. Then, he looked her directly in the eyes and with a low steady voice, he asked, "Do you love my son?"

Laila lifted her eyebrow in surprise at his inquiry. She did not think Kudar's father brought her to his house to ask her such a question. "Yes. Yes, I do love him." She nodded affirmatively when she found her voice.

"That's what I thought you might say," Amir said briskly, pivoted quickly then sat on a couch in the center of the room.

Laila turned toward him.

173

"Come. Have a seat," the imposing man instructed, nodding to the seat across from him.

Laila walked to the couch and sat down.

"Kudar is a good son," Amir began after she was seated. "He always has been. I'm very fortunate to have him as my son. He has so much to look forward to. His whole future is ahead of him. In our land, family, honor and tradition mean everything. Kudar is my family, my honor, my tradition. Without him, I have nothing. He is my only son. My future. The future of this family. Do you not want him to fulfill his obligations to his family?"

"Yes, of course I do."

"If my son does not have heirs, our family legacy ends. He cannot have heirs if he does not have a wife. He needs a wife of our culture and faith. He cannot continue to move upward socially without a proper wife. Do you want to prevent him from taking his proper place among our people?"

"Of course not. But, I must admit, I do not see what this has to do with me."

Amir brought the tips of his fingers together and placed them under his chin. Inwardly, he was seething as he looked at the beauty who had seduced his son. She was looking at him like an innocent helpless victim who could do no wrong. He wanted so much to slap her pretty little face. "It's time for my son's wild ways to end and you must help me," he said instead.

"Me?" Laila questioned.

"Let him go. You say you love him. My son is going to marry into the Sultan's family. There is no higher honor than that. But he will throw all that away unless you help him to take hold of his future."

"What do you mean?"

There was silence.

"I have learned some news I wanted to share with you." 'Bitch,' he wanted to add but didn't.

"What news?" This time Laila's voice was laden with curiosity.

"There is a passenger ship leaving Constantinople in two days."

Laila looked at Amir, befuddled.

"The ship will be sailing to the West Bank. When the ship docks, a convoy will be traveling through Egypt. Cairo, Egypt. If you're on it, you can be back with your family very soon."

Laila stared at Amir, not sure she understood him.

"You could be settled in your home in several weeks' time."

"Home?" Was there such a place? Was her home in the harem or was her home the place she used to dream about returning to? The place she had prayed a million times to return to.

"I don't know..." Her voice was weak this time.

"It's what you always wanted. You've been dreaming of it. Is that not so? Well, now your dream can come true."

"My home is here now. I can't leave."

"Kudar's home will soon be ruled by another woman...his wife. Do you think you will feel like this is your home when that happens? His betrothed is young and pretty. Do you think you can be happy seeing my son with his new *kadin*, watching him fall more and more in love with her every day? Do you think you can compete with a woman of royal lineage?

When the new *kadin* sees the special treatment Kudar gives you, she will no doubt be very angry. She is sure to make your life a living hell. And as Kudar's wife, she will have the power to do it. Think of it now. The women in the harem are already very envious of you, are they not?"

Amir was right. Her life in the harem was no longer a happy one due to the jealousy of the other women.

"You have a chance to leave it all behind and let Kudar start his new life. And you have a chance to be with your family. After all this time, wouldn't your family want to see you? Your mother. All of this time, she's had no idea where you are. She's had no idea if you

175

are alive or dead. Don't you want to see her to tell her you are alive?"

Yes, she wanted to see her mother. Her dear sweet mother had lived without knowing that she was alive and safe. Yes. She must see her mother. ...But Kudar?

"I need to talk with Kudar first. I need to tell him–"

"My son and I have already discussed this." The lie was a little one. "He knows I am meeting with you to ask you to leave."

"What?"

"I just came from seeing him and he agrees that this is for the best," Amir explained. The truth was, after his talk with Vashti he had stop by his son's quarters late that morning and he had seen Kudar preparing to leave. However, he had not talked to Kudar about Laila. But if he made Laila believe he had, it would make her decision an easier one. It would never do to let Laila know his son was in the dark on this issue. It was now past noon, Amir was sure his son had already left the palace. By the time Laila returned to the harem, Kudar would be long gone and could not stop her departure.

He continued, "At first Kudar resisted the idea. He thought about it for a long time. Once the war was over and you both came back to the palace, he finally agreed it is for the best."

Laila could not believe her ears. Kudar wanted her to leave. He had been thinking about it before they left for the war. "Nay. It can't be true."

"Oh, but it is. He feels really bad about everything, of course."

"He never told me."

"He decided he didn't want the confrontation. He agreed things would be easier if I handled it."

"But–"

"Look, my dear, the fact is, there is really no place for you in Kudar's life anymore. If you are honest with yourself, you will agree. Kudar knows once you go back home, you will have the chance to meet a nice young

176

man, marry and have a family of your own. If you stay here, you will always be one of many. Nothing but a number. My son may be able to squeeze in time for you when he is not with his wife and children. But you will never have him all to yourself like you have had. After a while, he will forget about you altogether. Is what I am saying not true?"

Laila lowered her eyes as anger, confusion and hurt filled her. It was all starting to make sense. Kudar had been contemplating getting rid of her for months. He had made up his mind to send her packing. He knew all along he had a new wife waiting for him, but couldn't face telling her. That was the reason he had not called for her. Now, he wanted her to return to her home so he could get on with his life. How could he be so callous?

"You see, my son has a way with the maidens. He always has. He woos women, then breaks their heart. I've seen it happen many times. That's why I was so angry at him when I saw it happening again. Look, has my son ever told you he loved you?" Amir asked gently, then chuckled, "Oh why do I ask? Of course he has. He tells every woman he loves her. That is part of his seduction."

Laila looked down at her hands laying in her lap. Kudar had told her he loved her. But were those words something he told every woman as his father suggested?

There was a silence so thick a spear could have been driven through it.

"I promised my son I would not force you to leave this house. I must keep that promise. So in the end, the decision to leave is one you must make. I have instructed Omar to pack your bags if you decide to go." Amir nodded to Omar, who still stood quietly in the corner. "Omar is good at doing what he is told. Kudar is not. If you love my son, you will not try to get him to change his mind and stop you from going. You will agree to leave and accept his decision. You will not make this harder on yourself or my son. I know you will make the right choice." With that said, Amir stood.

※

Irene stepped away from the door and back into the shadows when she saw her husband rise from his seat. She had been standing just outside the room listening to the conversation that took place within. She pressed herself deeper in the shadows as Laila exited the room followed by Omar. When they were gone, she stepped into the room they had just exited. Amir, his back to her, stood looking out the window.

"How could you do this to our son?" Irene asked accusingly.

Amir turned to her. "You were listening?"

"Yes. I heard everything. You never discussed the issue of Laila leaving with our son. How could you say such a thing? You could have at least talked to me first."

"I don't have to get permission from you before I act, woman!" Amir barked.

"No. But you promised Kudar you would not make her leave ever again."

"I am not making her do anything. I just offered her a trip home. That is all."

"How could you be so cunning?"

"Kudar doesn't know what's best for him. He's proven that."

"He loves that girl."

"What does he know of love? He's in love with what's between that *houri's* legs! He can get that anywhere. He doesn't need her around. As long as she's available to him, he will not get on with his life."

"He's done fine."

"How can you say that? Have you forgotten the scene they made at dinner? All my friends were there. I commanded him to stay away from her. It did no good. What else do you want me to do?"

"Kudar just wants to be with Laila. He cares for her. Is that so wrong?"

"Irene," Amir walked to his wife. He put his hands on her shoulders and softened his voice. "We have been too soft on our son. He has got to start focusing on his future. Getting that wench away from him is the first step."

"I just want him to be happy and I know he would not be happy if he knew you were going behind his back like this! He would be furious! If he knew–"

"He won't know. He won't find out because you are going to keep your mouth closed!"

"Don't threaten me!" Irene bristled. Turning her back she walked away from her husband.

Amir put his head in his hand and sighed. "You're right," he said. "I'm sorry I'm being disrespectful. I don't mean to treat you in such a manner. You don't deserve that. Look, wife, I know Kudar would never understand if he knew I spoke to Laila. But I don't know what else to do. I want what's best for our son and I don't know how else to give it to him. This is the only way I know. As your husband, I am asking you...telling you, don't tell our son what you overheard. It's for his own good."

Irene sighed and walked to her husband.

"Don't worry so much, dove. You know what? I will send off for a few of the latest fashions and have them sent to you directly from England. You would like that, wouldn't you?" Amir asked.

Irene nodded her head slightly.

"Of course you would. Everything is going to work out just fine. Trust me," he assured as he hugged her close.

❀

Kudar sat up in bed and noticed by the waning sunlight, he had slept too long. After Vashti left his chambers that morning, he realized he had a slight headache. But he ignored it when his father came to visit him. He and his father discussed his plans to finish his work in the city then at the end of the month travel to get his bride. As Omar began packing, his father hugged him goodbye then left the room.

However, as noon approached, Kudar found he was not ready to leave. It felt as if the room was spinning. He realized he had drank too much and feared he was in the midst of an alcohol-induced haze. He walked to his bed and lay across it. After closing his eyes, sleep quickly engulfed him.

Now, as he sat in bed, he realized he still was not ready to leave. Truth be told, he wanted to talk to Laila before he left. He had to explain his upcoming marriage, as well as explain why he had not called for her since they returned to the palace.

He climbed out of bed and called Omar.

When Omar appeared, he instructed the servant to tell Laila she was to come to his room for dinner. Omar looked shocked but did not say a word. He just nodded his head then left to do his bidding.

Kudar bathed and prepared himself for dinner.

As dinner was being set up on the balcony, he found he was very anxious. He was impatient to see Laila's beautiful face appear in his doorway. He practiced in his head what he would say to her when she arrived. The servant preparing the table asked if he needed anything else. When Kudar shook his head negatively, the servant left. Kudar looked toward the door hoping Laila would walk through it at any moment.

Thirty minutes later, she had not appeared.

Kudar began to pace as he waited.

An hour later, when Laila still had not arrived, Kudar realized she was deliberately staying away. Without further hesitation, he exited his room, marched down the hall and down a flight of stairs.

When he made it to the harem, he threw open the huge doors and stomped inside.

Chapter Fourteen

The women saw Kudar enter the harem and their conversations came to an abrupt halt. All eyes were transfixed on him as he walked to the middle of the common room and bellowed, "Laila! Laila!"

There was no answer.

He strode across the living area quickly glancing into the bedrooms as he passed them. When he looked into the *hamam* he saw Laila in the bathing pool bathing herself. Through the clear water, he could see her nude body was splendid perfection. Her round curves and shapely legs looked inviting. Her hair was wet. She was rinsing lather from her body.

"Laila!" he called again.

Undeterred, she continued her task and did not acknowledge his presence.

Kudar stomped over to the bathing pool, stood with folded arms and tapped his feet.

Continuing to ignore him, Laila leisurely finished washing the excess lather from her body.

When that was done, she reached for a towel and dried her hair. Once completed, she tossed the towel aside, stood and stepped out of the bath. She picked up another towel and slowly dried her body. All the while, Kudar stood staring at her without saying a word. Casually, Laila wrapped the towel securely around her chest and walked out of the *hamam*.

Kudar followed her to her bedroom. When he entered the chamber, he saw her sitting at the vanity table brushing her hair. Her towel was gone and she was dressed in a purple robe made of silk.

She continued to ignore him for several moments more.

When it was evident he was not going away, she spoke. "You still here? I thought you'd be gone on your trip by now. You know the trip. It's the one where you leave to get your new wife, isn't it?"

"I have to get married. It's my duty. I'm not going to let my family down," Kudar responded.

"How nice for you," Laila replied with words that dripped with honey yet held the sting of venom. "You won't let your father down…but you will let me down?"

"Laila, it's not that simple," Kudar protested.

"Then what is it, Kudar? I know your father doesn't like me because he doesn't think I'm good enough for you. But I never thought you would go along with him."

"It's not like that."

"Then how is it, Kudar?" Laila asked. Placing her brush on the vanity, she turned to him. "I'm good enough to sleep with? But not good enough for you to share your life with? I thought your feelings for me were real! But you never cared for me! Not really!"

"Laila, that's not true. I wanted to talk to you at dinner. I wanted to explain. That's why I called you to my room. You didn't come," Kudar countered.

"And I won't!" Laila assured him, her heart still heavy due to her earlier conversation with Amir.

"You won't come when I call?"

"You heard me! Now, lower your voice."

"I will speak as loud as I want!" Kudar raised his voice even louder. "You better start explaining why you ignored me when I sent for you to come to dinner tonight," he warned.

"You want me to explain?" Laila laughed sarcastically, then stood. "How about you do the explaining? Without a word to me, you decide to cast me aside, you promise yourself to someone else and you make love to another woman. Yet, you tell me to explain *myself*!"

"This is a harem, Laila, or have you not noticed that? In case you didn't know, sex is what goes on in a harem!"

"Fine! Go ahead! Have sex with whoever you like! Just remember, I do not want you to touch me ever again!"

"Damn it, Laila!"

"I don't know why you bothered to bring me back from Karamania. You don't love me. You've made that outstandingly clear. When it's all said, you don't think I am good enough for you. Not someone who is your equal. That's why you thought you could lie to me and tell me that you loved me. You used me and then discarded me because you see me as nothing more than your whore. Your love slave. Well, for the record, I belong to no one! I am no one's slave! And that includes you!" Laila spat back angrily.

"I could punish you for speaking to me this way!"

"I would curse you with every breath!" she pledged.

"Damn it, Laila! I want to explain everything to you…make you understand. You should have come to me when I called you tonight. When I call for you, you come to me. Now come."

Laila squared her shoulders but did not move.

"Come to me!" Kudar commanded again, this time with much more force. "You come to me whenever I want you!"

As her reply, Laila turned her back to him and started to walk away.

In two quick strides, Kudar was upon her. He put a staying hand on her shoulder and hurled her around to face him.

Laila glowered up at him. "Get your filthy hands off me! I don't know how many women your hands have touched! I'm sure Vashti and your new wife won't mind your hands all over them! But, I do!" she hissed.

Kudar scowled at her, his eyes blazing with fury. Impulsively, he shoved her backward onto her bed.

Laila landed in a sprawl across the bed, her purple garment an awesome contrast against the red satin sheets. Kudar fell on top of her. His huge hands clutched the soft cloth of her clothing. With ease he started to slide her robe from her shoulders.

"Kudar!" Laila protested, pushing at his shoulders. "What are you doing?" she questioned.

His response was to slowly and methodically rip the thin robe in half. Starting at the shoulder, he tore

183

the robe down her back until it fell off her shoulders. Laila gasped as the material fell around her waist, exposing her breasts to his view.

Instantly, Kudar was hard as a rock and Laila couldn't help but feel his response. She gasped in outraged dissent as his erect member burned the inside of her thigh, searing her with its touch. A glint came into his eyes and she shook her head in objection. She rolled her hands into fists and pushed them against his shoulders. "No! No! Not like this!" she objected.

Kudar quickly secured her hands in his. "When I call you, you come to me." His voice was husky. "And when I call you to my bed, you come to my bed and you like it no matter who has been there before!"

"No!" She shook her head in defiance.

Kudar growled and with one hand he ripped off his *gomlek*, exposing his muscle-carved chest.

Laila screeched in protest. "No! We can't! They will hear us!" she muttered loudly as she spoke of the women in the harem who no doubt could hear through the thin walls.

"Let them hear!" Kudar bellowed. "Let the whole world hear!"

"I hate you, Kudar! I hate you!" Laila hissed.

"Really, my dear," he replied, releasing his hold on her wrists. "Then slap me. Send me out of your room with my tail between my legs."

Laila made no move. She just stared up at him.

Kudar responded by removing his trousers and tossing her tattered robe to the floor. He stretched out beside her, his warm flesh pressed against hers. He let his hand run over her shoulders, breasts, stomach and the inside of her thigh. Finally, his fingers slithered to the warmth of her womanhood.

"Just as I thought. You want me!" he exclaimed when he felt the wetness between her legs.

"No!...No!...I don't..." Laila's words slurred as his finger entered her and he began to suck one of her breasts. "Stop!....Stop!..." she instructed strongly...

weakly as his finger rubbed the nub of her maidenhead.

"You want me to stop?" Kudar's voice was lusty and breathless.

"Yes...Yes. I want you to stop," Laila managed to say.

"Then push me away or else I am going to enter you and make love to you. ...Well. Go ahead. What are you waiting for?... You can't push me away because you want me as much as I want you."

"You belong to someone else. Your father has seen to that," Laila accused.

"You still want me. You want this." He lowered his head and kissed her hungrily. Then he moved on top of her, careful to rest his weight on his knees. His member prodded for the opening of her womanhood and found it moist and inviting. Without another word, he slid himself in her.

Laila found it impossible to resist him. She lifted her legs, drawing her knees to her chest to give him better access to her entrance. He pushed into her. Laila moaned uncontrollably when she felt herself being filled with his presence. He started to move inside her. She wrapped her legs seductively around him and pushed back, joining with him.

When he leaned down and kissed her on the lips, she found she could barely hold onto reality, for his touch sent her toward ecstasy. Kudar's lips trailed down her neck, his hands rubbed her stomach and traced the inside of her thighs, sending an urgent tingle through her. Laila wanted to explode from the pleasure of Kudar's touch. She found she had no choice but to give into his spellbinding touch...to him. His lips worshipped her. His body begged for her love. So she gave herself to him. All she had to give. She lay beneath him and he devoured her with love, gentleness and adoration. She responded by loving him in return. Soon, Laila found she was catapulted to heaven and she writhed underneath him as her insides accepted the seed he spilled deep within her. With a salient groan, he fell on top of her and she melted into the pillows on her bed.

Kudar rolled off her to lie on his back in the bed next to her. "Amazing!" he exclaimed.

Laila did not speak. She was too spent from desire to say a word.

Kudar pulled her to him so that her head rested on his shoulder.

The lovers lay still until their labored breathing returned to normal and they drifted off to sleep.

✾

The next morning when Laila awoke, the bed was empty. Kudar was already gone. Immediately, sadness washed over her. He had left and when he returned he would belong to another woman. She thought about the night they had just spent together. It had been beautiful. It had been something beyond her wildest dreams. Even though the night had been magical, he still had not said the words she was hoping he would say, had been hoping he would say for a while now. After all the things they had been through and all the love they had made, he still had not said he loved her and no one else. In the end, she had been living a fantasy.

When Kudar called for Vashti, she had cried until she was sure she had no more tears to shed. Vashti had told her once, what he did with her, he did with every woman. Vashti wanted her to believe she meant nothing to him, that she was just an object of his lust. Maybe Vashti was right. After all, Kudar had no problem ignoring her when it suited him. He had no problem leaving to get a wife because it pleased his father. If there was one thing Laila knew she wouldn't do, it was make love to another woman's husband.

When she found out from Amir that Kudar had decided he wanted her to leave the palace and return home, a million emotions had gone through her. She believed her relationship with Kudar had grown and deepened in the passing months. But the facts were, he had never told her she was the only woman he loved. And he would always have other women in his life. His father didn't want her around and he was off marrying another woman. She had prayed to one day be able to return home. Well that day was here. So, why was she not excited about it? She should be. The thought of one day going home was what had kept her from despair many a night. If only Kudar had told her he loved her and her alone as they made love the previous night, she would have stayed with him. But the facts were he had not. Instead, he had left that morning without even telling her goodbye.

Laila sat up in bed. She couldn't stay in bed for the rest of her life. She needed to get out of bed and begin her day. The first thing she needed to do was wash the sticky remnants of the previous night's loving from her body. Then she would go to the garden and prune the yellow and pink flowers that bloomed against green flowery leaves. Working in the garden always relaxed her. Besides, it would give her time to think.

She stood up and stretched. Her feet touched something cold and soft. She looked down and saw a tattered piece of purple fabric from her robe. She bent down, picked up the silk and rubbed it against her cheek as she thought about the scene she had made the previous night. If she could have seen herself, she was sure her cheeks would have been flushed red from embarrassment. Dear God! What the women must think of her? But there was no preventing it. She would have to step out of her room and face her detractors sometime.

By late afternoon, Laila finally made up her mind. "Tell Kudar's father I will return home. And please, tell Kudar where I've gone," Laila requested of Omar when he arrived in her room.

Omar looked at her. He could see the troubled storm that waged just behind her cloudy eyes. He nodded.

Laila continued, "Tell Kudar I love him and I wish I could stay. But I have to go home. His father is right. He is starting a new life and there is no longer a place for me in it. Make sure he knows I really do love him, will you?" Her eyes were pleading.

Omar nodded again. "I will tell Master Amir of your decision. I will begin to pack your things." Omar started to walk away but turned back to her after a few steps. "I, for one, will be sorry to see you go," he acquiesced. "I think you were good for Kudar."

"Thank you, Omar. My life with Kudar was good," Laila admitted. Then, her voice trailed off when she added, "...while it lasted."

�֍

Laila stepped into the courtyard. The evening air was chilly. A cool evening breeze tried to caress her. However, she wore a warm wrap which protected her from the crisp air. The sun was beginning to set. A burnt orange and deep yellow painted the sky. She walked across the courtyard toward Omar who stood at the gate. When she neared him, she turned around and took one last look at the place that had been her home in recent months: two palaces separated by the outdoor courtyard. *Goodbye home. Goodbye Kudar,* she thought.

She started to turn from the sight but paused when she heard a door open. Seconds later, Vashti stepped outside. When Laila's eyes met Vashti's, she saw a look of satisfied triumph idling there. Then, in an instant, the look of triumph was replaced by something Laila could only describe as hatred. A cold chill, not caused by the evening air, bolted down her spine. How could a friendship that started out so promising turn out so badly? Laila did not have time to ponder the question because Omar called to her. She turned and continued to walk to him. He opened the gate then he bent down and picked up her bags. Laila walked through the gate she had entered for the first time many many months before.

There was a small man standing by two donkeys. *"Merhaba,"* the man said in greeting.

"Merhaba," Omar spoke to the man and handed him the travel bags before turning to Laila. "Melek will take you to the ship."

Laila did not answer.

The man named Melek finished securing the bags to one of the donkeys then helped Laila on the other. "I am honored to have a beauty from the al Numan household accompany me on this journey. Shall we proceed?" he asked kindly.

Laila nodded as she pulled her wrap closed, not because she was cold, but because her hands needed something to do.

Melek spoke to Omar for a few more minutes then climbed on his donkey. Omar called a farewell to him and waved to Laila.

As Laila rode away from the palace, she refused to look back.

Chapter Fifteen

They arrived in Constantinople late that night. When Laila entered the city, she was amazed by the changes that were taking place. Though it was dark, she could see the results of the new construction underway. The minarets Kudar had proposed were going up around St. Sophia and other structural changes were being done to the church. Laila thought of Kudar. She wondered what he was doing that very moment. She tried to push thoughts of her lover from her mind as Melek led the donkeys to the harbor.

Once at the sea's shore, Melek pointed to a large vessel idling in the water and a man in a rowboat headed toward the bank. Melek dismounted from his donkey then helped Laila down. He walked to the water and began to talk to the man in the small boat when the man made it to shore. A few minutes later, Melek walked back to her.

"Abbas is going to row us to the ship. I told him that you are from the al Numan palace and you are going home to Cairo," Melek informed her as he led her to the craft.

"*Merhaba*. How are you?" Abbas asked looking at her as she stepped in the rowboat which rocked precariously back and forth.

"I am fine," Laila answered, showing Abbas a smile she did not feel.

"So you are from the al Numan palace?" he asked.

Laila nodded her head.

After her bags were loaded, Melek stepped into the boat and Abbas began to row them out over the dark water to the awaiting ship. The undulating waves were divided by the oars creating a tranquil sound. Laila thought once again about her life and how much it had changed once she met Kudar. She looked down at the sapphire ring she wore on her finger. She had not taken it off since Kudar had given it to her. She moved the ring back and forth on her finger. It was the only thing she had with her that directly linked her to Kudar. She glanced up then frowned slightly when she realized Abbas was looking at her. He smiled kindly at her. She was too heartbroken to smile back.

Once at the ship, a rope was lowered to the water. Laila was instructed to grab a hold of the rope, which she did. She was then raised up the side of the huge vessel. Once she got to the ship's rail, she was lifted overboard. When Melek and her bags were lifted up, a sailor walked to them and smiled. The sailor talked to Melek then bent and picked up her travel bags. Laila followed the sailor down a small flight of steps. When he walked inside an open door of a cabin, Laila followed him into the room. The cabin was only big enough for a bunk bed. However, it did have a huge porthole that undoubtedly let in a lot of sunlight. Now, the only light in the room came from a lantern in a holder on the wall.

"This will be your quarters. It's a little small but it should do." The shipmate squeezed her bags into a corner.

Laila smiled weakly.

The sailor left the room shutting the door behind him leaving her alone.

As light broke through the chilly mist the next morning, the ship began to sail out to sea. The journey to Egypt was slow and tedious. When Laila found she was the only female on board, she stayed in her small room as much as possible. The men were loud and un-bathed, and she did not feel comfortable walking on deck while every pair of male eyes followed her. Her days were lonely and the constant rocking of the ship made her nauseous.

With each day that passed, instead of her sickness getting better, it seemed to get worse. Laila found she spent most of her time lying in bed. There was not a moment that went by when she did not think of Kudar. She missed him so much even though he wanted her to leave his home. She wished with all of her heart that things could have turned out differently between the two of them.

Slowly, one day rolled into the next. The sun rose then set. Water stretched before the ship like a thick endless blanket. Before long, Laila began to suspect she was going to have a baby. *'No, it can't be!'* she told herself, even as her heart leapt for joy. If she was carrying Kudar's child, she couldn't help but be happy about it. Though she had left Kudar, he had not left her heart. Oh, why could he not love her totally and completely the way she loved him? Yes, she loved him! And she missed him terribly. But now it was too late. Kudar would never know about his child because he no longer cared for her and would no doubt not care for her child. No, there was no going back.

Finally, one day, land appeared on the horizon. Laila's heart jumped with elation when she saw it through the porthole. She gathered her things and went out to stand on the deck in order to watch as the city slowly came into view. The buildings of the city gradually grew from miniature structures to full-sized shelters. It was midday when the ship neared port.

The streets of Cairo were alive with the sound of controlled chaos. People scurried about. Merchants argued loudly amidst vigorous negotiations. Women in brightly colored clothing chatted loudly with each other while their children laughed and scurried about, careful not to lose sight of their mothers.

Donkeys pulling carts weighted with goods were slowly being driven through the streets, while their owners shouted instructions to the animals and prodded them forward with flimsy looking rods. All of these voices were mingled with the sound of squawking chickens, roosters and other fowl pinned in cages.

Cairo! She was home!

The ship finally docked and the sailors made preparations to disembark. Melek appeared and told her he would remain in town until his caravan was prepared for the journey south. He promised to drop Laila off at her home on his way out of the area. Laila shifted anxiously on her feet. In a short while, she would be able to see her mother. Would her mother look exactly as she remembered? And what had happened in her aunts' lives?

She thought of Kudar and her heart saddened. She wondered what he was doing at that moment. She missed him terribly despite everything, including the pain of his rejection. However, she knew she must push thoughts of Kudar out of her mind even as she carried his child in her belly. She felt as if she was half a world away from the palace and Kudar had done nothing to prevent it.

Sure, she could turn around and sail back to Constantinople and tell Kudar he was going to be a father. Even as she thought it, she knew it would do no good. He was undoubtedly married by now. Having a child with her was something he would probably not care about at this point in his life. He had started a new life. So must she. Life in the harem was her past. Life with her new baby was her future.

The ladder was finally lowered. Melek picked up her bags and Laila followed him down to the street. When her feet touched the earth, a feeling of peace filled her. Melek led her a few blocks then stopped in front of a merchant's cart. He exchanged words of greeting with the vendor and they began to talk.

From their conversation, Laila could tell the men knew each other. Each second that ticked by seemed like an eternity for Laila. She was back in Cairo. So close to home. She had to start out now if she wanted to make it to the hut before nightfall.

Unable to wait any longer, Laila took her bags from Melek, thanked him then told him she would find her own way home. He began to protest but Laila was already halfway down the street. She called a word of thanks to him for his assistance on her voyage, and then she headed home. She made it through the streets, amazed at how much things had changed, yet stayed the same. As she headed out of town, the noise and hectic commotion started to fade. The travel bags she carried began to feel heavy.

When the city was a miniature outline on the horizon, an old man riding in a wagon pulled by an even older looking donkey, stopped and offered her a ride. Because her travel bags were unbearable and she knew riding was faster than walking, she accepted the offer.

The ride was a pleasant one filled with small talk. The sun began to set and the air began to cool. Finally, the hut that had been her home came into view. As they advanced, they saw a woman and two children. Laila's heart began to pound with excitement. As they neared, Laila could see the woman was taking clothes off a line where they had been hung to dry. The two children, a small boy and girl, were chasing each other. As the old man prodded the aging donkey forward, the woman's features crystallized and Laila realized the woman was her mother. A sob caught in her throat. Her mother continued to work, oblivious of the approaching wagon.

When the wagon drew to a stop, her mother raised her eyes to see who happened by. Her hand fell to her side and she stared in complete silence.

Suddenly, she cried, "Laila!" Her voice was a shaky whisper. "Is that you?"

Laila climbed down from the wagon.

"Mother! It's me!" Laila answered. Before she could take a step, her mother sprinted toward her.

Tears were streaming down both women's faces as their arms wrapped around each other. The two women began to sob in each other's arms.

"My baby! My baby!" her mother cried happily.

"What is going on?" a voice asked.

Mother and daughter turned at the sound of a familiar voice to see one of Laila's aunts standing in the doorway of the hut. When the woman realized Laila was standing in the yard, she ran out to meet her with tears streaming down her face also. The kinswomen encircled their arms around each other as they cried and hugged each other close.

"Laila, where have you been?" her aunt wanted to know.

"Are you all right, angel?" her mother managed to ask between sobs.

"What happened to you?" came another question.

The two children in the yard had stopped playing and stood watching the scene unfold before them. They walked over and now stood looking up at the crying women. The children looked like they wanted to cry too.

"It's all right. Don't cry, little ones," Laila said to them.

"Laila, these are my children," her aunt explained.

"Auntie, these are your children?"

"Yes. They are orphans who needed a mother. They are the best thing that ever happened to me."

Laila was so excited at the news that a fresh batch of tears rushed down her face.

The old man cleared his throat and the relatives turned to him, suddenly remembering he was present. He held up Laila's belongings. Her aunt rushed to get them. "I'll take those," she said, grabbing the bags.

"Thanks for bringing her home," her mother called to the man before she turned back to Laila. "You're safe! I'm so glad! I've gotta know where you've been. How'd you get home?" Her mother asked one question after another, not giving Laila time to answer any of them. With her arm still wrapped around her daughter, she led Laila toward the hut. "I hardly recognized you when I first saw you. Have you been eating properly? Are you tired?"

When the women entered the tiny hut, the smell of roasting meat saturated the air and Laila's stomach growled. Things were just as she remembered.

"You hungry, angel?" her mother asked.

Laila was a bit hungry. But, due to her excitement, she doubted she could keep any food down. So, she shook her head negatively. Her mother continued to ask a million questions and she tried to answer them, though she suddenly felt tired. She sat down in a seat close to the hearth. When she did, a skinny brown cat with black stripes jumped in her lap and purred.

Her aunt walked in, looked at her, then said, "That's the children's cat. He likes you."

Laila smiled and stroked the cat's back. The cat settled in her lap then nestled its head against her stomach. Laila thought of the baby that grew inside her. She wanted to tell her family about her new addition. However, she decided to wait until their shock at seeing her had settled. She knew her family would be excited and her child would be loved. In the meantime, Laila tried to keep up with all of the questions that were thrown at her. Her aunt stayed a few hours more, then left for her own hut.

Alone, Laila and her mother embraced once again. Her mother asked her to tell every detail about what had happened to her. Laila began to tell her story. She told of her abduction, how she met Kudar and the time she spent with him. She left out the part about Vashti and the part about Kudar marrying another woman. She did not want to think about that, let alone talk about it. When she was done, her mother recounted the things that happened while she had been away.

Mother and daughter sat up and talked late into the night reminiscing over the past and revealing their hopes for the future.

The next day, Laila was happily reunited with her other aunt who returned from visiting a friend.

Once she was well rested, Laila decided to go back to her favorite spot along the Nile River. With a knife hidden in her pocket for protection, she made her way along the long winding path and over the bed of grass toward the river.

When she arrived at the waterway, she saw the stone formation jutting out over the water was just as she remembered. Carefully, she lifted herself up the side to the cool smooth center of the rock. She surveyed her surroundings just as she had the last time she was on the rock. Not much had changed along the river. The water was still a blue oasis for plants, wildlife and the villagers who fished in the distance.

Laila sat down and rubbed her stomach. Before long, she would not be able to hide the fact she was with child. She was happy to know she carried a piece of Kudar with her. She wished she could tell him she was going to have his child. She missed him terribly and wondered if he was thinking of her. She closed her eyes and thought of his face...his eyes...his lips...his touch....the last time they made love. Dear God! What was she doing? Why did she insist on torturing herself? Thinking of Kudar...of her past...would do no good. She had to forget the past and think only of the years to come...years without Kudar. *Things will be fine*, she told herself.

If only she believed it.

Chapter Sixteen

Kudar ran the back of his hand across his brow. For days, he had been busy assisting with the reconstruction of Constantinople, now renamed Istanbul. He had been reviewing designs and meeting with different councils. He looked up at the minarets that currently surrounded St. Sophia. They were almost done now that a layer of whitewash was being added to them.

Truly, there was no longer a reason for him to remain in the city. He was completely free to go get his bride. His excuses for not doing so had run out. Truth be told, he could have left the city weeks ago. But he had found reasons to remain close to home. He did not want to leave, not because he could not pull himself away from his work, but because he was dreading the journey he was to take once he did. He was already a month overdue at his soon-to-be bride's home.

If he waited much longer, winter would set in and he would not have enough time to travel to her home and return to his. He wondered for a moment what kind of woman his father had picked out for him. A twinge of resentment toward his father pierced his heart but Kudar suppressed it. He didn't like feeling such animosity towards his parent.

When he made it back to the inn where he was boarding, Kudar began to pack his belongings in preparation for his journey. That night, as he lay in a cold lonely bed, he stared into the dark toward the ceiling. As he lay there, he thought of Laila back in his harem and wished he could see her.

He remembered their night of passion with him intertwined in her arms. That night had been heaven, a place he never thought he would be. He had awakened early the next morning after he heard a few of the women rattling about. When he looked at Laila, she had been curled up invitingly under the covers. She looked like an angel sent from heaven. He had to fight the urge to stay beside her. He managed to resist and since she looked so peaceful, he left without waking her.

He regretted the argument they had that night. He hoped she was not still mad at him.

In his heart of hearts, he knew she would never accept him married to another woman. He also knew a life without Laila was not what he wanted. He would have to make a choice; Laila or his culture.

The choice was clear.

Quickly, Kudar got out of bed and picked up his travel bags. Stepping into the night, he threw the bags over his horse and swung his leg over the horse's back. Settling on his steed, he guided the animal away from the inn and out of the city. Smiling, he took the road that headed home... headed home to Laila.

✄

The ride back to the palace seemed to take forever for an impatient Kudar. As mile after mile dissipated under his horse's hooves, the burden on his heart lifted and his mood grew lighter and lighter. His every thought was of Laila. By the time the palace came into view, he was whistling. After all, it was only a few more moments before he saw the woman who had managed to capture his heart.

When he finally made it back to his room, Kudar was exhausted. However, he could not wait to finally see Laila so he decided to bathe and summon her. As he bathed, he thought again of the fight he and Laila had the night before he left. He did not know if she was still angry with him. Though it was rather late when he finished his bath, he called Omar and told him he wanted to see Laila. When Omar did not move to do his bidding, Kudar barked, "Are you daft, man? I said I want you to bring Laila to my chambers now."

"Master Kudar, with all due respect." Omar lowered his head. "Laila is no longer with us."

"No longer with us? What are you talking about? Speak up, man!" Kudar snapped when the eunuch hesitated.

"Laila…left the harem."

"Left the harem? What are you saying? When did she leave?"

"She disappeared the day you departed on your trip. No one has seen or heard from her since that time. She packed her belongings and no one knows where she went." Omar lowered his eyes as if pained at the expression on Kudar's face.

"What? Bloody hell! She's been gone for months! That can't be! Why didn't someone ride to the city to tell me when it was discovered she was gone?"

Omar did not answer.

Kudar cursed again. He stormed out of the room and down the dark hallways of the palace then barged into the harem.

"Laila! Where is Laila?" he bellowed.

The ladies, awakened by the commotion, came to investigate.

Kudar charged into Laila's old room. The room was dark when he stepped in, but he could see a form lying among the sheets on the bed. He rushed over, knelt down next to the bed and reached out to touch the still figure.

"Laila?" he questioned turning the figure to face him.

"Master Kudar?" a sleepy voice questioned.

It was Vashti. She sat up.

"Vashti? What are you doing here? In this bed?"

"This is my room now. Laila is gone. She has left you," Vashti answered.

Kudar lit a candle near the bed. Soft yellow light illuminated the room.

"I know this must come as a shock to you. When I heard she left you, I was no less shocked than you." Vashti swung her feet over the side of the bed. "You cared for her. You showed it countless ways. But she was ungrateful. She did not deserve you."

"Do you know why she left?"

"I have my suspicions," Vashti replied cryptically.

"When will she be back?"

"Why should she come back? She's been gone since the day you left, and that was after the night you forced yourself on her here in the harem. Remember it, Master? I wouldn't exactly say she was thrilled by it. In fact, I think she was humiliated."

"Humiliated?"

"Just think of how you used her that night. You took her by force. It probably made her feel bitter and start to hate you."

Kudar groaned as he thought back to that night. He had stormed into the harem and taken her roughly, in spite of the listening ears of the other women. He had sated his lust on her. In his fervor, he hadn't thought that she would hate him enough to leave. He sank on the stool in front of the vanity table. That had been a night of rough animalistic passion...of soft gentle caresses and butterfly kisses... He didn't want to think that Laila resented him. Yet, maybe what Vashti said was true.

"I don't understand. Why would she leave without telling me?" he questioned.

"She obviously did not care for you as much as you cared for her. Can't you see that? She left you because she didn't love you. She knew you had to honor your father's wish and be married. In the end, her pride was greater than her love for you. She betrayed you.

She wanted to hurt you because you were to marry a better woman. I mean, why else would she leave? I don't know why you ever trusted her. She should have never been brought to this palace. She never really cared for you. I just wish you could have seen that sooner."

"Vashti, that's enough! Do you have any idea where she might have gone?"

"Do you really think she would have told me? She doesn't want to be found or else she would have left a message. If it were me, I would have never left you. I would stay here and be with you. Isn't it now clear? She doesn't love you like I do..." Vashti's voice trailed off. She rose from the bed, walked to him and lovingly wrapped her arms around his neck. "Kudar, why can't things be like they were between us? I remember when I was your favorite. You used to love to make sweet love to me. You made me feel like a woman..."

"Vashti," Kudar reached out his hands and touch her arms in an attempt to pull away from her.

She pressed her cheek against his. "I want you to love me. I want your love. Do you still care about me? I am willing to forget about the past and start over. I don't care if you are married to someone else. You can have your wife. My life will still be dedicated to serving you."

"You don't mean what you're saying." Kudar pulled back and managed to unclasped Vashti's arms from around his neck before standing up.

"Of course I do."

"Don't be ridiculous. I've got to find Laila."

"Laila's gone!" Vashti stomped her feet. "She doesn't want to be found!"

"You're wrong! I will find her!" Kudar headed for the door.

"It's useless! She's not here. But I am." Vashti chased after Kudar and encased her arms around him in an attempt to hug him again.

Kudar brushed her hands away from his shoulders. "No, Vashti! Not now!"

"Then I'll visit you in your chambers. I won't give up on you."

"Vashti, what we had is over! Why can't you face that?"

"No! No! I don't believe it! Don't go!" Vashti flew to the doorway and stretched out her arms in order to block his path. "Don't walk away from me again, please! I'll do whatever you want."

"You'll do whatever I want? Then I want this to stop! Stop chasing me! Stop being so goddamn needy! And stop pressuring me to feel something I no longer feel!"

Vashti gasped. "How dare you speak to me like this?"

"Can't you see what we had *was* nice…real nice. *But, it's over!* I love Laila. I want to be with her, and I will do whatever it takes to find her!" Kudar assured before he shoved past his ex lover.

"Bastard!" Vashti yelled after him.

✵

Kudar was furious and frustrated all at once. Laila, gone. She was really gone. Was it really due to the way he had treated her the night before he left? Had he been such a brute? He needed to talk to his mother about it. She would know what to do. He also needed to finally stand up to his father and let him know the marriage did not take place.

Kudar crossed the courtyard to his parent's home. He decided he wanted to talk with his father first. He searched through the palace but did not see his father anywhere. As he searched, he became more frustrated. He felt everything was going wrong in his life. By the time he made it to his father's bedroom, he was fuming. He pounded on the door.

After a moment, a deep voice called, "Come in."

Kudar stepped inside the room. The bedroom was a large one. It was divided into sections by sheer curtains that hung from the ceiling. Candles flickered and the poignant smell of incense filled the room. His father sat on the side of the bed in the corner of the room. In the bed was a young girl sitting against a pillow with the sheet pulled around her chest and secured under her arms. Her bare shoulders remained exposed. She smiled shyly at Kudar then lowered her eyes.

"When did you get back, son?" Amir inquired as he pulled his robe together and turned to face his son.

"Laila's gone. Why didn't you have someone ride to the city to let me know when she left?" he demanded caustically.

"Can this wait? The hour is late. I was just about to retire." Amir nodded toward the brunette that graced his bed.

"No, Father! This cannot wait!" Kudar insisted. "I want answers!" he bellowed.

Hearing the distress in his son's voice, and seeing the fact that his son's feet were planted solidly in the middle of the room, Amir turned back to the girl and patted her legs. "Leave us, my dear," he instructed.

The girl exited the bed. Making sure to keep the bed sheet around her body, she scurried from the room.

Amir stood. "Son, why are you so upset? How did your wedding–"

"Wedding." Kudar waved his hand in dismissal. "I did not marry that girl."

"What?"

"I've had it, Father! I am not going to live my life by your damned rules anymore! I am your son, yes. And I do respect you. But, to try and force me to marry someone–"

"She's of royal lineage–"

"I don't want her!"

"It is our tradition once you are betrothed, you–"

"Well maybe it's time tradition changed! Now tell me, what have you done with Laila?"

"I don't know what you are talking about!"

"You know what I am talking about! You sent her away before. I swear, if you made her leave–"

"I've done nothing to that girl."

"Then, tell me, why wasn't I informed when she left?"

"What's going on here? Why are you two bickering?" Irene cantered into the room. She walked to

Kudar and rubbed her fingers against his cheek. "I heard you were back. Are you all right, baby?"

"Our son wants to know where that girl Laila went," Amir informed his wife.

Irene lowered her eyes and nervously removed her hand from her son's cheek. "Oh…" she mumbled, stepping away from him slightly.

Amir continued, "Look, son, I promised you before I would not force her to leave this house. I can stand here and tell you I have kept my word. She chose to leave on her own."

"Why didn't you send someone to the city to tell me she left? You know how I feel about her! Answer me!"

"Honestly, I didn't think about it because I was glad she was gone. You know I never liked the idea of you with her. What else do you want me to say?"

"Damn it, Father! You should have cared more about my feelings! What of you, Mother? Why didn't you send someone or come to the city? You've been to the city on shopping trips! How come informing me was not important to you?" Kudar scowled at his mother.

"Don't talk to your mother in such a disrespectful manner," Amir cut in.

"I….I…You were to be married. We…we thought it was for the best," Irene stumbled nervously over her words.

"Well, I didn't get married, Mother. I swear to the both of you… If I can't find Laila, I will never forgive either of you." With that said, Kudar turned and stormed from the room.

❁

Kudar talked to everyone he could about Laila's disappearance. No one seemed to know any details of her departure. Dismayed, he began to drink. Getting drunk seemed to be the only way to conceal the crater-sized hole in his heart. He began to drink so much his drinking soon became intolerable.

Consumed by bitterness, he lashed out at anyone who came near him. Within a week, he had managed to alienate everyone in his home. He went to the newest tavern in Istanbul to drink wine all day in hopes of drowning his broken heart. One night, after drinking all evening, he was so drunk he had to be helped home and put to bed.

As he landed on the bed, he opened his eyes, lifted his head and groaned. His head was pounding and the dark room appeared to be swirling. He laid his head back on the pillow. His eyelids drooped, fluttered slightly, then he closed them.

A sound caused him to open his eyes again. He turned to look toward the door in time to see a vision materialize in front of him. A woman appeared in his room dressed in a sheer covering and she floated toward him. As she did, the light within the room revealed the curve of her hips and her shapely legs. Her large breasts strained against the soft cloth that jailed them. Part of her face was covered by a veil. Kudar blinked and looked again. Could it be?

"Laila?" he called out and reached for the mysterious apparition in an effort to pull himself out of his alcoholic induced haze.

There was a movement beside him and a second figure appeared by his bed and placed a soft hand on his shoulders.

"Master Kudar, please don't worry yourself. You're intoxicated. We need to get you undressed and under the covers so you can sleep it off," a gentle voice said.

The voice sounded like it belonged to Bella. But he could not see her. Someone was pulling his tunic over his head. Soft hands delicately traced the ripple of muscles across his chest. He clutched the silky smooth arm and tugged gently. Bella fell across his chest with a laugh.

The shadowy figure that had entered the room was still advancing toward them. "Laila?" he whispered again hopefully.

The form moved closer to the bed and Kudar could see blonde hair and green eyes. It was Yasmine.

"Bella and I were sent to make sure you get in bed. It seems you got yourself drunk again," Yasmine said, after she sat on the side of his bed.

Bella, still sprawled across Kudar's chest, bent her head and kissed him on the lips. She pressed her body against him and sighed.

Yasmine took his hand and placed it against her heavy breast. The soft material covering her felt cool to his touch. She moved his hand in a circular motion in an attempt to have him caress her mound. "Oh..." she moaned.

Bella stretched her body over the length of him. She lifted the hem of her gown, took his free hand and placed it on her bottom before kissing him once more. Her lips left his and traveled down his chest and stomach. "Master," she began. "We know you have been unhappy lately. Let us take care of you."

Her words sounded muffled to his foggy brain.

Bella moved her hands from Kudar's and his arm fell to the bed. She clutched the string that tied his trousers. With her fingers, she began to unravel the knot on the drawstring that held his trousers around his waist.

Kudar shook his head, trying desperately to clear his mind. With much effort, he managed to sit up. "La...ladies...I am flattered. But that's enough. You wo...wouldn't take advantage of a drunken man, would you?"

"You just seem so unhappy," Yasmine noted.

"We just want to help you forget for a few hours," Bella explained.

"Beautiful Bella...you're sweet. Yasmine. You two have been very good to me. You ladies always know how to take care of me. However...this time...mating is not the answer."

The girls frowned.

"You two are good people. You deserve so much better than what I have given you lately."

"Don't be so hard on yourself. You've seen to it that we never go hungry," Yasmine replied.

"You're sweet...the both of you. But this is something I have to work through on my own." He tilted his head forward and kissed both girls' foreheads. "Now, go back to bed you two," he prodded. "I will be fine," he added when they hesitated.

Uncertain, the two girls stood up. Both glanced back worriedly at him as they walked to the door. Reluctantly, the young concubines exited the room and disappeared from sight.

"He got drunk again last night. He's been drunk every night for a week. This isn't good," Irene reported to her husband. "Our son is on a downward fall."

"He will get over it. He's not a babe. Besides, we both agreed it was for the best that she went away."

"I don't like seeing my child this way. He's so unhappy. I think we should tell him that we know where Laila is."

"He needs to start focusing on his work again and get his head out of the clouds."

"How can he do that when he's miserable?" Irene inquired.

"It's for the best."

"It's for the best that we lie to him? He thinks we know naught about Laila, when the truth is, you are the one who sent her away."

"Ssshh! Someone might hear you."

"We need to tell our son. He trusts us. I can't continue to do this to him. I can't watch him suffer like this." Tears crowded into Irene's eyes.

"Don't cry, dove. You know I hate to see you upset. If Kudar doesn't improve soon I will tell him. I promise," Amir assured, pulling his wife close as tears slipped down her cheek.

Kudar spent the day working in town. At the end of the day, he went to a tavern and ordered a drink. He alternated between sipping on the drink and staring into the cup.

"I feel the same way." A man turned around in his seat to face Kudar.

Kudar nodded half-heartedly to the man. He did not feel like being friendly or being disturbed. He wished the talkative stranger would just turn around and allow him to wallow in his sorrow.

Oblivious to Kudar's attitude, the man continued, "I should've joined Melek on his trip to Cairo."

Cairo? Laila had said she grew up right outside Cairo. Kudar looked up at the man. "You had a chance to go to Cairo?" he inquired.

"Aye. A friend of mine was headed that way. Once he arrived in Cairo, he was gonna gather a caravan and head further south."

"That friend of yours, does he head to Cairo often?"

"He travels all over. He will return in the spring. Oh…I've been talking but I neva introduced myself. My friends call me Abbas."

"Hello Abbas. My name is Kudar al Numan."

"Al Numan. I remember that name. You don't live in the al Numan palace outside of town, do you?"

"Yes."

"I remember now, Melek told me that lady that was with him was from the al Numan palace."

At the words, Kudar sat up in his seat. "What did you say? What lady?"

"She was a girl from the al Numan palace. I remember. Melek told me before they got in my rowboat. I rowed them both out to the ship that was sailing to Cairo."

Kudar plunked his cup down on the table. "So, you got a good look at the lady. What did she look like?"

"I remember her due to the fact she was pleasing to look at. She seemed sad though. She kept looking down at her hand and twirling a ring on her finger."

"Ring? What did the ring look like? Was it a sapphire ring?"

"Well, it was nighttime. Yet, I noticed it had diamonds 'round a dark colored gem."

"Laila!"

"Laila? I don't know. Can't say that I was ever told her name. Just know that Melek said he got paid handsomely to take the girl home to Cairo. He said the arrangements were made by a eunuch."

Omar? "Are you sure?"

"That's what he said. Hey, al Numan, are you all right?" Abbas asked when he saw the look on Kudar's face.

"I'm fine!" Kudar stood up from the table. "You have been very helpful. You don't know what you've just done," Kudar declared.

He paid for the man's drink then quickly left the tavern.

As Kudar raced back to his home, his heart thundered in his chest. He could not believe it. Omar had made arrangements to have Laila leave the palace? Omar had said he didn't know anything about Laila's disappearance. That was a lie. Why had he lied? Whatever the reason, Kudar planned on getting the truth from him.

"Omar!" Kudar roared as he stormed through the house when he arrived home.

He found Omar in the cooking area.

"You made arrangements for Laila to leave the harem!" Kudar accused, his voice seething with anger. "You've known all along where she's been because you sent her away! You lied to me!"

210

At Kudar's words, the eunuch did not protest. Instead, he said, "I didn't want to do it. I hope you will believe me."

"You betrayed me! You lied to me, you fool!"

"I had no choice!"

"You had no choice? Why, I ought to—"

"I was told to keep quiet. So I did. I was just following orders."

"Orders? Whose orders?"

Omar was silent.

"Tell me, Omar! Whose orders?"

"Your father's!"

"My father's!" The information was so devastating, Kudar had to take a step backward to stay on his feet.

"Aye. I hate to tell you. But it's true."

"Where did she go?"

"She returned to her home. Your father suggested she return to her family. He thought it was best since you were going to start a new life with a new wife. He paid Melek to escort her to Cairo and then take her to her home."

Of course! That's where Laila would be! Her home! How come he had not thought of it sooner?

Omar was speaking. "I've been with your family a long time. I've tried to be a good servant. I've done your bidding faithfully for years. Don't punish me for this," he pleaded.

"You betrayed me!" Kudar yelled angrily.

"I was just following orders!"

Unable to hold back, anger erupted in Kudar and he punched Omar across the jaw. Omar staggered away from him. "Damn you!" Kudar shouted. "I will deal with you later on this," Kudar promised. "Right now, I have to talk to my father!"

"You lied to me!" Kudar glowered at his father. "You lied and said you didn't make Laila leave, when in fact you paid to send her away!"

"Son, I have no idea what you are talking about."

"Don't lie to me!" Kudar snarled. "You know exactly what I am talking about! You're a lying, manipulative–"

"That's enough! I didn't make her leave. I promised you I wouldn't and I didn't. I just offered her a chance to return home and she took it. I just did what I thought was best for you!"

"No! You did what you thought best for *you*! You didn't want a son who didn't follow your plans! So you set about to destroy my happiness! I can't believe you've known all along where Laila is, and you deliberately withheld that information from me! You saw how much I was suffering! Yet, you insisted on lying to me every day! You even used Omar to lie to me too!"

"It's not like that. I only–"

"I wanted to. Just the other day I mentioned we should tell you." Irene walked into the room. Tears were in her eyes.

"Mother? You're involved in this?" Kudar gasped in disbelief.

"She wanted me to tell you. She's been worried sick about you."

"You've both have known about Laila all this time–"

"I know there's nothing I can say to make you understand why I did what I did. But, when I saw that you were headed down the wrong path–" Amir began.

"Wrong path? There was no wrong path! It was just a path you didn't agree with! Listen, Father, I will live my life the way I want! I am not going to be bound by tradition or anything else and do something I really do not want to do!

You've done everything you could to keep me from Laila! But I promise you, I will find her! I will search this whole earth if I have to! I will find her!"

"Please forgive us," Irene sobbed.

"Forgive you? Forgive you! Surely you jest! It was just by pure chance that I found out! If I hadn't found out on my own I would still not know!"

"We were going to tell you!" Irene cried ruefully.

"I loved you both...and trusted you both! But, you lied to me! You betrayed me! That's something I can never forgive!"

Chapter Seventeen

Kudar began preparations to leave town. Laila had gone into great detail about her home and he recalled every word she had spoken on the issue. So he felt like he had enough of an idea about where she lived. He knew it was just outside Cairo and he felt he could find it once he arrived there. However, reaching Cairo proved harder than he thought. He asked around but could not find information on any ship leaving for Cairo.

Kudar did not like the thought of spending one more day hold up with his parents close by. He upped his monitory offer and finally found someone willing to get a ship ready to sail to Egypt. Relieved that he would soon be on his way, Kudar packed his belongings for the long journey and made sure he had extra money if any unforeseen issues arose.

"I'm going to pack my things. I'm going with you," Omar told Kudar the day he was to leave.

"Go with me? I don't want you to go with me."

"I know you're angry with me. Let me make it up to you."

"As if there was anything you could do to make things up to me."

"I can help."

"I don't need your help. I can manage on my own."

"I can be of assistance when you get to Cairo. I may be able to interpret for you if needed which will make it easier for you to find Laila once we get there."

Kudar was silent for a while. Finally, he barked, "Fine. You can come. Just don't get in my way!"

Omar smiled and bowed. "Thank you, Master. I will prove to you just how sorry I am for what I did," he said contritely.

"Meet me in town when you are done with your packing. There is someone there I have to see," Kudar told Omar then dismissed him.

214

❈

What had once been Constantinople, now renamed Istanbul, was a city alive with change. However, Kudar had no time to admire his handiwork on several of the new building structures because his mind was on the mission ahead of him. He visited a magistrate who was in charge of legal affairs and ordered several matters resolved before he returned from his journey. When Kudar told the magistrate exactly what he wanted done, the man couldn't help but raise his eyebrows.

"I have never heard such a request from any man," the gaunt man began.

"Just do it!" Kudar ordered.

As the meeting was being concluded, Omar arrived.

"Let's go!" was all Kudar said to his servant before the men headed out on their journey.

❈

Kudar could not hide his disappointment at the ship that had been made ready to sail. Omar commented that he had not seen such a raggedy-looking sailing vessel in his life. The crew of the ship was a handful of men. But since the ship was not that large, the amount of men that were onboard to help sail seemed to be sufficient.

When the ship set off, sailing was slow going. The water was cold and as night arrived an acerbic wind blew. The wood that the ship was made out of seemed to absorb the cold, which caused everything on board to feel like ice. The large room set aside as the crews' quarters had a draft which caused Kudar's teeth to chatter.

As night fell, a ferocious storm arose. Dark clouds rolled overhead quickly and released torrents of rain. It seemed as if the sea itself came to life. The ship rocked back and forth. The boards underneath their feet creaked eerily and groaned in protest. Rain pelted down in sheets. Water rose into a solid wall before cascading over the ship's rail. The ship rocked violently. The captain of the mangy crew called all hands on deck to help battle the storm. Kudar and Omar were even called to help. The captain ordered the men about, shouting that the sails needed to come down before they were shredded to pieces by the storm.

The boat tilted and bowed again. This time, items not properly secured hurled across the deck. Several boxes slid across the deck in one direction. In a couple of seconds when the ship dipped, the parcels slid back the direction they had come. The boxes hit the side of the ship with a bang and split open. Their contents spilled out, creating an even bigger hazard of debris gliding aimlessly on deck.

Orders being shouted aloud were drowned out by the sound of crashing waves and raging thunder. Kudar was soaked with rain as he ran about to assist where needed. He was not holding onto anything when a wave crashed on deck and the ship lurched to the left side. He skidded across the cold wet deck and would have gone overboard if he had not managed to grab onto the rail.

Rain fell constantly for hours before it slackened a little. It never completely went away. As the night began to fade, the storm finally did subside. Suddenly, someone shouted, "We're taking on water!" There was a flurry of activity on deck and a rush was made to find the damage. It was soon revealed that the old ship was seriously damaged and the hull was quickly taking on water.

"We've got to get to land as soon as possible," the captain reported after he had examined the damage.

"We've been blown about. From what I can tell from reading the nautical charts, we should be close to the island of Cyprus," the man known as the navigation expert answered.

Everyone began to pray for land.

The ship continued to be tossed about. A short time later, with darkness blanketing the sky, the ship took on a slight list. There was no sight of land. Impending doom seemed inevitable. Just as the light of a new day glowed through the blanket of clouds, someone pointed to the east.

"There's land!"

A rumble of excitement filled the boat until they realized they were not headed in the direction of the land. The ship, weighed down with water, had stalled and they were too far from the island to swim.

"Break out the sails!" someone called.

"It's no use. The boat is heavy with water. It will never sail again, even if the sails are raised," came the reply.

"What about the rowboat?" someone asked.

"There's not enough room for everyone," was the response.

"Then, we'll make room. Lower the rowboat! It's time to abandon ship!" the captain bellowed cacophonously.

Kudar made sure his money pouch was tied securely around his waist as the rowboat was lowered. Omar came to stand beside him and the men found their way onto one of the boats. The rowboat wobbled precariously as one by one the men clambered on board. Eventually, everyone was loaded and they began to row toward land. Rowing was slow, but the ragged crew managed to put more distance between the sinking ship and less toward the land.

As the sailors neared land, one of the men said, "This looks like Cyprus! I think we made it!" Then, he stood up.

When he did, the boat rocked one time then pitched to one side before it flipped over. All the men were thrown out of the boat into the rimy gelidity. Kudar was no exception. In an instant, he was hurled face-first into the cold black water.

Chapter Eighteen

Sea waves blinded Kudar as the tenebrous water bit into his skin and tried to pull him under. He kicked his legs which were so strained they ached. His arms were beginning to feel like weights. Water filled his mouth. He spit it out. He managed to catch a glimpse of land. Despite the oppressive conditions, Kudar forced himself to focus on the land up ahead.

He stretched his arm over his head in a long stroke and started to swim. It felt as if he were fighting the current as he swam toward the island. Part of him wanted to surrender to the elements. But he willed himself to go on. *Just another stroke,* he kept telling himself.

When he felt sand mix with water in his mouth, he realized he had washed up on land. Soaked through and shivering, he heard moans and groans around him. He tried to raise himself so he could help the others, but he found he was too exhausted. He collapsed with a groan of his own as bitter pain engulfed him.

�֍

The next time Kudar woke up, he was shivering. His whole body seemed to be savaged by fire. He heard a voice over him and felt when something cold was placed on his forehead. He opened his eyes and realized he was laying in a bed. "I have to get to Cairo..." he mumbled and tried to lift himself from the bed.

A strong arm held him gently on the bed. "You can't go anywhere," a male voice said. "You've been through a terrible ordeal. You are sick. You have a fever. You must rest. I am the physician. I shall take care of you and the rest of those that made it."

"Omar? Did he make it?" Kudar asked before he broke into a fit of coughs and fell back on the bed exhausted.

"You need more rest," was all he heard before he fell into a restless sleep.

✄

The next time Kudar woke, it was because he had been awakened to eat. In between the times he was not coughing, he was fed soup and asked to drink water. He slept a lot and woke for brief periods of time. One day, he woke to find he was no longer burning with fever. However, he still had a small cough and he felt very weak.

Seeing Kudar sitting up in bed, the physician, who had been tending to another patient, came to hover at his side. "How are you feeling?" the old man asked.

"Like I just survived a shipwreck," Kudar answered flatly.

"I was worried about you for a while there. But you pulled through. I am glad to see you are able to sit up now."

"How long have I been sick?"

"Oh, about a week. You still have a little cough but that will subside soon."

"Is Omar all right? Is everyone else doing fine?" Kudar asked of his other roommates.

"I'm doing the best I can."

"When is the next ship leaving this island?"

"Ship leaving?"

"I have to get to Cairo."

"There is no way you can make it to Cairo in your condition. It is too dangerous for you to sail in your medical state. You should know that after what you've been through. Cairo is just going to have to wait. You are stuck here until you heal."

"Where is my money pouch? I want to pay you for your services. I really appreciate you helping me when I needed it most."

"My job is to help. No pay is necessary. Besides, you were found with no pouch. It must have gotten lost at sea."

Kudar frown. Not only was he sick but he was penniless.

"Don't worry about it. Don't worry about anything. You don't need to exert yourself too much. You need to preserve your strength and focus on healing. Now, I shall get you some soup to eat."

"Soup? If you don't mind, I need something a little more filling than that."

"Good," the physician smiled. "That means you are getting better. Soon you shall have your strength back." With that said, the old man walked away to get the meal.

Kudar thought about what the physician had said. He could not leave the island to find Laila and even if he could he had no money. Soon, he would have his strength back. But, how was he going to get to Laila?

�֍

A few days later, Kudar felt much better. He had reconnected with Omar, who was being treated by the physician as well. The two men were happy to see each other. Both men felt they had enough strength, so they left the sick house to explore the surroundings. There were single story buildings lining narrow meandering cobblestone streets. It was chilly out so the pair did not stay outdoors long. By the time they made it back indoors, the men had decided they would have to find some kind of job on the island in order to make the money they needed to purchase a spot on a ship headed for Cairo.

When the men returned to the sick house, Kudar asked the physician about getting work on the island.

220

The physician told him he would inquire around town and get back to him. The job Kudar was offered was in a bakery. He had never worked in such a position before but he took it. There was no good reason to be choosy. Omar found work in town as well. So, for the weeks that followed Kudar baked bread and prepared gyros for those who came by. He saved all the money he could as he dreamed of the day he would see Laila again.

When he and Omar boarded the ship bound for Cairo, Kudar smiled. Finally, he was back on his way to find his lost love.

❧

Laila placed her hand on her round belly. For the hundredth time that day, she thought of Kudar, the palace and her baby. Maybe after the baby was born she should go back ...No! She must stop thinking of him. With all of the women in Kudar's life, including a wife, there was no room for her. Besides, if she returned to the palace, her child would just be one of the many children Kudar was destined to have. She turned to look at her mother. They had come into the city to shop. Her mother was pointing to the cut of meat she wanted to purchase. The butcher wrapped up the meat and handed it to her.

"Are you tired, angel?" her mother asked as she turned to Laila while putting the package of meat in her large bag.

"Aye. A little," Laila answered.

"I want to buy bread. After that, we'll head home," her mother said.

Laila was relieved at her mother's words. The city was crowded with people scurrying about and there was too much haggling and too many conversations going on around her. She followed her mother to an indoor bazaar and to the bakery near the entryway.

Kudar was so happy to be on land once again. After sailing the Mediterranean and Aegean Seas, he was tired from the journey but too excited to rest. Half of the battle was over. Now was the hard part. If he had any hope of finding Laila, he had to find her village. At the moment, however, he was hungry. Omar said he was hungry also. So both men walked through the streets of Cairo looking for something to eat before they rented horses and started their search.

Kudar saw a bazaar ahead and he and Omar headed toward it since it was indoors and they wanted to be out of the sun.

Meanwhile, inside the bazaar, Laila and her mother ordered their bread and paid for it. As the bread was handed to them, Laila's mother said, "Oh, look at that!" She pointed to a pretty linen *kalasiris* hanging in front of a stand down the crowded walkway. The motherly woman grabbed Laila's hand and pulled her forward. The crowd swallowed the women from sight just as Kudar and Omar walked into the bazaar.

The first thing Kudar saw was a bakery. The bread smelled delicious and his stomach growled. So he stopped for a slice of bread.

Laila sat by the river as the sun slowly set. She and her mother had returned home from the bazaar hours ago. After they unpacked their goods, she headed to visit her favorite place on the Nile. She looked down at her stomach. Its curve was now very visible through her clothes. Being home with her family had been heaven

222

on earth. She loved being surrounded by people who loved her. But despite it all, part of her was sad. She carried a baby created out of love. But her baby's father would never know or see his child.

Laila had to admit she had secretly hoped Kudar would come after her. However, she had long since given up on that useless wish. She had told Omar to tell Kudar she loved him and that she was going home. Half of her had hoped that upon hearing the news, Kudar would have moved heaven and earth to find her. He had not arrived. Besides, even if he had wanted to come, he did not know exactly where to find her. On the other hand, she was sure she had told him enough about the nearby landmarks for him to find her village if he wanted to.

Laila had not wanted to keep thinking of Kudar. But as her stomach grew, so had her thoughts of him. No matter how she had tried, she could not push thoughts of him aside. Though he was hundreds of miles away…a lifetime away…she could not escape the memories. Oh, why couldn't she admit to herself then what she could admit now?

Why had she not been able to admit to Kudar that she loved him in return when she was lying in his arms and beg him not to marry that other woman? Somehow some way she had fallen deeply in love with him. All along she had wanted someone who loved her and only her. That was the real reason she wanted assurances from him that he would not be with another woman.

As Laila looked out at the Nile River she loved, a warm feeling curled through her. The setting sun reminded her she should already be on her way back to the hut. However, she did not want to leave her old hideout. She wanted to stay by the river and savor her memories of Kudar who had always been kind and gentle with her.

She thought about the first time she had seen him in the auction house. She thought about the way he looked the first time she saw him in his study. He had stood tall and proud and looked so handsome. She remembered the first time he called her to his chambers. She recalled the first time they made love and an uncontrolled smile curled her lips. She should be embarrassed. But she wasn't. She reminisced about the beautiful love they made, the picnics they took, the times they swam in the cool water, lay in the grass and fished. She remembered the very last time they had made love. It had been rough…it had been lusty…it had been good. It had been a mix of love, of lust, of anger and passion.

"Laila."

Kudar seemed to be calling her now. Her memories where bringing the past to life. It was as if Kudar was here in the dark calling her name.

"Laila." His voice came again. It was a voice that lived in her dreams and dwelt in her heart.

She must be imagining things because it looked as if Kudar stepped out of the shadows.

Laila froze for a moment. Barely breathing, she whispered, *"Kudar."*

Was it really him standing before her, his frame larger than life, against the pink and yellow of the fading sun? Had he once again appeared to rescue her? Or was he just a figment of her imagination? "Kudar? Is that you?" she asked as she stared in disbelief.

"It's me, lovely Laila," he answered before giving her one of his lopsided grins. "It's really me."

Chapter Nineteen

"What are you doing here?" Laila questioned as she descended from the rock she had been sitting on.

"I'm here to see you."

"How did you find me?" she wanted to know, still filled with disbelief.

"It took some work. But I remembered everything you ever told me about this place and I managed to find my way. Now, aren't you going to hug me?"

Laila walked into his awaiting embrace without further hesitation.

Kudar wrapped his secure arms around her. He pulled her close with a sigh and a gratified warmth spread through their bodies as they melted into each other.

"I found you. I really found you," he whispered softly, burying his head in her hair.

A cool breeze drifted over them as they held each other tight. The sound of crickets chirping in the pre-dusk light resembled music. There was the echo of something as it splashed in the river nearby. A fish, no doubt flipping through the air in celebration. Kudar pulled back slightly, seeming to notice Laila's swollen belly. The look in his dark eyes was one of confusion, realization, then excitement.

"You are..."

"Aye!" Laila giggled and nodded.

"With my..."

"Aye."

The biggest grin Laila had ever seen curled across Kudar's lips. He planted a wet kiss on her forehead.

"I'm going to be a father!" he exclaimed before he began to laugh.

Laila couldn't help but chuckle too. "How did you know I would be here by the river?" she asked when they had regained their composure.

"I didn't. Omar and I were riding along the countryside. Omar came with me. When we arrived in your village, we saw a couple of cute children playing in a field. I stopped and asked them if they knew a lady named Laila. They said yes. I was excited. They brought a lady to me and when I saw her my heart sank because it wasn't you. The nice lady told me she wasn't you. But she said she did have a niece named Laila. I told her my name and before I finished talking she took us to your mother's house...that's were Omar is now...with your mother. He is really taken by her. I think the man thinks he's in love," Kudar revealed delightedly, then continued, "Your mother told me you were at the river. You have a sweet mother, by the way. She told me how to find you here. So, wa la. Here I am."

Laila beamed blithely and touched his cheek with her hand.

"Believe me, I would have been here sooner if I had known where you had gone after you left the palace."

"Omar didn't tell you?"

"Omar said he was following orders by not telling me where you'd gone. He wanted to come on this trip to help find you...as a way of making atonement. I was very angry at him at first. It seems my father devised the whole thing...my mother went along with it too. It was by pure luck that I found out the truth. That sapphire ring I gave you was the missing piece to the puzzle." He took her hand in his and saw that she still had on the ring he had given her. He kissed her fingers. "I'll tell you all about it sometime, including my sailing adventures. But all that is over now. I am just glad I found you. Now we can return home."

Laila's heart skipped a beat. Home? When she was at the palace she had never really thought of it as her home. In the time she had been away, she realized it was more her home than any place on earth. She missed it. She wanted to return to it. But return to what? Being one of Kudar's many women? That just was not something she wanted. Sure he wanted her now, but how long would that last? How long until he decided to add another girl to his harem and then another? The thought of it hurt Laila's heart. She just couldn't do it.

"I can't go back with you, Kudar," Laila's voice was barely perceptible as she stepped out of his embrace.

"Can't go back? What are you saying? Of course you can go back."

Laila shook her head negatively.

"Are you still angry about the way things were the last time we were together? I know I shouldn't have been so rough with you–"

"No. That's not it. I can't go back knowing you are going to be with other women. My belief that love should be between one man and one woman is too much a part of me. That's why I can't go back. I know you could never be with just me in the harem. It isn't realistic."

"No, it's not," Kudar agreed.

"I know you have your harem and in your culture being with more than one woman is acceptable. That's why I can't ask you to go against the way you've been raised. You don't have to settle for one woman to love. You don't have to settle for just me."

"Laila, I always wanted you to fall in love with me. Not because of who I was or what I had. You want to know why I wanted you to fall in love with me? It was because I was already in love with you. Lovely Laila..." He gently gathered her back into his embrace. "I love you. There is no other woman I want. There is no other woman on the face of the earth who can ever take your place in my heart. You are the one for me."

Laila wanted to believe him. With all her heart she wanted to. However, she needed more than just words.

"The other women in the harem?"

"I thought you might be worried about that. That's why I relieved those other women of their service."

"What?" Laila gasped in shock.

"You heard me. They were let go…sent packing. Before I left, I made arrangements with a magistrate to send them all back to their homes…with a handsome financial settlement less there be any complaints."

"I can't believe it!"

"The money the women received will more than suffice. Their families won't be able to object."

"I can't believe it," Laila said again.

"Believe it!"

"What about Vashti?"

"She was sent on her way too. She thinks she loves me, but she is young and pretty. She will find a lad who will fall head over heals in love with her one day and I will be but a distant memory. But, you…I cannot live without."

"You can't be serious!"

"Oh, but I am." Kudar bent his head and kissed her passionately on the lips. "You and your strange ways. You want real love between one man and one woman. I didn't think…know it was possible, until you. Now I have a harem of one, and you are that one, my love."

"But your wife–"

"No, Laila, you still don't understand. I didn't get married," Kudar announced happily.

"What? Your father must be furious."

"Just before I left to find you, I told him I wanted naught to do with him. I told him I would never speak to him again for what he'd done. However, he trumped me."

"He trumped you? How?"

"My father said he realized he hurt me. He and my mother both said they were willing to let me live my life the way I want."

"But your father doesn't want me to be with you."

"He said he could see I really love you and he gave me his blessing to find you. Right before I left home, he told me he will accept you and my relationship with you on one condition."

"What condition is that?"

"That I marry you," Kudar declared.

228

"What?"

"It's a miracle, I know. ...Well, actually, I suspect my mother had a lot to do with him changing his mind."

"But your father always said he wanted you to marry a Turkish girl who is a Muslim. I'm not Turkish and I'm not Muslim."

"My mother is happy about that. She said she prayed to your Christian God and asked Him to help me find you. Since He did, I want to learn more about Him."

"There's no way your father could really want this. I was a slave. I don't come from a proper background like he wanted. We come from different cultures."

"None of that matters."

"How can–"

"No more questions. What matters is I've found you and I never want to be separated from you again. Now, for the last time, you stubborn beautiful woman, I love you. I want to love you and I want to marry you. We will stay here until after our baby's born and then we'll sail back to Istanbul."

"Istanbul?"

"The Sultan had the city's name changed from Constantinople to Istanbul. You can even see if your mother wants to come live with us. I'm sure Omar would like that. We're going to have that big palace all to ourselves. We'll have to fill it with lots of children. But, before all that can happen, you have to tell me if you love me and if you'll marry me."

"So you love only me?" Laila asked once more.

"For the final time...yes!" he affirmed. "Now, will you marry me?"

Tears crowded into Laila's eyes. He loved her just as she loved him. All of the obstacles that were between them were now removed. Any obstacles they still had to face, they would face together. "Yes! Yes, my love!" Laila ran her fingers through Kudar's hair. "I love you and I will marry you."

They kissed then.

Just as tears started to sprinkle down Laila's face, the baby inside her kicked. When they felt it, the couple broke apart and Kudar laid his hand on her stomach.

"Our son's glad you said yes," he gleamed. "I should get you home. Your mother is cooking dinner so we should head back. But before we do, I need one more kiss," Kudar whispered before lowering his lips once again to hers.

Laila felt safe and protected as she rested in Kudar's embrace. Her unknown wonderful and exciting future was about to begin. She fervently returned Kudar's amorous kiss with a moan. When he pulled his lips away from hers, it was as if the very air was taken from her. She looked up at him in protest.

Kudar looked down at her and nuzzled his nose against hers. "You bewitched me with one look. You captivated me with your peculiar beliefs. When I'm with you, I am deliriously content. I am so glad I found you for I see you were right, lovely Laila," he began.

"I was right?"

"Yes. You wanted me to believe it was possible to fall in love with and be faithful to one woman. I now see you were right, for you are all I need," he admitted with a smile.

After Thoughts

Author Bio:

Sheniqua Waters is a dedicated writer who loves to read and write and spends much of her free time doing both. She works to create characters with compelling qualities that enables them to overcome emotional and physical challenges.

For other books by Sheniqua Waters, check out her website http://www.TheWorldsBestBook.com

Discover These Books

Seduced by the Pharaoh by Sheniqua Waters

Latifa, the courageous daughter of the King of the Nubians, shuns her privileged life to take a vow of chastity and become a fierce female warrior. Her desire is vengeance against the Pharaoh of Egypt who she believes deceived and killed her father then destroyed her village.

Tariq, the newly appointed Pharaoh, has spent his life fighting against the Nubians as Commander of the Egyptian military. While journeying to Thebes, he unexpectedly confronts Latifa and makes a wager that he can conquer her hardened heart and make her willingly share his bed. Latifa vows to resist Tariq's advances and is taken aback when she realizes he is the man she has sworn to destroy.

After long days and nights spent traveling beside the Nile River, will love seize the hearts of these two sworn enemies? Or will Latifa refuse to be seduced by the Pharaoh?

Something to Hide by Sheniqua Waters

Southern belle Lily lives a life of privilege on her father's tobacco plantation before she marries the man she loves, a rancher named Brock. When Lily's enemies learn the secret of her birth, they enact an insidious ruse to have her abducted into the seedy world of slavery.

After years away, Lily survives the auction block and makes her way home only to find Brock has developed feelings for another woman. Can Lily make her husband remember the love they shared before it is too late? Or will the secrets she holds keep them apart forever?